THE ROAD TO FELLOWSHIP

Hindsfoot Foundation Series on the History of Alcoholism Treatment

Glenn F. Chesnut, Editor

The Road to Fellowship

▼

The Role of the Emmanuel Movement and the Jacoby Club in the Development of Alcoholics Anonymous

Richard M. Dubiel

iUniverse, Inc.
New York   Lincoln   Shanghai

The Road to Fellowship
The Role of the Emmanuel Movement and the Jacoby Club in the
Development of Alcoholics Anonymous

All Rights Reserved © 2004 by Richard M. Dubiel

No part of this book may be reproduced or transmitted in any form or by any means, graphic, electronic, or mechanical, including photocopying, recording, taping, or by any information storage retrieval system, without the written permission of the publisher.

iUniverse, Inc.

For information address:
iUniverse, Inc.
2021 Pine Lake Road, Suite 100
Lincoln, NE 68512
www.iuniverse.com

ISBN: 0-595-30740-X

Printed in the United States of America

In memory of my father, Walter Dubiel

Contents

Acknowledgments .... *ix*

Introduction: The Emmanuel Movement and the Jacoby Club xi

1. The Emmanuel Movement: Background and Beginnings 1
2. The Emmanuel Movement: Acceptance and Success 17
3. The Continuation of Therapy:
   Courtenay Baylor and Richard R. Peabody 35
4. Rowland Hazard and the Beginnings of A.A. 60
5. The Jacoby Club: Early Years 81
6. The Jacoby Club: Stasis and Schism 106
7. The Jacoby Club and A.A. 123

Appendix: Jacoby Family Genealogy 145

Notes *147*
Bibliography *173*
Index *183*

Acknowledgments

First and foremost my thanks to Ernest Kurtz and Bill White, who served as supportive colleagues, advisers and friends. With their help this work found its home with the Hindsfoot Foundation and Glenn F. Chesnut. Glenn's encouragement and expertise cannot be underestimated.

I would like to acknowledge my debt to and express my thanks to Bill Pittman for his help in fostering my interest in the Jacoby Club. His extensive organization of primary sources at the Massachusetts Historical Society provided the accessible core of material upon which this book is based.

Thanks also to John W. Crowley at the University of Alabama for his reading of my manuscript and his insightful comments. I am also grateful to Katherine McCarthy for her articles on the Emmanuel Movement and her conversations with me concerning this project.

A general thanks to my colleagues in the Division of Communication at the University of Wisconsin-Stevens Point for granting me periodic load relief. Specific thanks to Leslie Midkiff-Debauche and Jon Roberts of the UW-Stevens Point faculty for their conversations, book recommendations, and general input.

I am indebted to Ryan Reed, who served as my revision editor as I was rewriting the earlier version of this work. I am also indebted to the help of the staff at the Massachusetts Historical Society, the Diocesan Library and Archives of the Episcopal Diocese of Massachusetts, and the Rhode Island Historical Society, especially Rick Stattler.

Last but not least, thanks to the people at the Alcoholics Anonymous Archives in New York and at the Boston Central Service Committee.

And thanks to Reinhold Niebuhr for the Serenity Prayer.

INTRODUCTION

▼

THE EMMANUEL MOVEMENT AND THE JACOBY CLUB

This book traces the rise and decline of two early twentieth-century organizations that forged new approaches to the treatment of alcoholism and to sustaining the recovery of alcoholics. The Emmanuel Movement, founded in 1906 by the Rev. Elwood Worcester at Emmanuel Episcopal Church in Boston, attracted considerable attention in its early years, briefly spread to other cities, and served as the training ground for several important individual therapists before its decline in the 1930s. The Jacoby Club, launched by Emmanuel Church member and prominent rubber merchant Ernest Jacoby, began its "men helping men" meetings in the church's basement in 1909, with only six members at the beginning, but it grew rapidly and separated from the Emmanuel Movement in September, 1913. For several decades the Club sought out down-and-out men and pioneered the idea and practice of fellowship as a path to recovery.

Historians of Alcoholics Anonymous have recognized both of these organizations as important predecessors to A.A. Their contributions to A.A. are less direct than, say, the Oxford Group, which served as A.A.'s organizational birthplace. But there are several direct connections between A.A. and the Emmanuel Movement and the Jacoby Club. Cofounder Bill W. read books written by an Emmanuel-influenced practitioner. The Jacoby Club served to nurture the Boston A.A. during the chapter's first years. And the shadowy figure of Rowland Hazard, a patient of an Emmanuel lay practitioner, influenced the founding circle of A.A. at a crucial moment.

William L. White discusses other possible early influences on the development of A.A. in his recent paper, "Pre-A.A. Alcoholic Mutual Aid Societies."[1] White lists early temperance groups including the Washingtonian Movement, reform clubs, and moderation societies, as well as the Emmanuel Movement and the Jacoby Club, and points out the possible reasons for their demise, inviting a comparative study with A.A. itself. Indeed, White's comprehensive *Slaying the Dragon: The History of Addiction Treatment and Recovery in America* (1998) provides a further historical context for the study of Alcoholics Anonymous and its antecedents.[2]

If we are looking only for direct genealogical links to A.A., these two groups can remain essentially footnotes in that organization's history. In a broader sense, however, the Emmanuel Movement, Jacoby Club, and the approaches of practitioners influenced by them also form part of the cultural seedbed out of which the founders of A.A. gathered their ideas. They reflected the strengths and weaknesses of the early twentieth century's understanding of psychology, spirituality-based healing, and addiction. They can be viewed as false starts, as alternate paths that were not taken, or simply as artifacts of another time. But their story is of interest to anyone concerned with A.A.'s historical context.

Neither the Emmanuel Movement nor the Jacoby Club focused exclusively on alcoholism. Arising out of the great theological and intellectual ferment of the late nineteenth century, the Emmanuel Movement represented a grand experiment in synthesizing religion and the new science of psychology—or more accurately, in the employment of psychotherapy in the service of religion. Like other Progressive era movements, the Emmanuel Movement sought to uplift the urban poor; it turned to treating alcoholism only after finding that this frequently underlay the problems of its tubercular patients. Worcester brought a Progressivist's arsenal of weapons to bear: his academic training as a psychologist, his unflagging optimism, a willingness to experiment. He saw the importance of fellowship among his patients, and fine-tuned the rules for meetings; he tried out various measures of self-help; and he established spiritual conversion as the only lasting basis of recovery.

Worcester's client-turned-therapist Courtenay Baylor followed many of his teacher's psychological approaches and practices, even as the original religious framework withered away. But Baylor's very vocation was novel: neither clergy nor trained psychologist, and in fact a former alcoholic, he was, perhaps, the first lay therapist. Carving out a niche between traditional concerns of pastoral counseling and the medical methods of professional psychiatrists, Baylor pioneered the role of the therapist qualified in part by his very experience of addiction.

Richard Peabody, in turn a patient of Baylor who turned to alcoholism counseling, took the Emmanuel traditions further toward science and away from religion. A harsh and in some ways pessimistic taskmaster, Peabody's ideas about the cause of alcoholism and its treatment were quite influential, although they often contrast sharply with the A.A. philosophy.

A different lesson was taken from the Emmanuel Movement by members of the Jacoby Club. Although they allowed for clerical and professional therapy, the Jacobites stressed self-help, mutual aid (the reformed helping the unreformed), and fellowship. When one of the Club's officers, Lawrence Hatlestad, pushed his own agenda for the professional treatment of alcoholics, the club essentially split in two. For a brief, controversial period in the early 1940s, Hatlestad practiced a program that shared many ideas with the fledgling A.A. movement. After Hatlestad's departure, the Club became more devoted to its older members than to helping down-and-outers, but it remained a sterling example of the strength of fellowship.

What is striking about the Emmanuel Movement is not that it created an enduring, unified legacy but that it led to so many different practices. In different eras, in different settings, and guided by different personalities, the different approaches studied here each represent adaptations of the original Emmanuel idea. The spiritual element, central to the Emmanuelites, becomes peripheral to others. Fellowship, a tool for Worcester, is made a centerpiece at the Jacoby Club but is largely abandoned by Peabody. Where Worcester proclaimed a unity of science and religion, Peabody abandons religion to appear more scientific. Where the Emmanuelites assumed a unity of mind, body, and spirit, later therapists styled themselves more as doctors treating disease. Views of the alcoholic shift between benighted sinner and the sufferer of a fate determined in infancy. Self-help is alternately allowed, dismissed, encouraged. Some practitioners show great deference to the medical profession, while others created roles that brought into question the appropriate training for alcoholism work.

The variables were thus reshuffled, and the resulting practices informed by the ambitions and biases of the protagonists and by the mood swings of a nation shifting from Progressivist optimism to post-World War I practicality. These different approaches also played out against the rise of psychology, particularly Freudian psychology, both as a profession and a public obsession, and great changes in the incidence and patterns of alcoholism brought about by Prohibition and Repeal.

In addition to the brief treatments by A.A. historians, the Emmanuel Movement has been discussed in depth by Katherine McCarthy in a pair of 1984 articles.[3] I was greatly indebted to her scholarship in the early stages of my own research. Howard J. Clinebell, Jr. has also given an excellent short account of the movement which provides a number of valuable specific details about their therapeutic methodology, and Sanford Gifford has done a booklength study of their group treatment methods and the issue of lay psychotherapy.[4] In reexamining the story of the Emmanuel Movement I have sought not to replace their works but to emphasize particular themes that resurface in later approaches to therapy, including A.A. The story of the Jacoby Club, however, has remained largely unexamined. My research is based on previously unexamined materials at the Massachusetts Historical Society, recently catalogued letters at the Rhode Island Historical Society, and several other sources.

This consideration of the Emmanuel Movement and the Jacoby Club fits well with two earlier works on the history of Alcoholics Anonymous, Ernest Kurtz's comprehensive *Not-God: A History of Alcoholics Anonymous* (1979) and Mel B.'s *New Wine: The Spiritual Roots of the Twelve Step Miracle* (1991). Both works trace early influences on A.A., though in different degrees of detail. In any event it would be uneconomical to repeat the details of the Oxford Group, for an obvious example, or the various theological movements and sentiments that paved the way for the formation of Alcoholics Anonymous itself.

The Road to Fellowship will view the history it considers through the lens of Alcoholics Anonymous, pointing out similarities, differences, and direct connections. It will therefore be of interest to students of that organization, and to those recovering from substance abuse who wish to supplement their reading with historical background. Therapists, pastoral counselors, and health professionals will hear echoes of their present concerns played out against different cultural backgrounds. Finally, historians tracing the rise of psychology, the trajectory of American religion, or the many paths between nineteenth-century spiritual healing and modern self-help movements will find many connections here. For the Emmanuel Movement, the Jacoby Club, and the other practitioners all struggled to synthesize programs of recovery out of roughly the same elements at our disposal today: a more or less scientific understanding of the human psyche and addiction; the limited tools of somatic medicine; a spiritual understanding of the relationship between mind, body, and spirit; the role of discipline, ritual, habits of mind, and conscious mental retooling; the cathartic force of self-exploration and self-revelation; and, above all, the power of fellowship, the major theme of this study.

Chapter 1

The Emmanuel Movement: Background and Beginnings

The Emmanuel Movement began in the first decade of the twentieth century, a period of tremendous change and excitement. Technological advances came at a dizzying pace, and authors such as George Beard diagnosed the nation as suffering from "nervousness" brought on by modern times. The traditional foundations of Christianity were increasingly under assault from science, particularly Darwinism. A cultural divide was opening between science and religion.

Out of this conflict came a number of attempts at a new synthesis, including the Emmanuel Movement. As Katherine McCarthy points out, the Emmanuel Movement "was born in part as a response to Christian Science and the New Thought movements, both of which claimed to heal various diseases by Christian methods." Both of these movements were themselves earlier attempts to overcome the science-religion conflict.

Both New Thought and Christian Science can be regarded as what Sidney Ahlstrom calls "harmonial religion."[5] For Ahlstrom, harmonial religion "encompasses those forms of piety and belief in which spiritual composure, physical health, and even economic well-being are understood to flow from a person's rapport with the cosmos."[6] In other words, a person's happiness and immortality depend on "being 'in tune with the infinite.'"

Mary Baker Eddy founded Christian Science in 1879 primarily as an outgrowth of her search for health and well-being. Well-being ("wellness" in the current usage) was very much on the minds of Americans, likely an offshoot of public concerns for things scientific. It was during this period that John Harvey Kellogg concocted health foods, such as corn flakes, at his sanitarium in Battle Creek, Michigan.

Mary Baker Eddy eschewed both the stern Calvinism of her upbringing and the evangelism of the day, as well as liberal Unitarianism, transcendentalism, and Swedenborgianism. She also rejected all the assorted health cults, systems of quackery, and occult organizations that populated her world and intersected her life at various times. Hers was an age of healing spiritualists of many varieties. William James' *Varieties of Religious Experience*, especially lectures IV and V, "The Religion of Healthy-Mindedness," explored the cultural backdrop of these movements. Propositions regarding the immateriality of the physical world were not uncommon.

Mrs. Eddy's formulations began with an attempt to recapture the healing powers of "primitive Christianity." Her basic position was mind over matter: the spirit has power over material reality. The ultimate reality is the Spirit, referred to as God, which is infinite, universal goodness. The role of Jesus extends beyond his moral teachings. Just as his resurrection demonstrated his power over the physical world, so did his healing practices. A person who enters "the Mind of Christ" transcends the material world and reaches the spiritual dimension. The rightly attuned mind thus trumps the material world. Religion trumps science since science, being a creature of the material world, is based only on human perception.

It is noteworthy that in Christian Science, the unaided mind cannot attain spiritual insight or spiritual well-being: Jesus Christ must be included. In this sense Christian Science is not merely another variety of mind-cure (harmonial) religion.

A number of mental-healing sects, known collectively as New Thought, arose from the same late-nineteenth-century religious impulses as Christian Science. A thorough summary of New Thought is beyond the scope of this book, and Mel B.'s *New Wine* does an admirable job of outlining its impact on the future A.A.[7] For our current purposes we can say that most New Thought sects were offshoots of Christian Science, founded by dissenters who had problems with Mary Baker Eddy herself, the organization of her church, or the very underlying theories of Christian Science.

New Thought was less rigid in its approach to healing but did affirm the essential goodness of the universe and that "man is made in the image of the Good."[8] Critical to New Thought was the availability of the Divine Supply to its adherents. The basic beliefs followed the usual Christian virtues, with a decided emphasis on the individual, personal health, and well-being. The New Thought person was to be free from the principles of a declared belief, instead being in touch with the omnipresent Indwelling Presence of God. The favorable logistic of Divine Supply made God immediately available, and without meditation or long periods of study. The appeal to the harried American is obvious.

New Thought took many forms and assumed a variety of names, including the Divine Science movement, the Religious Science movement, and the Unity School of Christianity (1889).[9] For Mark Twain, all the various forms of New Thought, as well as Christian Science, were cut from the same cloth: "There are the Mind-Cure, the Faith Cure, the Prayer Cure, the Mental Science Cure, and the Christian-Science Cure, and apparently they all do their miracles with the same old powerful instrument—the patient's imagination. Differing names, but no difference in the process."[10]

Psychology and Religion

The Emmanuel Movement's first major contribution lay in its attempt to reconcile psychology, specifically psychotherapy, with Christianity. Though on a smaller scale, this endeavor to blend science and religion was not unlike St. Thomas Aquinas's reconciliation of Aristotle's thought to Catholic theology in the thirteenth century. In the first of her definitive articles on the Emmanuel Movement, Katherine McCarthy notes that the movement extended "the power and influence of the church by claiming religious authority over psychological ailments in direct competition with the medical profession."[11] This competition extended beyond the professional rivalry of clergy vs. physician. The legacy of scientific materialism, through all the influences cited earlier, was burrowing into the soul of humankind. With the rise of psychology, William James' humanistic impulses notwithstanding, reductionism posed a threat not only to religion but to the integrity of the human subject as a composite of body, mind, and spirit. The Emmanuel Movement attempted to provide the service of "free religious psychotherapy," an ambition that led to conflicts with the medical profession.

McCarthy also notes the importance of Worcester's employment of self-help techniques, used with tuberculosis victims in the slums of Boston. Whether through its use of auto-suggestion or its health class, the Emmanuel Movement challenged orthodox medicine.[12] But the missionary and evangelical impulse was not absent from the movement. Healing alternatives were already offered by various mind-curists and the more formidable Christian Science movement, and Worcester saw an opportunity for "the renewal of the power and influence of the Christian churches."

A third reason for noting the Emmanuel Movement was Worcester's "unique conception of the interrelations of the mind, body, and spirit." McCarthy points out that for Worcester the therapy could be conducted "for the healing of a wide variety of human problems—a quite different conception of illness from the somaticism of physicians in his time or in ours." The attending person did not have to be a physician, though this could be the case. Ministers could be equal players in the role of therapists, in conjunction with self-help techniques employed by the individual. The interplay of body, mind, and spirit in the Emmanuel Movement was a primary reason for its attractiveness, given the spiritual healing fads of the era. This very "unscientific" aspect for a time kept the medical profession at a distance, at least until the movement became too popular to be dismissed.

Social Work and Religion

The Emmanuel Movement reflected both secular and Christian impulses to social work. The movement began when its founders, Elwood Worcester and Samuel McComb of Boston's Emmanuel Episcopal Church, established a medical mission that focused on the treatment of tuberculosis in the city's slums. Their work soon took on a new dimension when they offered a "Class for the Treatment of Mental Disorders" with the help of a psychiatrist, Dr. Isador H. Coriat.

The movement's early successes owed much to its quiet pursuit of what would today be considered holistic practices, using what worked, but always in the service of society. The movement was strongly people-oriented, founded on an optimism that the Good would prevail and energized by the Progressive spirit of an age not yet darkened by the horrors of World War I. In this sense the Emmanuel Movement was a part of the Social Gospel movement; Walter Rauschenbusch published the most complete treatment of these themes, *Christianity and the Social Crisis* (1907), only a year after the founding of the movement.

Priests and Psychologists Joining Forces

Worcester was born in Ohio in 1863. He was educated at Columbia University and thereafter at the General Theological Seminary in New York. He later earned a doctor of philosophy degree at the University of Leipzig, where he studied under the eminent psychologists Wilhelm Wundt and Gustav Fechner and wrote a thesis, "Opinions of John Locke."[13] As we shall see, Fechner had a marked influence on Worcester. Upon returning to the United States Worcester lectured on psychology and the history of philosophy at Lehigh University in Bethlehem, Pennsylvania. He was later ordained to the priesthood of the Episcopal church. After serving in Philadelphia for eight years, Worcester became the rector of the Emmanuel Church in Boston on July 1, 1904.[14]

Dr. Samuel McComb, a Northern Irishman, had extensive training in Ireland, Berlin, and Oxford. His background included psychology, though "less thorough-going than Dr. Worcester's," and theology. He had been a pastor of Presbyterian churches in England, Ireland, and New York City as well as a professor of ecclesiastical history at Queen's University in Kingston, Canada. Approximately a year after Worcester's arrival, McComb was invited to join the Emmanuel staff. He was also later ordained to the priesthood of the Episcopal church.[15]

Treatment Techniques

The Emmanuel Movement never saw itself as engaging in the practice of healing without the attendance of physicians. In fact an alliance with medical practitioners, as the movement had in its early days, was seen as critical not only to healing the patient but also to establishing credibility with the public, though the leaders never quite put it that way. Worcester stressed that "There is no attempt to usurp the prerogative of the physician." In his work, nonetheless, he sought "to unite the functions of the priest and the medicine man: it is a new form of specialization...." The new specialization, he said, consisted of a variety of practices and techniques, all with some value, "but not one that applies to all persons."[16]

The basic technique involved reaching a state of dissociation of the personality by some means so that the power of Christ-inspired teachings could be imparted. These might include "hope, good thoughts, kindness, courage."[17] Hypnosis was the central technique of suggestion, but by no means necessary: "The subconscious mind is also suggestible without hypnosis; that is, it is subject to moral influence and direction."[18] For some patients simple conversation, always calm and soothing, was a technique by which this necessary guidance or suggestion could be delivered. At times Worcester wavered on the degree of "suggestion" employed. In recounting an attempt to soothe a woman about to undergo a serious operation, he states that "I went with her to the hospital and talked to her soothingly for some time. Then I relaxed her, induced a moderate degree of abstraction, and suggested to her that she would have absolutely no fear of the operation, but that she would regard it as God's means to restore her to health, and that no matter how long she was under ether she would not be nauseated...she made a good recovery."[19]

Suggestion and auto-suggestion were not the only methods of the movement. Classes and meetings were important components of the treatment, as well as recommendations of the ever-popular rest cure. As Freud became more established in the United States, Worcester admitted the occasional use of "psycho-analysis," but did not allow it to overshadow his own use of suggestion.[20] But regardless of the specific technique employed, the basis of the "cure" was the power of Christian faith to bring about a sense of serenity. A worrier, for example, should recall the words of Christ: "Be not therefore anxious for the morrow, for the morrow will be anxious for the things of itself." But quick to add the scientific component, McComb adds to this prescription: "It is not a theologian but our leading American psychologist, Professor James, who says, 'The sovereign cure for worry is religious faith.'"[21] In the specific example of the worrier,

McComb adds that "the root of the worrier's misery is lack of self-control. His greatest need, therefore, is moral re-education with a view to the coordination of his powers and the concentration of them on some worthy end." The role of morality blends with the religious reference, both directed to the service of society, reminding us that the movement was yet a creature of the Progressive era.

A vital component of the Emmanuel Movement was the Weekly Health Conference. The conference predated the clinic work and, according to Worcester, was the source of the movement itself.[22] The dynamics of the health conference are of interest to those looking for influences upon A.A., and, as we shall soon see, the Jacoby Club. After all is said and done, the health conferences reveal a good deal of what we may simply call fellowship, but a type of fellowship that could have well led to the success of the Jacoby Club and the easy association of A.A. in Boston with that group.

According to Ray Stannard Baker, the conference was essentially an old-fashioned prayer meeting, but apparently it went far beyond that. Worcester mentions that people as far away as New York would attend, leaving in the early afternoon and returning back on the midnight train. The average attendance of the Wednesday night meetings was 800 persons, representing a wide geographical distribution, including some "from the West and South."

Worcester described a typical meeting in his second Emmanuel Movement article in the *Ladies' Home Journal*.[23] Meetings began with "five or six hymns, hymns that have a certain uplift and power," and the singing was hearty. After giving notices of one sort or another, greetings of encouragement were offered by the physicians or clergymen present. But the key appears to have been "prayer for ourselves and for one another," an activity that began by reading specific requests that were handed in prior to the service itself. (Worcester refers to the conferences as "services" throughout.) Worcester offers several examples, including: "'A man struggling against strong drink asks you to pray that he may overcome his temptation.' 'A young woman troubled by remorse and dread asks you to pray that she may have a sense of God's pardon and peace.'" Spontaneous prayers were offered, "simple and heartfelt...followed with close attention and often with deep feeling." Often there was silent prayer.

The rest of the conference followed the order of a church service: a lesson, "usually of the words of Jesus in a new translation, which brings their meaning out more clearly"; the Apostles' Creed, inviting those who could "conscientiously do so" to join the recitation; and the "address," which should be "short, earnest, practical, and, as a rule...pertaining to right thought and the conduct of life." According to Worcester, many people took notes. An offering followed, for the usual reasons of maintenance of the class but including help for the poor. Worcester adds that the class "from the beginning has been self-supporting and not a drain on the charities of the church." This emphasis on the group's financial independence prefigures the practices outlined in the A.A. Preamble.

The meeting began at eight and ended an hour later. After the formal service an "after-meeting" of fellowship took place. Worcester tells us that three or four hundred people moved out into the parish house, where they could mingle in the "large, airy and plainly furnished" rooms. Food and drink were served to background music furnished by a pianist and violinist. Worcester states that "The motive of this meeting is purely social" but that the "social spirit" which is involved "means more. I attach an almost religious significance to eating and drinking with those I love." Both Worcester and McComb were present at the gatherings. Toward the end of the meeting, which lasted approximately three-quarters of an hour, some "young folks frequently ask to be allowed to dance for a little while, a request that is willingly granted."

Worcester adds two important conditions for the after-meetings: "At the beginning I laid down two rules which I have never had occasion to modify: 1. 'Those who come must come in an amiable spirit. We meet here as brothers and sisters in Christ.' 2. 'You may talk about anything you choose here except sickness, but no word in regard to disease.'"

These conditions are especially meaningful when we compare the Emmanuel "after-meetings" to the meetings of the Oxford Group, often cited as the precursor to A.A. Worcester's conditions kept the focus on conviviality and casual socializing, but with a reminder of Christ. The exclusion of "disease" from the conversations may have been intended to eliminate personal confessions and attendant intimacies. The format of a church service, as well as the physical location of the meetings in a church and parish house, may have also kept the religious tone intact, if not dominant. As long as the Emmanuel Movement stayed focused on the Emmanuel Church, elaborate parties in the style of the Oxford Group did not threaten the integrity of the organization. The religious nature of the movement seemed to be foremost in the minds of its directors. The cure was important, but not at the expense of the underlying Christian purpose.

The Weekly Health Conference was of great importance in the Emmanuel Movement as a whole. Worcester states that it is "one of the most valuable instruments which we possess. It was not planned; it has grown up, little by little, to meet the needs of our people." According to him, some people benefited from these services and social meetings and required little else in the way of treatment for their ills. Others, who had received various treatments and "who have recovered from serious disorders," claimed that the Health Conference was as valuable as any other part of their treatment.

Worcester offers a basic explanation for the effectiveness of the Weekly Health Conference. The first reason is the power of prayer. But he quickly adds, almost to the point of amending the statement, that "When the human is calm and impressionable and open to all good influence, I believe that a higher Spirit, the Spirit of all goodness, enters us, takes possession of us, and leads us in better ways." This is an important point in that it reveals two recurring tendencies in the thinking of the Emmanuel Movement: an unflagging optimism, and the linking of psychology to religion, even in the matter of a church service.

Worcester seems to regard the service itself as a type of mild dissociation, or as he put it elsewhere, "a mild abstraction." The very dynamics of the group in the church setting, the unity of purpose, the effects of music, hymn singing and the like, all produce a state that allows the infusion of "good thoughts." This, of course, is not very much different from the type of psychological state that might be produced at other church services, including tent revivals. But for Worcester this is science in the service of religion, of his church, even though he uses the locution "higher Spirit," once again suggesting the future direction of A.A.'s spiritual development.

Worcester's explanation of the service's effectiveness also testifies to his spiritual optimism. The idea of the demonic side of faith does not enter into his thinking; it seems to be an impossibility given the conditions he has set forth in the meetings. His assumptions are clearly rooted in the necessity of a purity of purpose, of a higher Spirit that will enter into the parishioners. Optimism flows from his thought. This type of optimism is similar to that felt at an A.A. meeting and read about in its literature.

Worcester does, however, talk about what he refers to as "mass impression." This is the feeling the people experience during the church service: the unity of purpose, the very "association with other men and women and the electric influence" of that purpose and faith. He does add, in deference to a possible wrong outcome, that this experience is not to be confused with "a lawless and ungovernable mob spirit of strong excitement. Here there is no excitement, no fanaticism, no sensationalism, but earnest faith tempered by sober thought." We can only hope that it was so. But why this is the outcome and no other depends heavily upon Worcester's estimate of the situation. His faith that the conference members would be uplifted during the service, given the "mass impression," is either a testimony to his ability as a religious leader or his inability to see an alternate set of possible outcomes. Once again, the demonic is absent. The sinful nature of humankind is nowhere addressed. His faith in the power of a purity of purpose is dominant.

And so it was with his evaluation of the after-meetings. The success of these functions was attributed to the laughter, "kindliness and gaiety." Worcester paints a before/after picture of the nervous sufferer. Before the service the person is sad, indifferent to others, melancholy, what we might think of as a depressed person. The after picture, more properly "during," is that of a panorama of faces in the church or in the parish house, "bright," "animated," faces with "happy smiles." If nothing else Worcester seems to be telling us that a certain lightness of spirit did the nervous sufferers well, that fellowship was in many cases as valuable as other modes of treatment. The after-meeting was a valuable addition in the arsenal of techniques that would come to bear on the formation of A.A. and, more immediately, had a strong influence on the Jacoby Club, a self-help group for men that began meeting in the Emmanuel Church basement after 1909. There can be no doubt that something new had been added to the often grim business of therapy. Charges of naive optimism notwithstanding, the tone of ease and simple fun brings a splash of color to an otherwise drab business.

The Curse of Alcohol

Worcester and his associates considered alcohol to be one of the chief problems confronting them, although its pernicious effects were often linked to other maladies. For example, drunkenness was regarded as the leading predisposing cause of nervousness.[24] In *Body, Mind, and Spirit,* Worcester and McComb list alcoholism as one of "the four curses of mankind."[25] In the second Emmanuel Movement article for *Ladies' Home Journal,* Worcester listed 661 cases undertaken by the clinic in the past year and indicated the number of each diagnosis. The largest was neurasthenia with 189. "Unclassified" was second with 106 cases, followed by alcoholism with 44.[26] Worcester deals with alcoholism proper (he does use this word) in the fourth Emmanuel article of the *Journal* series, although the discussion is set in the context of an "evil habit." While it seems that habit is the major cause for alcoholism, Worcester does not rule out the role of heredity in alcoholism.[27] His review of the disease also includes the more medical view, such as "the diseased nerve cell."[28]

In *Religion and Medicine*, Worcester's account of treating alcoholism is briefer and less detailed than either in the *Journal* article or the much later *Body, Mind, and Spirit* (1931). His discussion of alcohol treatment in *Religion and Medicine* is upbeat, telling of the successes of hypnotic suggestion. The reasons for the successes are more apparent in *Body, Mind, and Spirit*, when Worcester lists three rules he maintained as preconditions for therapy. From our current perspective we can see why he might have succeeded when others did not by virtue of his insistence on these three: Patients must wish to stop drinking "of their own volition," not by the insistence of family; patients must "seriously propose to themselves total abstinence for life"; and patients must be sober during treatment. Otherwise, "advice communicated to him...produces no effect."[29]

Worcester elaborates on the second point a good deal. His insistence on lifelong abstinence extends to recommending, if not demanding, that family members "show their sympathy with him by sharing his lot and by also becoming total abstainers." If the patient fails, he warns, they must share the responsibility. In the *Journal* article, Worcester is emphatic on this point, stating that "a drunkard cannot learn to drink in moderation. His only safety lies in total abstinence."[30] Tellingly, Worcester did not start from this position. He originally advocated moderation, attempting to teach men to "drink like gentlemen," but quickly reversed his position when it failed.

Hypnosis is mentioned, but it is by no means the only method used.[31] The mainstay of the formal treatment is a combination of what Worcester calls "analysis," not a Freudian variety of course, and suggestion, which he calls "synthesis."[32] The psychic condition of the patient revealed problems that included a "sense of inferiority, maladjustment to life, and psychic tension," issues that normally would have required "treatment by analysis if they had not happened to find a very imperfect sublimation in alcoholism."[33] The process of analysis was of little use in removing the psychic conditions described above, and we are to believe of similar inefficacy concerning the issue of alcoholism proper. Suggestion, on the other hand, provided an "immediate help and permanent immunity from a return of the habit."[34] It is important to remember that suggestion did not necessarily mean hypnotism. For Worcester the inculcation of good habits, the crowding out of evil, as it were, was the real goal of the overall treatment. This portion of the treatment included simple talk and often only "mild abstraction."

Not by Therapy Alone: Allow God

The issue of habit as a major component of alcoholism invited the usual Emmanuel bifurcation of the problem: one part "the mental or moral, and the other physical."[35] The physical aspects of alcoholism as a bad habit, including its deleterious effects on the bodily and mental functions, were duly noted. But Worcester, ever the priest, was eager to take the battle into the realm of the moral and the religious. At this point Worcester made a key observation that would become a mainstay later on of the A.A. movement. He notes that by using suggestion (and one would assume analysis) in order to "attack undesirable habits on the plane which they live" we might eradicate the habit, "but until the evil tendency is destroyed at its roots we are still enslaved."[36] Worcester did not regard the end of the problem to be the conclusion of therapy. For Freud a complete analysis is the best we can hope for, but for Worcester we are still enslaved. The bottom line, so to speak, is not reached until we engage the spiritual dimension and change the heart of the person. The signing of pledges, the swearing of oaths, and the making of resolutions were all fruitless for Worcester until the person truly overcame evil with good. And the source of that good is God, through Jesus. True healing, then, is a matter of conversion.

"We must go down to the depths of our natures and uproot evil from the place where it lives." For Worcester a "relatively deep abstraction, a cessation of our ordinary mental processes" was necessary for this new life to enter the person and set his life on a new course. Immediately, psychology joins religion. Elsewhere, Worcester wrote that "I personally attach a religious importance to this state of mind."[37] The full force of this religious element was seen in the conversion experience itself, during which evil would be overcome by good. The effect, predictably, produced statements from patients that included: "Something has died in me, and something has been born within me. What has died has been the old habit, the old evil desire; what has been born has been a new life in God." Lest Worcester sound too much like a tent revivalist, he quickly added "This [the foregoing statement] is strictly in accordance with the suggestion given." He continues by informing the reader that he also includes a negative suggestion, one that we might call an aversion statement, in order to create a "distaste" for the habit in the mind of the patient.[38]

Worcester did not see the therapeutic process as the end in itself. Just as a physical rehabilitation of the person was needed, so was the psychic, the psychological component. But Worcester went beyond that by insisting upon the inclusion of the soul, and in no unimportant way. The spiritual dimension required nothing less than a type of conversion, a dedication to the good that was offered by Christ. Here is the element of powerlessness. The person, even with the aid of therapy, cannot achieve a state of sufficient power to resist the return to alcohol. The person and the therapist by themselves simply are not enough to conquer alcoholism. Not only is the treatment tripartite, but it includes an admission of the necessity of God, in Worcester's case a Christian God and his Son, Jesus.

Worcester was well aware that his patients might not stay free from alcohol. A new way of life, involving a total abstinence, was not easily achieved. Although at times he sounds naively optimistic, he was aware of the need for prayer and for continuing moral reeducation as a necessary part of rehabilitation. Worcester also acknowledged that the close degree of contact required between the pupil and the teacher, whether cleric or therapist, was problematic, and that the latter's personality and philosophy might be imposed on the patient.[39] He offered no explicit solution to this dilemma, but one might guess that he felt that further Health Conference meetings, associations with new people and places, and prayer would keep the person sober and on the right track.

The Emmanuel treatment also included an after-care component. Each patient received twelve blank cards "containing printed questions as to the most important facts of their present state," that is, pertaining to the person's specific illness. By responding to these, the person kept in touch with the clinic and provided feedback to the staff. A second aspect of after-care was urged on alcoholic patients. This is simply the second half of the Twelfth Step of A.A. In the words of the Emmanuel clinic it said "Saved thyself, save others. Having gained the farther shore, bring others over. Redeemed thyself, redeem. Having found peace, make peace."[40] Here is the A.A. slogan "Pass It On."

CHAPTER 2

THE EMMANUEL MOVEMENT: ACCEPTANCE AND SUCCESS

The Emmanuel Movement rose to its height with the publication of a series of six articles that appeared in the *Ladies' Home Journal* between October 1908 and March 1909. According to his autobiography, Worcester was reluctant to write the articles owing to the labor involved, but conceded to the insistence of the publisher.[41] The first article was not a part of the Emmanuel series itself, and was entitled "What Suggestion Can Do for Children" (October 1908). The Emmanuel articles were each entitled "The Results of the Emmanuel Movement" (November, December 1908; January, February 1909). The final article appeared in March 1909 and was entitled "The Emmanuel Church Tuberculosis Class." The series did much to promote the movement and produced, according to Worcester, over five thousand unsolicited letters requesting help, "to most of which I replied." He added that "These articles more than anything else, brought our work before the whole country."[42] By

1908 the movement had its own journal, *Psychotherapy*, and Worcester and McComb were active on the speaking circuit. By 1909 the Emmanuel Movement was instituted in New York, Cleveland, San Francisco, Detroit, Philadelphia, Baltimore, and Seattle.[43]

E. Brooks Holifield credits the Emmanuel Movement as the "first serious effort(s) to cure souls" in light of the new psychology synthesized by William James.[44] It was here that formal religion first tried to appropriate the new science of psychology, recognizing its usefulness in the mission of the church. For Donald Meyer, this meant "adding modern scientific psychology to the armamentarium of Protestant pastors," contributing to a marriage of psychology and religion that entered a crisis in the late 1950s.[45]

There is no doubt that Worcester and McComb began their work as a result of the rise of Christian Science.[46] Mary Baker Eddy experienced tremendous success and energetically expanded her own brand of religion into the realm of health. But New Thought and Christian Science, both healing and harmonial religions, using those terms loosely, were not Christian in the tradition upheld by Worcester. New Thought and Christian Science appropriated elements of Christianity as they saw fit.

A Spiritual Basis

The Emmanuel Movement was an attempt at establishing a new direction for the Christian mission as much as it was an accommodation and application of the rising science of psychology to an existing religious tradition. While it may be that psychology was being added to the arsenal of the Protestant minister, it is also true that Progressivism was a palpable force in the social mission of the church and that psychology was a vital tool not to be overlooked. Both Worcester and McComb were ministers with pastoral experience who "turned Emmanuel Church into a social settlement offering camps, clubs, and a gymnasium." The psychological component, that is, therapy, was an additional means of advancing the mission of the church.[47]

Worcester's religious dimension is apparent when he says, "As a student of the New Testament and of early church history, I knew that something valuable had been lost from the Christian religion, and that Christianity had not always been so unsuccessful in its appeal to human nature as it is now. What has been lost is chiefly Jesus Christ .... A sense of this loss brought me to the healing ministry of Jesus, in which we come most directly into contact with his personality, his compassion, his understanding of his mission."[48] Here we can see signs of Worcester's theological training and his exposure to the "higher criticism" of the Bible he undoubtedly encountered while a student at Leipzig. The minister does not concern himself with trying to defend all early Christian beliefs and practices, but rather with the essence of Jesus' central purpose. He states: "As a student of history and of human affairs, I was aware that a return to the first century, in either fact, knowledge or our outlook on life was impossible." Worcester sees that his mission is to "try, however humbly, to introduce a new conception into the life of the Church which would aim at combining the disposition and power of Jesus and a sense of the reality of the Spiritual world with the views and practices of modern science."[49]

In almost direct anticipation of future critics, Worcester states that the role of the church and the Emmanuel Movement is to examine the situation of its people and address their needs. He underscores the need for a powerful spiritual basis lest the church overemphasize the social work aspects of its mission. In the last portion of *Religion and Medicine* Worcester reviews the reasons humankind was "swept into the Church": "an ardent love, a living faith, the source of innumerable moral regenerations." He speaks of the "enormous sense of spiritual power" and how "he that was in Christ felt himself a new creature."[50]

The active dimension of charity in the Church—which for Worcester and his staff included working in the slums—was one of the distinguishing features of the Christian religion: "no sullen muttering about altruism can supplant divine love." Divine love translates into dealing with the reality that confronted the early church: "a colossal task in the reclamation of the sunken and in consoling the griefs of mankind."[51] Yet Worcester is aware of the dangers of the busy day-to-day routine of work, social or not. He states how the social movement in the Church "is not sufficiently personal, spiritual, and ethical. It [active social work] can change the environment, but as yet it seems to have no means of changing the heart." This leads to a "weariness of a continued sectarian existence," a condition that is with us but that can be overcome.[52]

The Role of Christ

The Christology of Worcester envisions a Jesus well suited to the Progressive movement, the liberal church, and the Emmanuel Movement. Jesus "united men in the only two points of view in which they can be united—in love and trust of a good God—and in affection to one another."[53] Worcester reminds the reader that Jesus toiled daily, "surrounded by human beings with human needs." This is not a reclusive Savior, not a contemplative. Revealing his breadth and scope, Worcester tells us that along with Kant, Jesus "declared the problem of the universe insoluble to speculative reason, but soluble to practical reason." The manner in which Jesus spent his time gives us the ethical dimension of life: "He had not thought except for the passing day, no care except for the sick, the sinful, the sorrowful, the seeker who claimed His every hour."[54]

Although few Christians would deny the social dimension of the life of Christ, the Emmanuel Movement viewed Christ in its own image. Neither Barton's businessman nor a self-absorbed follower of Trine, their Jesus was a man of action. But the Emmanuel Movement does what it hoped to avoid. In distilling the essence of Jesus as a man of charity and good works, the Emmanuelites begin to read into their view of Jesus, the image of a person who would better fit their own age, someone who would embody their sense of Christian action. Jesus provides the model of the healer who sees the unity of the mind and body, and exemplifies the "essential unity of human nature."

Whether these claims are true or not is not the task before us. What is interesting is the staunch Christian stand of the Emmanuelites even though this position reflects their will to see the unity of man in light of the science of psychology. Of course, there is nothing wrong with this, not in theory or in practice. It does, however, distinguish the Emmanuel Movement from aspects of New Thought and certainly Christian Science. The Emmanuelites are not asserting the unity of all life as emanating from God, or the existence of Divine Mind of which we are but specific instances or "individualizations," to use Meyer's term.[55]

Emmanuel and New Thought

For contemporary readers the insistence on the unity of body and mind and the rightful place of psychology in healing may seem like an exercise in the obvious. But this was in fact an attempt to distinguish the movement from various cult movements and what Worcester would regard as aberrant Christian beliefs. When Worcester says that "the plain truth is that the Church is not bringing the whole force of the Christian religion to bear upon the lives of the people," he is not simply pleading for more social action.[56] Rather, he is insisting that the spiritual dimension be realized along with the bodily, the physical. He sets his view of the "essential unity of human nature" against "the older materialism," Christian Science, and what Worcester refers to as the "so-called New Thought," which mistakenly represents the body as a "garment of the soul."[57]

Worcester and his colleagues were aware that the Emmanuel Movement was often placed by the side of the New Thought organizations and Christian Science,[58] and the comparison haunted the group from its inception. Parallels can be drawn, especially because various movements, cults, and denominations, influenced by similar forces, often overlapped and intersected. E. Brooks Holifield summarized some of the similarities between the Emmanuel Movement and New Thought. The parallels included counseling and lecturing in cities, places where people were "swept by social uncertainties." Both also depended heavily on "the cooperation of women," apparently to the extent that "some of the movement's critics charged that it was simply a ploy to attract neurasthenic women."[59]

On the ideological side, Holifield takes the Emmanuel Movement to task. Emphasizing ideological parallels to New Thought, Holifield first notes the movement's praise of writers such as Horatio Dresser and Ralph Waldo Trine. He then adds that "both movements were revolts against philosophical materialism" and "both promised health and harmony."[60] It is true, for example, that the New Thought books of Dresser, Wood, and Trine were regarded as "of inestimable value."[61] But Lyman Powell, an Emmanuel Movement practitioner in Northhampton, Massachusetts, whose *The Emmanuel Movement in a New England Town* was published in 1909, reminds the reader that the Movement is indeed in revolt against materialism, but by "evolution, not revolution." Further, he decries the "nebulous and invertebrate" theology of Christian Science and New Thought and chastens the New Thought practitioners for attempting to cure physical ailments with either words or insufficient medical knowledge.[62] But the fact that the Emmanuel Movement shared in the revolt against materialism and pursued health and happiness in no way establishes an ideological link. The association is coincidental, an association no doubt shared with other historical movements.

Holifield's second line of criticism is one with which we will have less disagreement, but it still needs qualification. This criticism maintains that Emmanuelites held "two conflicting visions of the healing power of nature." Nature could be either energy or resistance; one could benefit from its powers through either surrendering to or struggling against it. At one point Worcester and his associates suggest "relaxation," allowing the energies within the subconscious to express their power. But yet, they also tried to introduce positive thoughts, "healing suggestions," into the mind of the sufferer. Although not harsh, these exhortations were nonetheless a kind of moral lesson.

The issue of control or surrender cannot be avoided.[63] Is the true power of suggestion to influence and to change faulty ideas or to allow the true healing power of nature to prevail? At what point would rationality in the service of reeducating the mind clash with the healing power of nature? McCarthy makes a critical point in stating that New Thought wished to "control the world by controlling the mind." New Thought essentially wanted to crowd out evil and flood the mind with positive thoughts.[64] But importantly, Worcester regarded the unconscious as a repository of positive potentiality and "in a more traditional Christian way felt that the mind should be made open to beneficent spiritual influences from without."[65] Nevertheless the unconscious itself is not Divine; it is still an aspect of the creature, not the creator. And this critical link to Genesis (and Christian orthodoxy) keeps the Emmanuelites distinct from their New Thought neighbors.

The Positive Unconscious

Evidence of the positive nature of the unconscious, its beneficent nature, can be seen in Worcester's account of "sleeping on a problem." This is related to the idea that "sleep brings wisdom," as demonstrated by moments of inspiration when we finally hit upon a sought-after solution, and finally receive the burst of energy and insight to create as a "poet, philosopher, artist, composer, or writer of fiction." The Muse was really a "higher power" that can be distinguished from "the studied efforts of conscious reason."[66] We can only do so much, but can do more when we allow our subconscious to aid in the task. Similarly, the goodness of nature can be seen in the very tendency of the body to grow towards health and normality, "one of the accepted commonplaces of pathological investigation."[67] Apparently Worcester and McComb had not yet heard of entropy.

Such unrelenting optimism was in part a reflection of the age, which was experiencing what Ray Stannard Baker called "a great wave of idealistic philosophy," a hope that the materialists of the nineteenth century had had their day.[68] Although much of this spirit was based on the philosophy of Josiah Royce (1855-1916), a consideration of his thought would lead us in another direction. More to the point is a brief look at Gustav Fechner, who influenced both Worcester and William James.[69]

Gustav Fechner: Panpsychism

Gustav Theodor Fechner (1801-1887) was a German scientist and philosopher who is credited with at least two notable contributions: the founding of psychophysics and a strong defense of panpsychism. He was a pioneer in experimental psychology, although his psychological studies were intended to support his metaphysical views.[70] If nothing else, Fechner was a versatile thinker. He began his career studying electrical currents, later branching into the human perception of color and subjective afterimages. After recovering from a serious illness, Fechner developed a considerable interest in philosophy, particularly the task of refuting materialism. To this end he published a work arguing for nothing less than the mental life of plants.[71] This established the basis for his later belief in panpsychism.

Fechner's psychophysics attempted to empirically prove the unity of mind and matter: the two are different ways of regarding the same reality. He conducted a number of studies concerning physical stimuli and sensation as well as the perception of weight and distance. His work in perception later led him to explore aesthetics, seeking to subject this traditionally elusive area of philosophy to the rigors of science and empirical investigation. These studies resulted in his psychological laws of aesthetics. This was typical of Fechner's general approach, that is, to reconcile diverse aspects of reality to the scientific method as he understood it.

Fechner's most notable contribution for our purposes was in his panpsychism, for it is here that his influence on both James and Worcester can be most clearly seen. His basic view initially sounds like New Thought, but Fechner's ideas belong to his own unique system. The universe is comprised of spiritual reality. Even atoms are spiritual and are the basic elements that lead up to God. The material world that we see is but "the external manifestation of this spiritual reality." Only certain "systems," which he called "organic wholes," possess souls. "God is the soul of the universe." He referred to the earth as "our mother," an organic whole with a soul of its own.[72] It is important to note that, by and large, consciousness is an aspect of all that exists. His qualifications of this statement become rather technical.

Fechner paints a picture of a nonmaterialistic universe that is alive with spirit and consciousness. His view of the universe is decidedly friendly, as contrasted to the materialist's universe of cold and soulless matter. He referred to his view of the spirit-infused universe as the "daylight view," as opposed to the "night view." At this point Fechner attracted the interest of James and, one can presume, Worcester. Fechner asserted that the "daylight view" of life and the universe is the preferred option. He maintained that any hypothesis that cannot be proven but which does not contradict scientific evidence ought to be accepted if it produced happiness. Lest we construe Fechner as less than rigorous, we should add that he supported his position with various analogical arguments. But his reasoning bears a strong resemblance to James's pragmatism, notably the Will to Believe.

Just how Fechner's position meshes with any version of Christianity does not concern us here. It seems reasonable to assume that Fechner did in fact influence Worcester's ideas of the unity of body, mind, and spirit.[73] But Fechner may also have been the source of Worcester's almost stubborn optimism and his avoidance of the question of evil—tendencies that contributed to his disfavor within the church and the demise of the Emmanuel Movement. Worcester avoided theodicy, the reconciliation of the existence of evil in the world with God's infinite perfection and goodness. While Worcester and the Emmanuel Movement, unlike many competing "cults," did acknowledge pain and suffering, the reasons for the existence of this evil never entered into their writing.

Optimism over Evil

Despite the "Boston craze" and easy associations with one cult or another, the Emmanuel Movement maintained its identity and its distinctive Christian orientation. Although Worcester and his associates maintained their close associations with the leading neurologists and psychologists, they were unwavering in their ethical and spiritual orientation: "Our work is essentially ethical and spiritual. Our chief interest in the men and women who seek our care is a moral and religious interest. In other words, we desire not merely to give them temporary relief, but to do them permanent good, to open to them the possibility of a new life, not merely to restore them to health but to give them motives for living."[74]

This openness to the Divine, while acknowledging the life of the sufferer, affirmed the traditional separateness of the creature and creator of traditional Christianity. This underlying distinction is a critical difference between the Emmanuel Movement and other varieties of New Thought.[75] New Thought needed to bridge the gap to eliminate a Willful God, a Sovereign Creator. The mysterious powers of God were removed in New Thought, an idea that the Emmanuel Movement, for all its problems, could not allow.

New Thought explained evil away by claiming it was illusory or a symptom of negative thinking, insisting that we simply had a wrong picture of the truth. Evil and pain were things that tested us when we did not completely apprehend the fullness of the good. Sinfulness was related to making mistakes; in fact "sin" and "mistake" became well-nigh synonymous.[76] But for the Emmanuel Movement pain and suffering did exist, under the power of God. Once again, operating from its traditional Christian stance, the Emmanuel Movement could see good conquering evil, the power of Christ prevailing over Darkness. Certainly no Manicheans, Worcester and McComb were confident in the triumph of good. Far from living in Freud's metaphorical murky cellar of horrors, the Emmanuelites saw only greater possibilities through science, a study governed and directed by their religious views. "Does not the whole moral and religious life of man testify to the existence of unseen spiritual powers which are friendly to us? Such unquestionably was the belief of Christ."[77]

Worcester adds that we will discover the mechanical aspects of this Power through science first, as he believed science was indeed accomplishing in his time. The second aspect of the Power would come in the future, "so our moral and spiritual life is destined to be evermore profoundly transformed. We shall learn the secret of Christ's personal life." As if this promise were not enough, Worcester assures us that the future discoveries will bring us a "a faith which opens our heart to the universe" and "possession of an inward peace which the world cannot take from us…."[78] Later on the same page of *Religion and Medicine*, Worcester expounds on the practical application of suggestion techniques on a sleeping child, as it would remove "many childish faults and nervous weaknesses." This is pointed out not to disparage Worcester, but rather to illustrate how the book is written on a wave of religious fervor followed by a trough of practical application. But the whole rhythm is one of sincerity, commitment, and deep belief. All this is underscored by an unwavering optimism.[79]

It is this combination of attitudes and beliefs that constitutes the Emmanuel Movement's answer to evil and suffering. Adherents did not doubt the existence of these aspects of life, they simply assumed that good would prevail and that the action of the day was to imitate Christ in the prompt and efficient healing of the ills that surrounded them. Not unlike the liberals, or later Harry Emerson Fosdick, they wished to take on evil as they saw it, but assumed that the task can be accomplished by a set program, their eclectic approach notwithstanding.

But their optimism engendered a set of problems that brought opposition to the Emmanuel Movement in theological circles. As with the liberals before and after them, the Emmanuelites felt the power of Christ but ignored the passion of Gethsemane. They slighted the Cross, the doubt, the agony. There is no place for Christ's words: *"Eloi, Eloi, lama sabachthani?"* (Mark 15) Theirs was a religion of certitude that offended the orthodox with its system and its program. Sin was treated ambiguously at best. Was it a malady to be cured? Or was it an aspect of humankind that would eventually be overcome through a better environment?

A more Old Testament view would see the sins of a hubristic Israel in the face of a demanding God. The Emmanuelites took their position too much for granted. The cries of the prophet were not heard, only the triumphal joy of the saved. But the doubts that necessarily accompany faith have no place in the Emmanuelite world. If doubts persisted, there might be a therapeutic solution: suggestion, or autosuggestion, or class instruction. Perhaps these criticisms are too much an interpretation and anachronistic in that they reflect some of the later neo-orthodox thinking, similar to Reinhold Niebuhr's criticisms of the Social Gospel. There were more specific criticisms in Worcester's own time.

Detractors and Decline

Worcester and his associates were anything but insensitive to the criticisms that they would inevitably draw. Soon after the publication of *Religion and Medicine* (1908), the press coined the term "The Emmanuel Movement" and controversies ensued. He writes, "All of this was surprising and most distasteful to us."[80] Because Worcester and McComb did not fit the usual stereotype of "faith healers," their work stimulated curiosity on the part of the press. As Worcester further notes, he and McComb had no choice but to let the news and public interest run its course.[81]

Just what would constitute this interest was no doubt a source of displeasure. For one, there were accounts of Worcester raising a woman from the dead, all stemming from the wish of the "sensational press" to see the movement as an "unending source of weird stories and of caricature."[82] Worcester was aware of these difficulties and wondered how they as a group would be able to sustain the criticism and "abuse" except by "the Spirit of God." Throughout he was aware of his pastoral responsibilities to the Emmanuel Church and was "anxious that the parish should suffer no injury from our new interests. So I threw myself with redoubled enthusiasm into my parochial duties."[83] In spite of this, the Emmanuel Church parishioners and Bishop William Lawrence of Boston remained cool towards the movement, although they did allow him to continue to use the church as a headquarters for this work.[84] And there were theological criticisms, some of which stemmed from theological positions of the sort already mentioned, while others were more particular to the age.

Holifield points out that the Emmanuel associates were moving in a direction in which the individual was invited to trust in the creative forces of nature as a "precondition of the active assertion of the will." Whereas the early days of the Emmanuel Movement itself had relied upon mild exhortations, "masculine" advice, the later days of the movement were headed more and more into the darker workings of the subconscious. Indeed, Worcester himself stated his inclinations: "the first half of the twentieth century promises to be mystical and spiritual. Already we are conscious of a general revolt in the name of the soul."[85] But this direction for Worcester would move in the direction of automatic writing and the dynamics of prayer.[86] For his contemporaries, sinfulness and sin, in various conceptualizations, were to gain the attention of the church leaders.[87] The point is that the belief and interest in a positive and beneficent subconscious out of which an optimistic outlook could flourish was losing ground.

Specific theological criticisms of the Emmanuel Movement in the early years of the twentieth century were more or less diffuse, coming from a more general questioning of the mixing of religion and medicine.[88] Another line of criticism leveled the charge of "hedonism" at the movement, the idea that one should not seek too much relief from pain lest this counter resignation to the will of God.[89] The Rev. Dr. Robert MacDonald, although himself an Emmanuel practitioner from Brooklyn, criticized his fellow Emmanuelites for downplaying the evil in the human soul too much, and with that, neglecting the need for a divine atonement for human sinfulness: "The Emmanuel Movement knows nothing about and cares less for either original sin, or any other such theoretical redemption."[90]

A rather well-publicized remark came from the Rev. Dr. George Gordon, a minister in one of Boston's more prominent churches. Gordon apparently referred to Worcester and McComb as "two crazy fools" in a sermon that was covered by one of the papers. The Rev. Gordon later apologized, stating that he meant "loons," not "fools." Worcester later wrote that this correction "made little difference" to him because he knew that Gordon was not a sportsman and would not know the true nature of the loon "as one of the cleverest and most socially minded of birds."[91] Worcester was a dedicated outdoorsman and indeed would have known and appreciated this fact.

The charge of shallowness of thought that is often brought against the movement is perhaps best summarized by a quote from Josiah Royce: "Whoever, in his own mind makes the whole great world center about the fact that he, just this private individual, once was ill and now is well, is still a patient."[92] Cunningham, in his article in the *American Quarterly*, adds the more general skepticism of William James towards "systematic healthy-mindedness" as another kind of criticism brought against the Emmanuel Movement.[93] These charges were yet slight compared to the attacks that arose from the medical profession.

During his visit to the United States, Freud's comments regarding the Emmanuel Movement did not do any immediate damage but were one of the first open statements of the doubts that had already started in the medical profession. These doubts were to prove more troublesome than those coming from the theological arena, as previously discussed. Freud's comments were published in an interview in the *Boston Evening Transcript*, September 11, 1909, reported by Adelbert Albrecht. The article was in keeping with the new journalistic interest in matters pertaining to psychotherapy, psychoanalysis being the latest "news" in that area.[94] Freud predicted that the popularity of the Emmanuel Movement would soon abate and that there was a certain danger in having men "without medical, or with very superficial medical training" practicing in an area with "many physicians who have been studying modern methods of psychotherapy for decades…." Continuing, Freud was not surprised that the combination of church and psychotherapy had wide appeal. He attributed this to the sense of mystery "and the mysterious" which he apparently believed was fostered by the association of psychotherapy with the religious. People are always attracted to the mysterious. Alas, ever the skeptic, Freud maintained that psychotherapy had "absolutely nothing mysterious about it."[95]

Despite the fact that Worcester always claimed to be linked to the medical profession with the best of relations, this situation was never exactly stable. The movement maintained ties with physicians, Worcester's early associations with Dr. Joseph H. Pratt in their tuberculosis work being most notable. *Religion and Medicine* itself was co-authored with Dr. Isador H. Coriat. The series of addresses that were given in the parish house in November, 1906, to begin their new work with the "nervous," featured well known medical doctors, in addition to Worcester's assurance that they did not wish to intrude into the physician's work.[96] The first speaker was the notable Dr. James J. Putnam, professor of neurology in the Harvard Medical School. The second speaker was Dr. Richard C. Cabot, who later served as one of the movement's medical advisers.[97] But this early relationship with the medical community rested upon the role of the clergy in the moral and ethical guidance of the patients. There was more or less a clear distinction between the medical treatment and the moral, that is, religious. As Worcester and McComb became more interested in psychotherapy as a technique, this clear distinction became blurred and criticisms from the medical profession became more frequent and more intense.[98]

As the movement extended beyond the Emmanuel Church and its popularity grew, so did criticisms and the concerns of psychotherapy being placed in the hands of any and all clergy. The public seemed to approve of Worcester and McComb and their immediate Boston associates, but as more people began to try their methods, doubts arose and confidence eroded. "The great majority of the medical profession felt that the extension of the Emmanuel methods was highly undesirable. To their genuine fear lest the standards of the therapeutic art be lowered, was added, perhaps in many cases, the fear of losing patients."[99] Added to this was the possible loss of professional status that affected physicians who were associated with the movement.

Dr. James J. Putnam attempted to disassociate himself from the movement in a letter to the *Boston Sunday Herald* in 1908. He wrote, "I consider the whole affair an injury to the progress of scientific medicine, especially to neurology, and to the intelligence which made possible the recent discoveries in this delicate branch of medical science." His other points included the possibility of clergymen less trained than Worcester in psychology becoming involved in psychotherapy.[100] For at least one observer, the cause of the eventual demise of the Emmanuel Movement was directly related to the struggle between physicians and ministers of the church: "back of it all lies a real struggle of the two professions to attain a greater influence over the lives of men."[101] The more aggressive medical profession made great advances in the science of therapy as well as promoting its use through a variety of university programs. In this sense, the church-based movements were crowded out of the market. Further, the medical profession was not convinced that the role of the religious in therapy was sufficiently justified. In fact, "the movement had irritated them."[102]

Perhaps because the issue of psychotherapy itself was beginning to be accepted, the press began to lose interest in the Emmanuel Movement, and by 1911 it had disappeared from public view. Magazines had ceased to be interested and "little or no serious reference to the work was to be found."[103] Greene adds that the decision of Worcester and McComb to avoid controversy was a second reason why the heat of publicity was off. Nonetheless, the work went on, though without the tumult of the earlier years. In 1912 Courtenay Baylor joined the Emmanuel staff, and the movement became more involved with working with alcoholics.

To ensure that the Emmanuel Movement existed after Worcester's retirement, Baylor and Worcester founded the Craigie Foundation in 1925, established as an organization that would carry on the movement's work independent of Emmanuel Church. Worcester retired from the church as rector in October, 1929. He continued his health work with the Foundation, in addition to authoring *Body, Mind and Spirit* with McComb, an update of *Religion and Medicine*, and an acknowledgment that his earlier psychological principles had been refined. In 1932 he wrote his autobiography, *Life's Adventure*, and a year later wrote *Making Life Better: An Application of Religion and Psychology to Human Problems*, essentially a popularization of his previous work.[104] Worcester died in 1940, and the movement apparently dissipated soon thereafter.

The Emmanuel Movement and A.A.

There is little doubt that the contributions of the Emmanuel Movement were significant in terms of the formulation of Alcoholics Anonymous. If nothing else, the widespread public notice which the movement had received had strengthened belief in the connections between body, mind and spirit, and in fact had helped save this idea from the disrepute that various mind-cure movements and revivalists had cast upon this approach to health. The idea of alcoholism as an illness gained ground, the movement adding to the later A.A. supposition that alcoholism is not a moral failing. Yet, Worcester and his associates did emphasize the moral and ethical dimension, tied to religious commitment in no small way. The Weekly Health Conferences of the Emmanuel Movement, complete with their "after-meetings," established the role of friendship, fellowship and joviality as a part of the total therapeutic package. While perhaps A.A. would not want to regard fellowship as "therapy," there is little doubt that it serves this vital function for the suffering person. The immediate offshoot of the movement, the Jacoby Club, was the direct beneficiary of the fellowship component.

While the relationship between the Emmanuel Movement and the medical profession was strained at best, there were ties established between therapy and religion, and, for the alcoholic, between the illness and medical treatment.[105] In employing Courtenay Baylor as a specialist in therapy with alcoholics, the movement took another step toward the serious professional treatment of the alcoholic, saving the suffering person from quackery, irresponsible experimentation, and further degradation.[106] The movement's direct legacy therefore includes both the work of Baylor and his student, Richard Peabody, as well as the Jacoby Club.

CHAPTER 3

THE CONTINUATION OF THERAPY: COURTENAY BAYLOR AND RICHARD R. PEABODY

Courtenay Baylor

Courtenay Baylor began working with Elwood Worcester in the Emmanuel Movement in 1912, focusing on alcoholism—a field, according to Worcester, "in which he has no equal."[107] In 1925 the two men founded the Craigie Foundation to continue the movement's work after Worcester's eventual retirement from the church. The physical headquarters of the movement now became 176 Marlborough Street, "five doors from our dwelling [the rectory], a beautiful and perfect house exactly adapted to our needs."[108] Worcester explained that he and Baylor decided to change the name, since the press had coined the term Emmanuel Movement to begin with.[109] Worcester and his associates had long since tired of the controversies surrounding his work, and the new name might shelter them from linkage with that in any future publicity.[110]

Baylor first consulted with Worcester for his own problems in 1911, and the following year joined in the doctor's service. He was a worldly and successful businessman, but came to feel that his life had been changed, that he had acquired a new life and a new attitude.[111] Baylor stayed with Worcester out of a desire to help others as he had been helped. Worcester apparently never regretted accepting his offer. In his autobiography he praises Baylor for "his originality, his psychological insight, and his extraordinary ingenuity as a teacher." He adds: "His strength lies, partly, in his ability to impart his wholesome philosophy of life so unobtrusively as to arouse no opposition. In a short time the pupils begin to announce his principles as their own convictions."[112] Baylor's greatest successes were with alcoholics, but Worcester also cites his abilities in "adjusting and arranging marital infelicities"; he may well have been one of the first paid marriage counselors.

Remaking a Man: Baylor's Reasons for the Book

The primary source for Baylor's thought and work is his 1919 book, *Remaking a Man: One Successful Method of Mental Refitting*. Baylor makes several qualifications regarding his own credentials, tied to his purpose in writing the book, and defends his and Worcester's past work as having achieved very positive results. In the book's foreword he apologizes for not using the latest "technical vocabulary" and hopes that this will not be held against him. His hope is that his "method and results" will not be overlooked because of his layman's vocabulary. Baylor then gives his reasons for writing the book. These reasons help place Baylor in the changing context of therapy and illustrate both the parallels and the differences between his ideas and those of the later A.A. movement.

First, Baylor wishes to tell us about his methods to establish the claim that "it is logical, legitimate, ethical, and safe for one who has *no medical or surgical knowledge* and who has *no psychological degree* [my italics] to do a certain type of psychological work in conjunction with skilled physicians," provided that person has sufficient competence and experience in dealing with "certain types of neuroses."[113] He offers the parallel to the soldier who receives his officer's commission in the field ("the practical school") and deserves a place alongside those officers with "theoretical training." Second, Baylor wants the book to provide instruction for the "practical application" of his methods, for either helping others or for self-help. Finally, Baylor wants to "to suggest to the physicians in authority" a method for treating returning soldiers who might be suffering from "shell-shock" or other "neurotic conditions" that resulted from "war-strain."

Baylor's first reason was enough to ensure the medical profession's continuing animosity over the Emmanuel Movement's intrusions in the medical arena. Baylor's wording was imprudent at best, though today we might term it insensitive, with regard to the Emmanuel Movement's precarious position vis-à-vis the medical establishment. With the rise of Freudianism and other new medical and scientific theories about the causes and proper treatment of mental disorders, and the concern of the physicians over their own professional image, this statement was likely regarded as nothing less than a challenge to battle. It bore out the medical profession's worst fears with regard to the spread of the Emmanuel Movement, namely the rise of hordes of untrained practitioners. While Baylor was safely under the wing of Worcester, the latter's status as a clergyman and hence a trained professional (even if of a different kind) kept the debate concerning their lack of medical or psychological credentials from escalating.

The further reasons he gives for writing the book might be considered presumptuous in light of the first reason. Baylor, while tipping his hat to "physicians in authority," still assumes, fully confident, that his method will be of use to the medical doctors. But as with the first reason, he allows for others to use the method on what might seem to be a casual basis in order to help others, or even worse, for self-administered help. Once again, the professionalism of the medical profession is compromised. Unqualified (that is, uncredentialed) people were literally being invited to use his therapeutic methods without professional direction.

Baylor did establish evidence, however contested, that therapy could succeed without the direct supervision of medical doctors or even formally trained psychologists—with important implications for the development of A.A. later on. For better or worse, Baylor did his part in making the Emmanuel Movement a success, however limited in duration. Regardless of the continued development of new treatment methods by the psychologists and the medical establishment (including the rise of the controversial new Freudian theories), Worcester and Baylor's work would remain an annoyance, proving in its own fashion that therapy was possible without the formal training the medical profession would come to demand and cherish. Even worse, the Emmanuelites were talking about self-help. The later Alcoholics Anonymous movement would elevate this idea to the level of a fundamental principle: the A.A. Twelve Traditions would state unequivocally that their own system of self-help "should remain forever non-professional."

A last point should be made. It is difficult to tell whether Baylor's conviction that alcoholism was just another form of neurosis was a positive step or not; it can be debated either way. But it is reasonable to assume that his putting this idea in print was an important part of the process of removing the moral degeneracy stigma that had been so firmly attached to alcoholism. A moral degenerate deserved only punishment of the most severe sort, whereas a neurotic was someone who was ill and who needed a kind of treatment that was designed to heal that illness. Baylor was in this way an important precursor of Mrs. Marty Mann (the first woman to obtain long-term continuous sobriety in A.A.), who later on formed the National Council on Alcoholism to propagate the disease concept of alcoholism on a nationwide basis, and devoted her life to the attempt to further remove the stigma attached to pathological drinking.[114]

The Therapy: Concepts and Technique

A main reason why Baylor could so boldly distance himself from the medical profession was based upon the very nature of this method and his attendant self-regard. For Baylor the task that lay before him as a therapist was not a matter of what we would today call "hard science." Rather, for Baylor, therapy was "more than a science; it is also an art" (24).[115]

Just why Baylor's adaptation of the Emmanuel-style therapy was an art involved his key notions of the process itself. The explication of this process is the major subject matter of *Remaking a Man*, first the concepts involved, then some of his actual techniques. The book concludes with a section titled "Illustrative Cases." Throughout his explanation Baylor underscores the necessity of working with the patient closely, by first getting to know his "alcoholic environment," which meant his background as well as his thinking processes. The therapist and the patient will get to know each other and eventually will be thinking at the end in tandem, as the artful process of therapy unfolds (63).

Baylor's beginning point is the assumption of an underlying "alcoholic neurosis." But this neurosis is fundamentally no different from the one experienced by the non-alcoholic neurotic (4). In fact, shell-shocked soldiers share this state with the alcoholic. The actual taking a drink is "a temporary but recurrent mental condition" which is best understood as "a combination of wrong impulses and a wholly false, though plausible, philosophy" (7). The drink, then, is but a symptom, no matter how powerful and devastating it may be. The actual taking the drink is a loss of reason, a type of seizure of the mind, which Baylor calls a "tenseness." In this moment there is a "peculiar shifting and distorting and imagining of values." The state of "tenseness" is in a metaphorical way a type of demonic possession, overthrowing one's true nature and true self. It is the old story of Dr. Jekyll's mind suddenly being taken over by the destructive alter-ego of Mr. Hyde.

Underlying the alcoholic neurosis, then, is the patient's dual system of values. There is always a "secondary and false philosophy," composed of different and destructive values that are ready to replace the normal operating system of the sober individual. Given the tenseness, given the drink, the "false philosophy" will prevail. This conflict is always there, just not evident—most of the time. But this tension-producing conflict does reside within the individual and is evident even with moderate drinking. In these instances, the observer can see Mr. Hyde and his alternate view of the world for a short period of time. However, with regular drinking the "false philosophy" gradually replaces the normal system of values completely. The alcoholic philosophy may include what A.A.'s refer to as "stinking thinking," that is, a destructive way of attempting to deal with one's current life problems, based on resentment and rage and self-pity. But in Baylor's sense it no doubt included much more. The alcoholic philosophy refers more to a self-concept, a set of attitudes that include the rituals of drinking, coupled with a certain amoral system which places the individual at the center of the universe, thereby allowing the usual moral laxity that accompanies the "drinking life." Abandoning this whole mindset will require the science and art of the therapist, first to relax the patient, and then to re-educate him. The relaxation will remove the condition which gives rise to the seizures of tenseness that allow wrong values to prevail.

In that Baylor describes "mental tenseness" as the "underlying cause of the neurotic condition" (29), his task is to remove it permanently. He is careful to point out that the "relaxed state" is not a state of "mere limpness." While it is the opposite of tenseness, "relaxation to me suggests a combination of suppleness, vitality, strength, and force.... It is always the condition behind good work, physical or mental" (20-21). Baylor points out that successful athletes, musicians, writers and so on are at their best when they are relaxed and able to "coordinate all their powers." For Baylor, the relaxed person is at the apex of the human condition, functioning fully and functioning well. In that state of mind, the person will be able to recognize the danger signals and avoid tenseness. In order to do this the patient must be "re-educated in his whole mental process so as to know how to recognize and dissolve certain tendencies at their very inception…for it is only by doing this that he can prevent the recurrence of his tenseness" (21).

The re-education portion of treatment sounds as if it were straightforward Emmanuel-style therapy. The first task is to induce relaxation, then to re-educate. "It is of little avail to feed logic to a tense mind, for such a mind cannot digest it" (22). The real "psychological work" of re-educating "is done though logical analysis and explanation and definite instruction." This is what Baylor states "might be called the inspirational phase of the treatment." Whereas Worcester elaborates on the Spirit and the Divine at this point, Baylor quietly writes on without using any heavily religious language, stating the importance of giving the neurotic "a new point of attention, a new philosophy of life, and new courage with which to face life" (23). The point here was to focus on the good, bringing a kind of generalized natural goodness to the forefront of the person's life. Alcohol was not a thing to be avoided; it would simply fall from its primary place in a person's consciousness when supplanted by a positive attitude and value system.[116] Free from his "false philosophy," he can look forward to the day when "those things which seem to be problems to him in his illness will cease to be anything more than mere incidents of life" (18). The reader who is familiar with the A.A. Big Book will recognize in the foregoing a similarity to one of the Twelve Promises given there: "We will intuitively know how to handle situations which used to baffle us." We will have more to say in this area in a moment.

Baylor reflects some of Freud's insights throughout his book, knowingly or not. His description of the relationship of the patient to the therapist shows awareness of what the Freudians called the transference process. And in another section Baylor reminds us that the patient is not all that willing to give up his illness, that is, there will be what the Freudians called resistance. A feature of the neurotic condition, he reminds us, is the lack of any genuine desire to "reach a point of complete normality" (17). The patient is not completely willing to let go of his "false philosophy" or "dream-values." The person when relaxed will freely acknowledge the foolishness of his false values, yet is capable of succumbing to them once again if tenseness returns and "gains control of his brain" (16). However, once the patient recognizes that he is hiding behind his illness, not unlike a reluctant convalescent, "recovery can become rapid" (17). The game-playing of wanting a "cure" but not wishing to let go of the "old ways" is familiar enough to the recovering alcoholic. The reluctance to completely surrender is so critical a step that it can never be easy to carry out. In a slightly different way, Baylor seems to realize the nature of these dynamics completely.

By the time Baylor was writing *Remaking a Man* (1919), an awareness of Freud's theories was clearly beginning to be felt within some medical circles and in Boston in particular. Freud had made his famous trip to America in 1909, ten years before Baylor wrote this book, and had given his much-publicized lectures at Clark University in Worcester, Massachusetts, which was close enough to Boston to allow influential people like the Harvard psychologist and philosopher William James to attend.

There is certainly the possibility of a generalized Freudian influence that could have affected Baylor on some of these issues. We can observe some of these possible linkages but must not overemphasize them.[117] There were many other competing models and systems at that time in addition to Freudian psychoanalysis: Freud himself characterized the principal competing groups as the psychoanalysts, the neurologists, the psychiatrists, and the psychotherapists (as he called them), four fundamentally different kinds of systems, all making different claims and utilizing different methodologies.[118] Even more importantly, despite passing similarities in places to some of Freud's concepts, Baylor's therapy remained solidly Emmanuelite at the most basic level.

Baylor and Worcester: Whither God?

One of Baylor's basic presuppositions came directly from Worcester's thinking, which should not be surprising. Simply put, this assumption was that something has gone wrong in the mind of the patient that has caused what we might call a "problem," either in thought, attitude, or some form of aberrant behavior. The patient will correct the problem not by virtue of psychology alone, or medicine alone, but rather by being placed in a state or condition that allows *something else positive* to replace it. For Worcester this will involve the subconscious, and will ultimately be connected to religion. As noted earlier, Worcester wavers between letting the Spirit reach the patient in a passive way, and taking a more active role and "suggesting" or "educating" the person with regard to correct and moral views. But in any event, a religious dimension is present.[119] For Baylor, the *something else positive* that replaces the old destructive ideas, attitudes, or behaviors is discussed much more vaguely, the subconscious not being used as a category, and the religious element being mentioned hardly at all.[120] But in both cases re-education in one form or another remains a key factor in therapy. While Worcester ultimately centers his transformation on the power of the Spirit, making references to the Divine, Baylor's *Remaking of Man* mostly ignores that element, despite some occasional passing references to the "inspirational phase" and the necessity of a spiritual element. The power of the transformation in most of the book is scarcely identified as anything more than the power of the therapist.

Baylor did not however ignore what he called "the spiritual element" when considering his reasons for failing to get a patient to respond. The failure is the result of Baylor's inability to get the "attention" of the patient so that he will see the need for "prompt relaxation" and the "immediate elimination of wrong tendencies at their very inception" (68). The failures were hopeless for all intents and purposes. In each case they involved patients who lacked the true desire to change their lives and had no "spiritual element out of which to build such a desire." Or they had an "actual mental defect," or, worse, their illness was "so-deep seated " and their "spiritual side so buried" that the treatment methods were ineffective. Only an inordinate amount of personal attention might get through to these persons. Since this was not possible, they were among the lost souls. But the important consideration is Baylor's admission of the term "spiritual," at least in this context, so that at this level at least he recognized the necessity of referring to some spiritual dimension in describing his methodology for the total "remaking" of the person.

The Emmanuel Movement (from Worcester to Baylor) and Alcoholics Anonymous

The following list summarizes some of the main parallels between the principles and beliefs of the Emmanuel Movement and those of the later Alcoholics Anonymous movement:

1. The introduction of a formal program of therapy to the treatment of alcoholism. A positive stance toward modern "science" and its medical and psychological contributions, and reference to alcoholism as a disease.
2. The paradigm of full health as involving the necessary healing of spirit (and mind) as well as the body, producing a linkage between science and religion.

3. The use of therapists who are not medical doctors. The introduction of the idea that medical doctors are not necessary in the treatment of alcoholism (apart from the treatment of the obvious physical aspects of the disease).
4. An opposition to some presuppositions of Freudian psychology, especially the avoidance of any great emphasis upon discovering the deeply buried subconscious "causes" of the illness.
5. The patient is "mainstreamed" by not being singled out as worse than other neurotics or "nervous sufferers."
6. The role played by the Spirit, including actual reference to a "higher spirit."
7. The positive role of prayer in recovery.
8. The weekly health conferences, used as group sessions for the formation of fellowship among recovering people as a value in therapy.
9. The emphasis on positive living as opposed to the mere avoidance of alcohol alone.
10. The emphasis on the need for those under treatment to develop a total plan for living, a new philosophy.
11. The importance of after-care, including work with peers in recovery, and continued attendance at weekly health conferences.
12. The role of the family and other aspects of the "environment" in overcoming the illness.

Given these many overlapping themes, it should come as no surprise that Baylor, in his later years, attended an A.A. meeting "and loved it," enthusiastically recommending it.[121] Perhaps Baylor's most prominent patient-turned-lay therapist, however, deviated from many of Baylor's ideas. Richard Peabody took the Emmanuel tradition in a very different direction.

Richard R. Peabody, Child of Boston Society

In one sense Richard Rogers Peabody belongs to the Emmanuel Movement by virtue of lineage. Just as Baylor was Worcester's patient, so was Peabody a patient of Baylor. Peabody no doubt played an important role in the formation of A.A., especially as a contemporary of Bill Wilson and his wife Lois, both of whom had read[122] Peabody's *The Common Sense of Drinking*.[123] But the connecting thread to the Emmanuel Movement stretches thin and eventually breaks, leaving him with his own contributions to the larger movement of treating alcoholics.

Richard Peabody was born into wealth and privilege, distinguishing himself from the more modest backgrounds typical of Emmanuel patients, however relative this may be.[124] Peabody graduated from Groton preparatory school and later attended Harvard, but did not complete a degree. The Rev. Endicott Peabody, his uncle ("Uncle Cottie"), was the headmaster of Groton and a distinguished force in that institution. Richard was also the godson of J. P. Morgan, the industrialist and financier.

In 1915 Peabody married Caresse Crosby, a young girl he had met while still at Groton; his uncle, the Rev. Endicott Peabody, officiated at the wedding. From her earliest recollections of Richard at Harvard, drinking was a part of his life.[125] On the birth of their son, Peabody exhibited a rigidity of temperament that apparently had been a part of his own childhood upbringing. "Dick was not the most indulgent of parents and like his father before him, he forbade the gurgles and the cries of infancy; when they occurred he walked out, and often walked back unsteadily."[126] Caresse Crosby's depiction of Peabody's family is one of militaristic emotional repression and "tiptoe discipline." "My father-in-law was a stickler for polish, both of manners and minerals." Her mother-in-law was an invalid who wore "nun-like dresses, and in bed or out wore starched collars and cuffs as severe as piping." The house was, in fact, "unjoyful."[127] This background hardly exhibits the signs of the kind of over-permissive childhood indulgence that Peabody later theorized lay at the root of alcoholism.

Peabody served in World War I as a captain in the field artillery. After his return to civilian life, his continued drinking, along with severe depression, soon landed him in a sanitarium.[128] The marriage also failed. It was at this point that he came in contact with the Emmanuel Movement.

A Student of Baylor

His ex-wife Caresse Crosby speaks of his "remarkable recovery" after their divorce, ascribing his success to Dr. Worcester and the Emmanuel Church, although in fact Peabody's treatment was actually with Baylor. She adds that he began attending the classes of the church and soon began to style himself as "Dr. Peabody," complete with an office on Newbury Street.[129] Her summary of the Peabody treatment was his "advice" which he customarily gave to the alcoholics who came to him: "When you need a drink you need a friend. Come to me then, we will talk it out at any time, day or night."

According to Katherine McCarthy, Peabody attended the Emmanuel Church clinic and weekly health classes in the winter of 1921-1922. He seems to have worked as a volunteer in the church for several years before opening his own office on Newbury Street, when he apparently first became known as "Dr. Peabody." McCarthy suggests that Baylor likely had more clients than he could accommodate and Peabody handled the overflow.

By the 1930s Peabody was publishing articles in both medical and lay journals. By 1933 he was practicing in New York. The influence of Peabody extended into leading hospital treatment programs of the day, later including clinics opened under the auspices of the prestigious Yale Center of Alcohol Studies (1944).[130]

Peabody, from a most proper Bostonian background and privileged status, differed from Worcester and Baylor both in temperament and social orientation. If Baylor had been more worldly than Worcester,[131] Peabody was unashamedly secular even compared to Baylor, and was eager to appear "professional" at all costs. Where Worcester stressed a spiritual foundation in his work, spiritual language and concepts are entirely absent from Peabody's writings.[132] Worcester and McComb had also made much of their credentials as doctors in psychology and their standing as members of the clergy, but they began during an era when medical doctors like the Freudians were only first beginning to take over the area of mental illness and neurosis and the treatment of nervous disorders and psychotherapy was still more or less an open field.[133] By the 1920's the situation had changed dramatically.

The Issue of Professionalism

While some criticisms of the Emmanuel Movement did arise from its intrusion into medicine, this hostility was minor compared to what Peabody and his associates encountered in this new era. Jim Bishop's account of Peabody and William Wister, one of his lay therapists, cites instances of such confrontations, including threats of arrest.[134] Wister's practice was haunted by fear of the American Medical Association, yet he had to rely on the willingness of physicians to refer patients. Wister's dream was to be appointed to work in a sanitarium.

By the 1920's Freud had become sufficiently well known to cause consternation among many of the professionals in the United States who treated mental disorders. Many of them disagreed vehemently with Freud's theories, and they feared that the popularization of Freud would result in irreparable distortions.[135] They could not prevent the general public from becoming aware of some of these controversial ideas however. While Freud was often a topic of sometimes quite shocked conversation—the sexual nature of his concepts attracted considerable attention—few people actually read his books. Yet because of the popularizations of these concepts through the mass media, this new role and image of the professional "psychiatrist" became accepted by the public. Freud came to stand for virtually all the new developments in psychology.[136] The consequences of this popularization worked both for and against self-proclaimed psychologists such as Peabody. On the one hand, psychology in general was starting to become accepted into the mainstream of American culture. But there remained strong ties between the medical and psychoanalytic communities, and the well-organized medical profession stood ready to exclude marginal practitioners such as Peabody.

A Secular Practice

In an attempt to gain the respect of the doctors with whom he had to work, Peabody and his followers, as McCarthy points out, "essentially gutted their method of the vital substance that had made Worcester and Baylor so successful in earlier decades."[137] Peabody's method centered on staying "professional" and avoiding the emotive excesses, as he saw it, of the early Emmanuelites. Recognizing the attitudes of the medical community, including the Freudians, Peabody knew that divinity credentials would carry little weight toward acceptance. But abandoning the spiritual dimension of his inheritance cut into his success, and lessened, though it did not totally negate, his impact on the later development of Alcoholics Anonymous. (Peabody's *The Common Sense of Drinking* came out in 1931, and the A.A. movement began four years later, when Bill W. met Dr. Bob in 1935.) Whereas Worcester, McComb, and Baylor had the justification of pastoral work behind their therapy, Peabody did not.

Having only the most tenuous association with the Emmanuel Movement, Peabody proceeded in his venture despite being neither a physician nor a psychologist, except by self-declaration. He closely adhered to his own system, a practice that was designed to fit in with the medical treatment of the day through a kind of mimicry. He also emphasized an American ethic of hard work, discipline, and above all, efficiency.

The Glass Crutch: On the Road to Common Sense

A valuable portrayal of Peabody's approach comes in Jim Bishop's *The Glass Crutch*, a biographical novel of William Wynne Wister. The book sweeps the reader along from 1900 to 1945, illuminating the spirit of the times and adding a bit of drama. Much of the book concerns alcoholism and various theories and treatments of it during the period. At the book's center is Wister's meeting with Richard R. Peabody in 1934, which leads to him becoming one of Peabody's lay therapists.

Early chapters of *The Glass Crutch* portray the protagonist enjoying his membership in the Philadelphia aristocracy. The book takes the reader on an F. Scott Fitzgerald-like joyride through the first part of the twentieth century. Wister's hitch in the RAF, love affairs, divorces, bootleg booze, speakeasies, an interlude on a Western ranch, and a new Stutz Blackhawk four-seater with a tan top, all lead up to his encounter with Peabody's practice. Along the way we are privy to the extravagances of a person who gets out of tight situations by means of family money and connections.

The sustained theme throughout the journey is drunkenness and irresponsibility, marked by periodic and ineffective treatments. Some more fictionalized episodes are comic: Wister visits a Freudian therapist, Dr. Sigmund Wertenbacker, who tells him after six visits that he has an Oedipus complex. In an accent that must have reminded readers of the day of the Katzenjammer Kids, the doctor explains that this means "you vere sexually in luf wit' da mutter and dot you vont to kill da fodder. Dis, uf course, would be subconscious, uf course."[138]

On a more serious note, it appears that Peabody had the attitude that psychoanalysis was simply another minor subvariant of ordinary psychotherapy, albeit of uncertain value. Better informed people had already begun to realize the radically different basic underlying principles of the new Freudian psychoanalytic method at least as early as the mid-1910s, according to one historian, placing Peabody a bit behind schedule.[139]

A sardonic 1945 review of *The Glass Crutch* in the *New York Times* treats the book with impatience, and concludes with the hope that "the subject of the anti-social or problem drinker has been exhausted for the next five or six years."[140] While we may today regard the subject of drunkenness seriously, such was not always the case. The tone of the article suggests that Wister was a self-important bore who was lionized by Bishop. Rather than achieving some success, the article states that Wister, after having been "a considerable souse," fell "into the hands of the psychotherapists, reformed and became a sort of lay witch-doctor himself and one of the great bores of our time."

Wister's total submission to alcohol, his repeated failures, and the horrors of the sanitariums and all, set the stage for Peabody's entrance as Wister's savior, offering a hope that seems sane, logical, and reasonable. According to the book, the seeds of Wister's family background and critical early experiences underlay his later alcoholism. At the age of two Wister underwent a dangerous operation for a double mastoid. Upon coming out of the ether, he showed an overpowering attachment for his nurse, who "cradled the baby against her bosom, laid him down, pulled his covers up, and watched him wiggle himself comfortable and go off to sleep. The seeds of Bill Wister's alcoholism had been planted."[141]

Such simplistic and tenuous assumptions reappear in Bishop's descriptions of Peabody's beliefs, as well as in *The Common Sense of Drinking* itself. Unable to accept the condition of alcoholism as a given (this would be unscientific), Peabody posits a psychic cause, but then proceeds to construct a cure that avoids the seemingly overwhelming impact of early conditioning. He speaks the language of a determinist in one moment, but turns around in the next and offers a cure that is reminiscent of the earlier mind-cure practitioners.[142]

When Wister sees Peabody in *The Glass Crutch*, it is not until after he had seen a medical doctor (Dr. Walters) and sought a physical explanation and cure. The psychological approach was to be Peabody's domain. Wister first learns that he must never drink again, a conviction that Peabody inherited from Worcester. Second, he must do this for himself, an idea that Peabody would elaborate on in the coming visits. Peabody also invokes the word "honesty," a word that would become critical in later A.A. thinking. The issue of making amends (which was to become so important in the later A.A. twelve step system) is also approached in the early stages: Wister is asked to notify creditors and tell them that he plans to repay them.

Underlying Ideas

As portrayed by Bishop, the meetings between Wister and Peabody are cut and dry. The exchanges are formal and the information regarding alcoholism and its treatment are given in a flat, matter-of-fact manner, without affect. "He spoke objectively, as though he were discussing the proper treatment of a broken leg."[143] Wister, an ideal student, takes in the information and is on his way to recovery. He learns that the cause of his alcoholism is environmental: he was overprotected to an extreme degree as a child, "overly spoiled and undisciplined." This situation "produces a nervous condition which ultimately leads to alcoholism. After all, alcoholism is nothing more than a disease of emotional immaturity."[144]

Heredity has no direct importance, but family background does play a part in that "a nervous system which proves to be nonresistant to alcohol…is more often acquired from neurotic parents who have expressed their nervousness in some other manner than that of chronic intoxication" (15). Peabody explains that just has one inherits weak lungs that make one susceptible to tuberculosis, "so I believe is a nervous system transmitted which is highly susceptible to alcohol." Note the word "believe"—Peabody is not in the realm of hard science. This idea, incidentally, is taken from Worcester and McComb, who affirmed that many cases show how "nervous conditions in parents repeat themselves in children, frequently in severer form."[145]

Peabody places himself in a difficult theoretical position. In *The Common Sense of Drinking,* he asserts that the explanation of alcoholism ("excessive drinking") lies in the realm of abnormal psychology rather than either physiology or ethics. "As a background to almost every case of chronic alcoholism there exists an inner nervous condition that is akin to the 'unreasonable' feelings of anxiety and inferiority suffered by the abnormally nervous" (xii). We can forgive him for living in a time when the notion of abnormal psychology differed from ours, but Peabody seems unaware of his true disciplinary and theoretical orientation.

For one thing there is the issue of causation. On the one hand, he wants to have individuals only *predisposed* to a certain set of conditions that will lead to alcoholism. On the other hand, these conditions, at least in the case of Wister, *sowed the seeds* of the malady. As recounted in *The Glass Crutch,* the events of Wister's early life seem to flow from the initial episode with the nurse and set a pattern that leads to near destruction. But it seems that Peabody would have us recognize that these conditions are not absolute determinants and do not negate free will. Although the individual is fighting against the odds, given his early environment and possibly inherited nervous condition, he can effect a favorable recovery and enjoy a cure. How this is possible is problematic indeed, especially given Peabody's theoretical stance against physiological treatment and his aloofness toward religion.

It is clear that Peabody does not want to lock the alcoholic into a hopeless and determined world of alcoholic oblivion. Despite downplaying the physiological element, a knowledge of "abnormal psychology" seems to be sufficient to accomplish the task.[146] Just how this knowledge alone will counter the weight of heredity and early conditioning is never convincingly demonstrated. Such a demonstration would be difficult for a practitioner who avoids working with the body and spirit, and restricts the "mind" portion of therapy to a process of secular exhortation that in its military and business-like stress on efficiency also severely restricts the emotional component. Peabody paints a grim deterministic picture but then offers a cure, one that reflects a curious combination of the earlier mind-cure techniques with a form of what would later be called reality therapy, that seems to have been authored by a person with severe affective disorders. In other words, in order to be "professional," the Peabody program avoided emotional support, empathy, and fellowship. In this regard the program Peabody offered was a long way from the Emmanuel Church.

What Richard R. Peabody did offer was expressed directly in *The Common Sense of Drinking*, and indirectly as advice to Wister in *The Glass Crutch*, which offers a sense of context and personality to Peabody's ideas. The spirit of his method is expressed in a passage from *The Glass Crutch*. After telling Wister that his trouble is psychological, Peabody asserts the primacy of the task of living sober by stating that it is going to be done "for your own benefit."[147] A key idea follows: "Whatever will-power you use will be applied to following the treatment, not in trying to overcome a drinking habit." Here of course is Worcester's idea of crowding out evil, or in McCarthy's words, "Resist not evil" in a direct confrontation, but replace it with positive alternative goals.[148] Peabody adds in no uncertain terms that "the system will take care of your drinking."[149]

The system assumes that the patient's immaturity needs correction, something that will be done by a schedule and the inculcation of sound habits of living. The program offers a kind of boot camp for alcoholics, consisting of a schedule that must be "thorough," "not only work and duty, but pleasure and rest, though the rest should be of a definite nature and not just be loafing about" (159). Peabody hopes to "reintegrate" the person's character. The schedule, based on "sound psychological principle rather than magic" (167), instills in the patient a sense of doing something positive about his alcohol problem and achieving a sense of accomplishment by carrying out his own schedule (160-161).

The goal of the program is to achieve a state in which the patient masters his emotions and "will sit, intellectually, in the driver's seat." Bishop states the essence of this when he discusses Peabody's ideas on "thought control." By controlling thoughts, the patient controls actions.[150] Peabody states: "This is the most important element in the work—*the control and direction of thoughts toward the ultimate logical goal*" (109). In Bishop's novel, Peabody explains to Wister that we are all comprised of two selves, the intellectual and the emotional. "The intellectual self is the good," while the emotional self wants to keep drinking. By practice the good self will be built up and the emotional self diminished. Thought control will "shrink down" the emotional self so the good, logical, intellectual self can make the decisions. While Peabody allows that the two sides must be reconciled, "you must permit the intellectual side to dominate."[151] The logical side must guard against glamorizing the past, that is, the old drinking days, and put them in proper perspective, emphasizing the miseries of alcoholism and sanitariums and other treatments. Similarly, all social activities, in fact any activity that might trigger a drinking thought, must be monitored by the ever-alert intellectual self. Well and good, but the thoughtful person might still yearn for the joy of the Emmanuel Weekly Health Conferences and references to fellowship.

Peabody's strongly dualistic insistence that logic and reason are good, whereas emotions and feelings are inherently dangerous and destructive, and must be kept under rigid intellectual control at all times, is reminiscent of some well-known ancient Greco-Roman philosophical biases. One can see this deep fear of our natural human emotional life in many places in the later Platonic and Stoic philosophical traditions as they developed during the Roman imperial period, along with the attempt to totally de-emotionalize our thinking processes.[152] "Salvation" in these ancient pagan systems was often tied into the attempt to cease feeling any ordinary human emotions at all. After the fall of the Roman empire, for another thousand years medieval Christian teaching often continued this deep hostility toward the natural emotional component of human thought[153] and mixed it with a soul-body dualism which denigrated many emotions (like sexual desire for example) as simply a sinful entanglement in the inferior materialistic world and the lure of the pleasures of the flesh.

Peabody's insistence that we can only find salvation by practicing "thought control" and putting reason and logic "in the driver's seat," is part of a two thousand year old western tradition of fearing and fleeing from emotions and feelings which, when it becomes too moralistic and repressive, can create more psychological problems than it solves.

The later sections of Wister's treatment as described in *The Glass Crutch* allude to Peabody's use of Emmanuel methods, especially those promoted directly by Baylor. Relaxation is advocated, as is the technique of suggestion (134). Even though Peabody sometimes used suggestion to "penetrate the subconscious" (236), this was an area he largely left alone. When encountering the unconscious, as in discussing the alcoholic's inner tensions and the need to relieve them, the subject is skirted. Peabody acknowledges that we must "educate the unconscious so that it will function in harmony with the desires of the conscious" (132).[154] But his discussion is fraught with the fear of raising negative thoughts, the ever-present temptations, the pull of the darker emotions toward destruction. Whereas Worcester wished not only to educate the unconscious but also to draw out its latent positive potentials, Peabody regarded the unconscious as more of a boiling pit of demons, ever ready to spew up dark forces with frightful visages that would lead the patient to ruin. This concern is not a passing one; it appears throughout *The Common Sense of Drinking*.

The Appeal of Peabody

Peabody's method was attractive perhaps not so much for its success with alcoholics but because his treatment involved harshness. No one particularly liked alcoholics—drunks—and the idea that they are morally flawed in some lasting way has never completely disappeared. While Peabody states in his summary at the end of *The Common Sense of Drinking* that "the individual is only an inferior person as long as he continues to drink," the tone of his book says otherwise. Peabody's terse, unemotional, no-nonsense prose and frequent militaristic references to the battle against alcoholism (161) suggest that, although a therapist, he will not be coddling drunks.[155] His methods achieved a kind of revenge against drunkards.

Despite Peabody's claim that he was not moralizing, it is hard to see where his use of "abnormal psychology" leaves off and moralizing begins. His plan, his schedules, and his emphasis on efficiency sound like a moral program for better living delivered by a humorless Puritan taskmaster. This may be a harsh characterization, but there is in fact little cheery sentiment in *The Common Sense of Drinking*. As Mel B. points out in *New Wine,* his notion of "surrender" was not the surrender of Bill W., a spiritual turning over of one's will to God. Rather it was merely the surrender of the idea that one could some day safely drink again.[156] It was also, of course, a surrender to the Peabody method.

Another aspect of Peabody's appeal was, in fact, common sense. His generation had its ideals shot apart on the battlefields of the Great War. The optimism of a Worcester did not resonate in the post–World War I years. It was a world of the "Lost Generation," the sparseness of Hemingway against the excesses of F. Scott Fitzgerald. This was a time that brings us back to the changing mood of the 1920s and 1930s. Meaninglessness was a real concern in the world, and when such a specter hovers over the world, the beauty of the simple task done well is appreciated.

This common sense was Peabody's bottom line, the idea that the alcoholic is not getting a good deal in life by being intoxicated. To make his point Peabody uses words like fool, stupid, farcical or, more mildly, misguided. In the name of efficiency, drunkenness is not a good use of time (176-177). As Alfred Adler might have put it, excessive drinking is a sure sign of an inferiority complex. Peabody exhorts his patients to have self-respect, be productive and, incidentally, prosper. But his is no gospel of success. It is a cold and plain plan for survival.

Contributions to A.A.

The Peabody method, despite its shortcomings, contributed much to the development of A.A. It continued a type of therapy that further removed alcoholism from the back wards of the sanitarium. The dialogue Peabody established with the medical community, for good or ill, furthered scientific interest in the pathology of the disease. By the 1930s the Emmanuel Movement had all but disappeared, whereas the Peabody method was very influential in the establishment and practice of other clinics.[157] More directly, Peabody was the most likely source of Bill Wilson's phrase, "half measures availed us nothing."[158] Peabody wrote, with italics, "*halfway measures are of no avail*" (99). Further, Peabody prescribed reading, journaling, and the use of platitudes "as if they were profundities" (75). Repetition can be the cement of an organization, and Peabody was not afraid to employ this element. "Bring the body and the mind will follow" is one such A.A. slogan that may well have applied to Peabody's patients.[159]

As with the Oxford Group, one of the greatest contributions of the Peabody method to A.A. may have been to show, in negative fashion, what an alcoholism treatment program should *not* omit to provide. This missing piece may have been apparent to more than one early A.A. member who had also read *The Common Sense of Drinking*. The fatal omission in

Peabody's system was the lack of any method to supply the warmth of fellowship, a theme taken up earnestly by the Jacoby Club, which had begun twenty years earlier, in 1909, as an offshoot of the Emmanuel Movement. In the last three chapters of this work, we will need to go back in time and see how the Jacoby Club was organized to provide the kind of fellowship and group support which was necessary for recovering alcoholics.

CHAPTER 4

▼

ROWLAND HAZARD AND THE BEGINNINGS OF A.A.

Rowland Hazard III was a wealthy Rhode Island businessman who had become an alcoholic, requiring hospitalization on more than one occasion. He is well-known to the A.A. tradition as one of the Oxford Group circle who rescued Ebby Thatcher and got him sober when Ebby was threatened with commitment to the Brattleboro Asylum in August 1934. Three months later, in November 1934, Ebby visited Bill Wilson, the co-founder of A.A., and they sat in Bill's kitchen talking for hours in the famous scene which is reported in the first chapter of *Alcoholics Anonymous*.[160] Ebby was the messenger to Bill W. of victory over the alcoholic compulsion through a new spiritual way of life.

But even if Ebby was the one who actually talked with Bill, Rowland Hazard is recognized in the A.A. tradition as "the messenger behind the messenger," and two things about him are normally highlighted: He was a member of the Oxford Group, and he had been a patient of the famous psychiatrist Carl Jung in Switzerland. In the traditional A.A. version of the latter story, it was said that Hazard had been unable to stop returning to the bottle in spite of extensive Jungian therapy, until finally Jung told him that with alcoholics of his type only a spiritual conversion of some sort, which would enable him to radically remake and remold his inner spirit, would ever give him freedom from his overwhelming compulsion to drink.

But there was a third factor involved in Hazard's story, one that up until now has been omitted in A.A. accounts of his role in their history. During both 1933 and that especially crucial year 1934, he was also a patient of the Emmanuel Movement author Courtenay Baylor, whose contributions and methods were discussed in the previous chapter. So early A.A. was influenced by the Emmanuel Movement from at least two different sources. Bill W. read Richard R. Peabody's *The Common Sense of Drinking*, which taught a secularized and intellectualized version of the Emmanuelite methods (as was explained in the previous chapter), but he was also in secondhand contact (via Ebby) with Rowland Hazard and hence the ideas of Courtenay Baylor, who taught something much closer to the original spiritually based Emmanuel therapy as devised in 1906 by the Rev. Elwood Worcester in the basement meetings he conducted in the church he pastored in downtown Boston.

The discovery that Rowland Hazard was deeply involved with Courtenay Baylor and the Emmanuelite tradition in addition to his Oxford Group activities was in fact only made quite recently. The present chapter will discuss the way this new information can be documented in the Hazard family papers which are preserved in the Rhode Island Historical Society. It will also attempt to sort out some of the perplexing issues surrounding the story of Rowland's therapy with Carl Jung in 1931, because materials contained in that same archival source make it clear that he was only in Europe from June to September of that year as part of a Hazard family trip, and that the dates and places given in the family's letters from that period would have given Rowland two months at most to spend in Switzerland with Jung. In fact, as will be seen, even that may be pressing the matter: Rick Stattler at the Rhode Island Historical Society, who did the primary research, sorting through all the family papers searching for relevant items, has stated that he believes that Rowland would have found it very difficult to have spent more than two weeks at most talking to Jung in any great depth during that trip to Europe.

Rowland Hazard III

Rowland Hazard III was born in Peace Dale, Rhode Island, on October 29, 1881. (Bill Wilson was born in 1895 and Dr. Bob Smith in 1879, so he was closer to Dr. Bob's age, and fourteen years older than Bill W., who likely seemed to him but a brash young man.) Rowland ("Roy") represented the tenth generation of his family in Rhode Island. The first American Hazard, Thomas, was born in 1610; he came over to the New World after the British had begun settling in Massachusetts, taking up his residence first in Boston, then the Massachusetts Bay Colony. Roy was the eldest of five children born to woolen manufacturer Rowland Gibson Hazard and Mary Pierrepont Bushnell. Hazard graduated from the Taft School in Waterbury, Connecticut, and Yale University (1903) with a B.A. degree. He sang in the Glee Club and University Choir and was a member of Alpha Delta Phi fraternity as well as the Elihu Club.

After graduation Hazard worked at family businesses in Chicago and Syracuse briefly, then entered the woolen textile trade in Rhode Island, where he joined the Peace Dale Manufacturing Company, which specialized in woolen and worsted fabrics. The firm had been founded circa 1801 by his great-great-grandfather and his great-grand-uncle, Rowland Hazard and Joseph Peace Hazard respectively.[161] He began work in the wool-sorting department and worked his way up, eventually being elected treasurer of the firm. The firm was sold in 1918.

Hazard served in the Rhode Island state senate between 1914 and 1916 and spent World War I as a captain in the Chemical Warfare Service of the Army. Shortly after the war a number of family deaths left Hazard the eldest member of his generation. In 1919 he effected a plan originally formulated by his father and uncle and formed the Allied Chemical and Dye Company. By 1920 he was a director and so remained throughout his career.[162] By 1921 Hazard had also joined the New York banking firm of Lee, Higginson and Company and remained there until 1927. Throughout this period he remained active in Rhode Island politics.

In the fall of 1927, Hazard went on a hunting expedition to Africa for big game and specimens for American museums. He contracted a tropical illness, and on his return to the United States in 1928 settled on the West Coast. He established a ranch in southern New Mexico, at La Luz, and shortly organized the La Luz Clay Products Company. He had discovered substantial deposits of high-grade clay for the manufacture of items ranging from roofing tiles to decorative urns and vases. Upon establishing La Luz, he returned to the East Coast to pursue other ventures. By 1931 he had transferred his residence from Peace Dale, Rhode Island, to a family home in Narragansett, Rhode Island, originally built in 1884 by his great-grand-uncle, Joseph Peace Hazard, and known as Druid's Dream.[163] "He also kept residences intermittently at 52nd Street and other addresses in Manhattan; in La Luz, New Mexico; at 'Ladyhill' in Shaftsbury, Vermont; and at 'Sugarbush' in Glastonbury, Vermont."[164]

In his later years, following his move to Narragansett, Hazard served as the executive vice president of the Bristol Manufacturing Company, Waterbury, Connecticut, manufacturers of precision instruments. He also served as a director of the Allied Chemical and Dye Company, the Rhode Island Hospital Trust Company, and the Interlake Iron Company. From 1935 to 1938 he was in a general partnership with the New York brokerage house of Taylor Robinson Company, Inc. At one point he was director of the old Merchants' Bank in Providence.

In 1910 Hazard married Helen Hamilton Campbell, the daughter of a Chicago banker. The couple were divorced on February 25, 1929, and remarried on April 27, 1931, little more than a month before the trip to Europe during which Hazard was supposed to have had his crucial encounter with Carl Jung. Rowland and Helen had four children, Caroline C., Rowland G. III, Peter Hamilton, and Charles B. Of these four, it was Charles who lived the longest, dying in 1995.

Rowland Hazard III remains somewhat of a mystery, cloaked in a silence that was partly a feature of his times and his class, but a silence that is especially impenetrable because he left behind almost no extant letters of his own. We have to read about his life for the most part through the letters of other family members. In addition, much of the information concerning Hazard's relationship with early A.A. is anecdotal, very little of it documented.

On the surface, Hazard's life is mirrored effectively in the descriptions of some of the characters in F. Scott Fitzgerald's novel *The Great Gatsby*, though Hazard was more like one of the East Egg crowd, the established wealthy class, than the upstart Jay Gatsby himself. When Fitzgerald (in a remark to Ernest Hemingway) spoke of the very rich as being different from you and me, he might have been speaking of the Hazard family and Rowland. Hazard moved from place to place with apparent ease, tried his hand in this business and adventure and then that. His success was seemingly always assured, his position never tangibly threatened. His alcoholism was spoken of in hushed terms, if mentioned at all. The information about exactly where he was and when during his trips to Europe or Africa is vague and not well documented.

And this has bearing on the claim that has been long accepted: that Hazard met with Carl Jung and was in therapy with him for an extensive period of time ("over a year" in the version frequently seen in the later A.A. tradition). Since Rowland's own letters are no longer in existence, the correspondence between his mother and his brother, Thomas Pierre Hazard, provide the bulk of what we do know about "Roy," but they do not ever mention him going to Jung for psychiatric treatment. This may have been a matter which he did not fully share with his mother and brother, or they may have avoided talking about it in their letters out of embarrassment that a member of a family so solid and distinguished as theirs would need a psychiatrist. But these letters do provide enough information about where Rowland was during the period from 1930 to 1934 to make it clear that the only opportunity he would have had to see the Swiss psychiatrist Jung in Zurich in any kind of extensive fashion was for a couple of months in 1931.

Hazard clearly struggled with alcoholism throughout his life, even though mentions of it in the letters are scant. It embarrassed the family and it made them uncomfortable to acknowledge his drinking problem even to other family members. We do know that he eventually became acquainted with Ebby Thatcher, a friend of Bill Wilson's from their days as classmates at the Burr and Burton boarding school. And we know that Hazard's connection to A.A., that is, to Bill W., came through his meeting Ebby and helping rescue him from commitment to an asylum in August 1934.

Hazard and Courtenay Baylor

Whatever his relationship to Jung—an issue which will be discussed in more detail later in this chapter—Rowland Hazard had considerable involvement with Courtenay Baylor, establishing a direct link between the Emmanuel Movement and the formation of Alcoholics Anonymous. The documentation of Hazard's treatment by Baylor is contained in the list of Hazard family documents prepared by Rick Stattler.

The relationship between Hazard and Baylor, though provable, is lacking in detail: ample evidence at the Rhode Island Historical Society documents that Hazard was a client or patient of Baylor during 1933 and 1934. The Hazard family papers also show that after January 1933,

Rowland went through a long period when he was virtually incapacitated by his personal problems. He ceased being actively involved in the ventures he had begun in New Mexico, and his brother-in-law Wallace Campbell had to take over all his regular business. Rowland's canceled checks showed only routine payments (although they were still signed by him) for many months afterward. Finally in late 1933 he completely stopped writing any checks at all. During most or all of this period, he seems to have been in Vermont under the care of Courtenay Baylor, and only occasionally made trips to New York to see family and sign checks. He was unable to return to his normal high level of activity until October 1934.[165]

So the period when Hazard was Courtenay Baylor's patient corresponded to the deepest slump in his life, the time between January 1933 and October 1934, when this normally aggressive and continuously active businessman, industrialist, and entrepreneur seems to have been rendered almost totally nonfunctional by his psychological and alcohol-related problems.

Baylor may in fact have been first called in when Hazard was hospitalized for his alcoholism in February and March of 1932, but this would be merely supposition. We do know that Baylor visited the family and worked in some fashion with other family members also during 1933 and 1934. But the lack of full detail means that though we know that their continuing relationship existed during this period, we know little else about it. The available documents thus do not allow us to discover whether Hazard's enthusiasm for the Oxford Group was aided by his work with Baylor or diminished by it. We do know that Hazard did not remain sober throughout his life, and did drink again after 1934.

The first mention of Baylor in the surviving family documents occurs in a list of acquaintances compiled by Hazard on April 13, 1933. Hazard was attempting to sell maple syrup from his farm in Vermont and a "C. Baylor" is listed. According to Stattler's notes, Baylor responded but did not order syrup.[166] The next reference to Baylor occurs on July 24, 1933, when his mother writes to Thomas Hazard from Vermont: "Mr. Baylor just arrived. Am to have a talk with him today, Roy goes to N.Y. and Baylor will go to Burlington tonight and come back here tomorrow."[167] The first therapeutic contact, as mentioned previously, may of course have arisen much earlier, and may have been related to Hazard's hospitalization for alcoholism in February and March 1932.[168] Perhaps the severity of that episode triggered a serious recovery effort on Rowland's part, or caused his family to call in Baylor for an intervention. But this must be conjecture. And it is also possible that Baylor may not have become involved in trying to help until after Rowland's further breakdown in January 1933.

Of the fourteen letters in the RIHS material pertaining to Baylor, most concern bills from him paid by Thomas Hazard. As Stattler summarizes, "It collectively indicates that Hazard hired Baylor from at least December 15, 1933 to October 16, 1934 for unspecified services." There is also reference to the fact that Baylor worked with the entire family, not simply on a personal basis with Hazard alone. In one letter (November 20, 1934), Thomas Hazard wrote: "Inasmuch as throughout 1933 and 1934 you were working with Helen, Carol and Rowley as well as Roy, it seemed to me that it would be proper to estimate that one-third of your remuneration could be considered as a gift to my brother."[169]

Baylor seemed to have become rather a part of the family in some ways. While brother Thomas was signing checks, he was also a potential business partner, or so it seemed in Baylor's eyes. On Feb. 2, 1934, Baylor sent Thomas Hazard a long letter detailing the opportunity to buy into a Nevada gold and silver mine. Baylor referred to the deal as one which he believed to be as "clean a proposition as could be found in mining."[170] Thomas checked this out with business friends who advised him against the deal. On February 13, Thomas's secretary curtly informed Baylor that "Mr. T. P. Hazard has directed me to advise you that all the individuals have been heard from, in connection with your letter, and are not in favor of going into the venture." The letter concludes with a reference to an

Internal Revenue tax matter covering payments to Baylor by Hazard's mother.[171]

The RIHS packet of Hazard-Baylor letters concludes with a rare document of Emmanuel Movement history. In 1949 a letter was written to Thomas Hazard at Peace Dale, the family home, by the Courtenay Baylor Memorial Committee, so indicated by the letterhead. The letter is a request for donations for a memorial to Baylor, consisting of lighting fixtures at the entrance of the Parish House of the Emmanuel Church. They were to be wrought-iron lanterns, "one to be fixed to the outside of the Parish House entrance, and the other to be placed inside the entrance porch. A dedicatory inscription will be carved into the stone wall of the porch." The author of the letter preceded this description with the comment that "the idea [of the lighting] is a particularly happy one as it is symbolic of the light shed by him on the paths of so many people."[172]

The bills from Baylor to Hazard document the continued existence of the Emmanuel Movement, renamed the Craigie Foundation, as manifested in Baylor's work. The full nature of the foundation's activities during this time are not easy to document. The bills do not explicitly specify that Baylor was paid this money for treating Hazard for his alcoholism, but it is difficult to see anything else Baylor could have provided them for which payments of this sort would be due.

Baylor knew that a person had to rethink and reformulate himself, that is, "remake himself," if he were to escape from alcoholism. Attempting to bring this message to a person of Rowland Hazard's stature and accomplishments could only have been a vexing task.

Just how Baylor related to the rest of the Hazard family raises questions the surviving documents cannot answer. Baylor believed "every alcoholic came from what might be called an alcoholic or neurotic atmosphere" and that "we can hardly expect a patient to become or stay cured if he must remain in an environment which has in all probability contributed to his own abnormal nervous condition. This environment must in its turn be 'cured.'"[173] So in terms of Baylor's normal methodological assumptions, it would make sense if, in the process of attempting to treat Rowland for his alcoholism, he also made some efforts to change the way the other members of his family interacted with one another. Nevertheless, given the accomplishments and self-confidence of the Hazard family as evidenced by their letters to one another, it is difficult to believe that Baylor would have remained a popular guest if he had pushed too hard on the other members of the family to change their ways also. Hazard's mother in particular does not appear to be the type of person who would take kindly to the suggestion that she too needed to be cured.

Hazard was also participating in the Oxford Group during this same period. The earliest reference in the Rhode Island Historical Society collection is a letter from Thomas P. Hazard to his mother in February of 1934 which refers to Rowland as being a member of the Oxford Group, but he could in fact have joined them much earlier.

Whether from his therapy with Courtenay Baylor or his participation in the Oxford Group (or both combined), Rowland Hazard was ultimately apparently able to achieve at least significant periods of continuous sobriety; whether he achieved real serenity and happiness we cannot know.

A linked chain did however exist, starting with the Rev. Elwood Worcester at Emmanuel Episcopal Church in Boston, and linking him to Courtenay Baylor, who in turn worked with Rowland Hazard during the years 1933 and 1934. Hazard in turn was linked, through Ebby Thatcher, to Bill Wilson at the decisive moment at the beginning of the A.A. movement. Hazard also knew the people at Calvary Church in New York, where Bill W. started going in 1934 for further spiritual help with his alcoholism. So he definitely moved in the same orbits as the early members of A.A. and was present during the time period when Bill W. was first getting sober.

How and to what degree Hazard influenced events must remain more conjectural, beyond a few bare bones facts such as his major role in helping to rescue Ebby Thatcher and get him sober in August 1934. Nevertheless A.A. historians must take seriously not only his continual and important presence behind the scenes during that key period, but also the possible ways that he could have been of major influence.

Hazard and Jung

Ernest Kurtz's definitive history of A.A. regards Hazard as instrumental in one of the four founding moments of Alcoholics Anonymous, the point where Bill W. learned from Ebby Thatcher about what Carl Jung was supposed to have told Hazard, that is, that alcoholics could not recover without some sort of spiritual conversion. Bill W. interpreted this kind of conversion experience as necessarily involving a major ego deflation.

> One-half of the core idea—the necessity of spiritual conversion—had passed from Dr. Carl Jung to Rowland. Clothed in Oxford Group practice it had given rise to its yet separate other half—the simultaneous transmission of deflation and hope by "one alcoholic talking to another"—in the first meeting between Bill and Ebby.[174]

Kurtz quotes Bill W.'s own words on this issue (where the "Oxford Group friend" is of course Rowland Hazard):

> *Deflation at depth*, yes that was *it*. Exactly that had happened to me. Dr. Carl Jung had told an Oxford Group friend of Ebby's how hopeless his alcoholism was and Dr. Silkworth had passed the same sentence upon me. Then Ebby [Thatcher], also an alcoholic, had handed me the identical dose."[175]

Carl Jung (along with the American psychologist William James) was frequently cited by Bill W. and the early A.A.s as a way of legitimizing their emphasis on the spiritual dimension of recovery. For James, religion embodied a perfectly valid kind of experience, one that could be studied and said to have its own objective reality. It could be demonstrated that certain kinds of religious experiences could produce extraordinary life changes. For Jung, religion was a way of expressing in symbolic fashion certain key components within the human psyche, using archetypal images which were part of the makeup of all human minds at the unconscious level. This material had to become integrated at the conscious level, he stated, to produce full mental health.

Conventional psychiatry by itself could not bring freedom from the alcoholic compulsion to a certain type of chronic alcoholic, as Bill W. had heard the story of what Jung told Hazard. So as Bill interpreted what he believed to be Jung's opinion, he saw this at first as a decree of hopelessness just as severe as the one imposed on him by his own American psychiatrist William D. Silkworth. The psychiatrists, even the best in the world, could not help a certain kind of chronic alcoholic by conventional psychiatry. But Jung had said to Hazard, according to the story Bill had been told, that a real spiritual conversion could provide the power to stop drinking.

So conversion then became the only hope. This necessity of conversion became a key ingredient in the formation of A.A. For the history of A.A., the connection with the ideas of Carl Jung was extremely important in this way, and in a variety of other ways also.[176] Kurtz goes into considerable depth on this matter, including long discussions of the way Bill W. regarded Jung (and William James too) and appropriated their material.

All these observations remain valid. Carl Jung stated in a letter to Bill W. many years later that the A.A. understanding of his theory of alcoholism was in fact correct, and those who have studied Jungian psychiatry can easily see how that understanding fits smoothly into his overall theoretical structure. Jung praised the A.A. movement in that letter and indicated that he wholeheartedly approved of their approach. But the fact is that there was at the very least a considerable exaggeration of the length and depth of Rowland Hazard's contact with Carl Jung in Switzerland. Part of the Hazard-Jung story, as recounted in later A.A. sources, was clearly more legend than historical reality.

The Traditional Account of Hazard's Therapy with Carl Jung and Its Influence on A.A.

The official story regarding Hazard goes something like this, as stated by Bill's early biographer Thomsen and quoted by later A.A. historians.[177] The story begins with the assertion that Hazard "wound up in Zurich, a patient of Carl Jung," and that he worked with him in therapy of some sort for "over a year."[178] This was supposed to have happened in 1931. Hazard apparently thought that he had seen the depths of his unconscious and understood himself to the extent that he could rest easily in a sober life. According to the basic Bill W. biography, Hazard then left Zurich but soon found himself drunk once again. He returned to Zurich and once more sought the counsel of Jung. At this time the psychologist told Hazard that he was hopeless in his alcoholism, insofar as conventional psychiatry was concerned, and that religious conversion seemed the one hope for such cases.

After this second meeting, Hazard is said to have discovered the Oxford Group and to have begun to flourish in the program it provided.[179] Hazard then came to Ebby Thatcher's rescue in August 1934 when Thatcher was threatened with commitment to the Brattleboro Asylum. The intervention of Hazard, along with Cebra G. and another Oxford Group member, Shep C., was apparently fortuitous. The three members happened to be vacationing at a summer home near Bennington when they heard of the impending commitment. So they decided there on the spot to make Thatcher a "project."[180]

After his rescue, Thatcher took to the program of the Oxford Group with a good deal of enthusiasm. Their zeal and evangelical fervor appealed to him, granting him an extended period of sobriety. Three months after the Oxford Group people had saved him from the insane asylum, he passed the message on to Bill W. in the latter's kitchen in November 1934. The standard A.A. tradition regards this as the context in which Ebby told

Bill W. the story about Rowland Hazard and Carl Jung. And then, according to the time-honored story, the account of what Jung had told Hazard continued to sit and ferment in Bill W.'s mind, and was one of the more important things that Bill learned from Ebby in that meeting in his kitchen in November 1934.

The importance of Jung to Bill W. is not in doubt. But the detailed account given for many years by A.A. people of Rowland Hazard's activities from 1931 to 1934 clearly contained some legendary elements. Hazard could not conceivably have seen Jung for more than two months, perhaps less, in 1931. There is no evidence in the Hazard family papers that he joined the Oxford Group at that point. In fact, the earliest documentary evidence of him being a member did not appear until February 1934, six months before he helped rescue Ebby Thatcher from the asylum. Although this does not mean that he could not have joined the Oxford Groupers much earlier, all our evidence so far of any deeply committed involvement on his part in that group's activities comes from 1934. Furthermore, we have now considerable evidence of Hazard's contact with the Emmanuel Group author Courtenay Baylor during 1933 and 1934, presumably as Baylor's patient, which is a key factor which was left out of the traditional A.A. legend.

So to understand the actual role which Rowland Hazard may have played in the development of early A.A., it will be necessary to go beyond the legend and see what the Hazard family papers reveal of what may or may not have actually happened.

The Problems with the Traditional Account of the Hazard-Jung Contact

Two scholars, Rick Stattler and William L. White, have recently investigated Hazard's role in the founding of Alcoholics Anonymous, in part by examining materials at the Rhode Island Historical Society (RIHS) in

Providence. This author likewise examined selected Hazard material at the RIHS, focusing largely on Hazard's connection with the Emmanuel Movement, but also reading materials discovered by Stattler which might pertain to the Carl Jung question. Scholars must be warned that the nature of these papers means that many important questions still cannot be answered. They give us evidence which is in many ways partial and sometimes frustrating.[181]

In recent correspondence with the author, Rhode Island Historical Society Manuscripts Curator Rick Stattler summarized the findings of a 1998 research project which endeavored to document Hazard's whereabouts during the period 1930-1934.[182] Stattler's scholarship as summed up in this letter and seen in an accompanying six-page document list (1930-1934) is thorough and germane to the subject at hand: Hazard's involvement with Courtenay Baylor.[183]

Stattler himself best summarizes his main point: "I can state with confidence that Rowland Hazard did not undergo any counseling in Zurich for more than a couple of months between 1930 and 1934. I can also state that the records examined, which are very suggestive on other matters, do not so much as hint at any treatment by Dr. Jung, at least not as I have interpreted them."[184]

The Stattler letter is accompanied by a document list, an annotated list of letters from the Hazard Family Papers between 1930-1934. The letters either place Hazard in a specific locale or refer in some way to his alcoholism. The letters verifying his 1931 trip to Europe also substantiate Stattler's claim that "there is no way he could have spent an extended period in Europe between 1930 and early 1933; he was intimately involved in several business ventures in New York and New Mexico." When he did visit Europe from June to September of 1931 he was with his wife and children. Stattler adds: "it seems very unlikely that he could have spent more than a couple of weeks in Zurich."[185] This author examined the letters on Stattler's document list and can attest to the reasonableness of Stattler's conclusions. The letters during the 1931 trip do in fact give the feel of a family adventure. In one such letter Hazard's mother, Mary, writes to his brother Thomas from Florence, Italy,[186] wondering if Roy (Rowland) won't bring her LaSalle automobile over when he arrives so she can take it to England. When the itinerary is discussed in several places, a familial feeling pervades, at least in the heart of the mother. There is an expectation that all the family members will be in contact and will meet at some point.[187]

Examining the family correspondence, however, still leaves a few mysteries during the overall period that ran from 1930 to 1934. In a March 9, 1930, letter to Thomas, the mother asserts: "I think Roy has had a spiritual awakening which makes him ready to do anything which he feels incumbent upon him. That is why I think those about him should try to prevent a sacrifice which is not to the best good of all." She recognizes his vulnerability at this point, particularly with regard to his ex-wife. At that time he would have been considering remarriage to Helen after their divorce a year earlier.[188] The point is that this spiritual awakening would have been in advance of meeting Dr. Jung or being introduced to the Oxford Group or any contact that we know of between him and Courtenay Baylor. What was this awakening? At this point we do not know.

A second mystery surfaces in letters written on February 3, 5, and 13 of 1933, in which his mother mentions Roy's "successes" with a "patient" and later refers to other "patients," presumably while he was in Vermont. The "patient" could not have been Thatcher at this point, since Hazard and Cebra did not carry out their intervention with him until August 1934. Was Hazard attempting to be like Baylor, emulating his own doctor and trying to take on patients himself as a lay psychotherapist? This would be interesting in itself since the first actual documentation on any connection between Hazard and Baylor does not occur until December 15, 1933, ten months later. But as has been noted, there is the possibility that Baylor may have first been called in when Hazard was hospitalized for his alcoholism in February and March of 1932, so his apparent attempts to play

lay psychotherapist in early 1933 could have occurred under Baylor's influence. There are no other mentions of this practice in the collections, so the references to Hazard having "patients" of his own in early 1933 remain a mystery.[189]

It is important to note that these investigations do not conclude that Hazard had no contact with Jung. It is possible that the two had a brief encounter, and that it was of such a force that the meeting turned into a legend which, in the retelling, was expanded into the tale of a course of extensive psychotherapy that soon encompassed a full year or more. The news from Jung that so impressed Bill Wilson might also have affected Hazard in a similar manner; such is the nature of "good news." Apostles, stricken as they are with the revelatory nature of the message, are more interested in passing the message along than in documenting times and dates. And so it may have been with Hazard and Jung. A cynical interpreter would also note that alcoholics tend by their nature to exaggerate and boast and inflate the stories which they tell. Such is the nature of the disease.

The Correspondence between Bill W. and Carl Jung

On January 23, 1961, Bill Wilson wrote a letter to Carl Jung referring to the psychiatrist's encounter with Rowland Hazard thirty years earlier, and on January 30, 1961 Jung wrote him back.[190] Jung said that he remembered working with Hazard, and that Bill's account of what he told Rowland at that time was "adequately reported" and completely correct.[191] Jung's letter also gives the only perhaps potentially deep insight we could possess into Hazard's personality and character. The psychiatrist seemed, on the basis of his remarks in his letter to Bill W., to have had other experience in trying to work with alcoholics, and made the interesting observation in that letter that the kind of spiritual conversion he was referring to when he spoke to Hazard could take one of three forms.[192] It could be produced by "an act of grace," but Hazard, the hardheaded businessman, apparently had too many mental blocks in place to ever allow himself to have anything like the vision of divine light, for example, which Bill W. experienced in the Charles B. Towns Hospital not long after his meeting in the kitchen with Ebby Thatcher, or any equivalent to that sort of spiritual experience.[193] Conversion could also be produced, Jung said in his letter to Bill W., "through a higher education of the mind beyond the confines of mere rationalism," but the pragmatic industrialist and banker Hazard did not seem to have had any ability to explore the Jungian interpretation of religious ritual and art in a way which would involve the deeper feeling levels. Hazard's mind apparently was too prosaic for that.

But a spiritual remaking could also be produced, Jung commented, "through a personal and honest contact with friends," that is, through joining in a fellowship of people who were attempting to lead the spiritual life and then becoming totally immersed in the activities of that group. And on the basis of what Bill W. had reported in his letter, Jung said that he believed that Rowland had chosen that way, "which was, under the circumstances, obviously the best one."[194] Fellowship among recovering people—that vital part of both the Emmanuel Movement method and the Oxford Group's practices—had been the only one of these threes routes through which a man like Rowland Hazard could be reached and freed from his alcoholic compulsion.

The Rhode Island Historical Society material requires us to regard part of the later A.A. account of the meeting between Rowland Hazard and Carl Jung as legendary expansion. Whatever specific conclusion a reader of those documents might reach, their contents cannot be simply ignored. Yet we also have this 1961 letter from Carl Jung affirming that he had in fact had some sort of significant contact with Hazard thirty years earlier, and that the A.A. account of what he had told the Rhode Island businessman at that time was substantially correct. And it seems unquestionably the fact that Jung came into the thinking of the A.A. founders in 1934, and exerted a profound influence on their ideas during the years following.

Additional Emmanuel Movement Influence on A.A.: the Emphasis on Fellowship

Hazard's later years seem to have been prosperous enough, although he never did join Alcoholics Anonymous.[195] In 1936 he became a member of the Episcopal Church and remained active in several of its organizations. Throughout the latter part of his troubled life, Hazard relied on the fellowship of the Oxford Group (including activities such as his work with Ebby Thatcher in 1934) to aid and comfort him in his struggle with alcohol. It was fellowship that helped him even toward the end of his life, when he was being returned to New York after his 1936 binge. The comment Carl Jung made in his letter to Bill W. seems to have been correct, that a saving encounter with the healing quality of the spiritual life could in fact be brought about "through a personal and honest contact with friends," and that this route had been "obviously the best one" for someone of Rowland Hazard's personality.

It was fellowship between recovering people that was a vital part of the approach which the Emmanuel Movement and its offshoot, the Jacoby Club, began developing in 1906-1909. We do not know whether Courtenay Baylor was one of the people who was encouraging Hazard to participate in the activities of the Oxford Group in 1934, but since Hazard lived at a great distance from Boston where Emmanuel Episcopal Church and the Jacoby Club were located, the Oxford Group could have appeared to Baylor as a useful alternative to suggest to the businessman.

Fellowship with recovering alcoholics was also one of the most important features of the A.A. method of freeing people from the compulsion to drink. There have been voices to the contrary: Linda Mercadante, in her book *Victims and Sinners*, claims that the original intention of A.A.'s founders was to have the Big Book the central point of recovery. She insists that "meeting attendance was not seen as 'vital to sobriety.'"[196] In her analysis, the rise of meetings was accidental, more or less an afterthought that later took over the very character of the movement. This seems a very strained interpretation. While it is true that the Big Book was seen as the central point, capable of evoking reverence both then and now, this does not diminish that fact that fellowship, the idea of one drunk helping another, sprang forth almost immediately as one of the key ingredients in the movement. A person cannot get sober alone: this became an axiomatic and vital A.A. tenet. Fellowship became indistinguishable from the movement itself. This was a situation in which one could not tell the dancer from the dance.

Rowland Hazard's own personal experiences made the importance of fellowship clear to the early A.A. people who knew him. And he was a patient of Courtenay Baylor, who came out of the fellowship-oriented Emmanuel Movement tradition. Rowland himself was very active in 1934 in the Oxford Group, which was a strongly fellowship-based spiritual program, and as a result of this, seems to have recovered from his almost two-year total breakdown and returned to his normal business activities by October of that year.

Although Hazard did not get along with Bill Wilson and the other early A.A.s, never joined an A.A. group, and may not have even liked its program, the fact is that he knew from personal experience the power of the fellowship he had seen, felt, and witnessed in other contexts. And he must have had some sort of influence on early A.A.s who knew about him, whether at first or second hand.

Could one imagine that some small portion of the power of the early Emmanuel meetings, held by Elwood Worcester in the church basement in Boston back at the beginning of the century, was somehow carried through time and was conveyed to Hazard by Courtenay Baylor when he ministered to and influenced him in 1933 and 1934? We cannot know. But it is clear that behind Ebby Thatcher, the messenger who brought the word of salvation to Bill Wilson in the kitchen of Bill's apartment in November 1934, lay the figure of Rowland Hazard III, the mysterious messenger behind the messenger.

Chapter 5

The Jacoby Club: Early Years

We need to go back several decades now, to the beginning years of the twentieth century, and take a detailed look at the most important force for successful alcoholic rehabilitation which emerged from the ferment of ideas linked to Emmanuel Episcopal Church in Boston. This was a group which continued to work with alcoholics until the early 1940s, and was for a brief period regarded by many responsible observers (including the New York A.A. office) as the only group other than A.A. which seemed able to get alcoholics sober and keep them sober in any large numbers.

The Jacoby Club began in 1909 as an offshoot of the Emmanuel Movement, first as an informal auxiliary meeting for people who were affected by drinking problems to meet and help each other. Ernest Jacoby, a parishioner and rubber merchant, began the group as an adjunct to the social service work of Emmanuel Church. The group stated its purpose in various ways, ranging from men helping each other, to a place where men "who lost their grip" could get together, to a place for "down and outers" to gather and reconstitute themselves. As McCarthy mentions, the fact that these people were concerned with drinking as their primary form of "nervousness" was concealed from church records, but there is no doubt that the main purpose of the group was to provide self-help among the newly abstinent patients of the Emmanuel program who had alcoholism as one of their most important problems.[197]

The Jacoby Club's purpose became formalized in a slogan that appeared whenever the group advertised itself or its meetings: "A Club for Men to Help Themselves by Helping Others." Such advertisements also stated a good deal of the orientation of the organization. One read, for example: "Its working principle is sympathy and encouragement. Its club room is a place where the man who wants to break the habit is encouraged to believe in himself and to do what he can to help others fighting the same battle." The "habit" is identified as "the drink habit."[198] Other newspaper ads in the 1913-1916 period become more open regarding the mission of the Jacoby Club, stating that this is a place where men could make "the fight against rum" or "the fight against alcohol," and "overcome the drink habit."[199] What began as a meeting place for "down and outers" became more openly an arena of struggle against alcohol.

Elwood Worcester and the Club

The tie between the Jacoby Club and the Emmanuel Movement was acknowledged and clarified in "The Parish News" of the Emmanuel Church (May 1910) by Elwood Worcester himself. Worcester acknowledged Ernest Jacoby's "unassuming, but truly Christian work" in helping "men and women who are struggling to escape from the slavery of drunkenness." Worcester stated that it was "advisable to form them into a permanent club, the first as far as I know which has been attempted by any church in christendom" [sic].[200] In the spirit of his own weekly health conferences, Worcester praised the group for its effort to "remind men of their good resolutions" and "to surround them with good influences and to supply them with good motives."

Worcester was careful to add an Emmanuel dimension to the Jacoby Club in stating that the club was not to be "an ordinary temperance society" but rather a place "to see that careful scientific treatment by qualified physicians and clergymen is administered to those who need it." And perhaps the key aspect of the club was seen as a manifestation of "personal religion": "that every man who is cured shall undertake the reformation of one other person." This was regarded as a critical function in creating "a spirit of service," which would later become the twelfth step of the A.A. program. But here we see mutual support as evidence of Christian charity. As we shall see, the ministering of physicians and clergy became secondary in the philosophy and operation of the program, with self-help and fellowship looming larger. Perhaps herein lies a cause for the eventual split with the Emmanuel Church.

The Jacoby Club was not in fact the first organization to invoke the spirit of self-help and mutual support for dealing with alcoholism.[201] The most notable was the Washingtonian Movement, dating back to the pre-Civil War era. Nevertheless the foregoing "Parish News" quote indicates that whether or not Worcester or Jacoby knew of these historical precedents, they indeed saw the club as original, if for no other reason than by virtue of its ostensible connection to the Emmanuel Church and its rejection of the temperance approach to alcoholism.

Publicity and Growth

The combination of the self-help method, the Emmanuel name, and frequent press coverage spurred the growth of the Jacoby Club. The club started with just six members in 1909, and by 1913 reportedly had helped 500 men.[202] In its 1915-1916 annual report the club claimed to have helped over 1,400 men since its inception. This figure reappears in several newspaper articles concerning the club during this time. The club met in the Emmanuel Church basement during its early years, with summer quarters on the Riverside Recreation grounds, at Riverside on the Charles River. This location was used for Saturday and Sunday meetings, when there were "opportunities for all kinds of sports and games."[203]

By 1913 the Jacoby Club was ready for new quarters, and was also prepared to weather a split with Emmanuel Church. The exact reasons for the separation, although referred to as a schism in one newspaper article,[204] were almost totally glossed over in the press and absent in the archival material reviewed by this author.

The *Boston Globe* article last cited gave one of the few insights available into some of the issues which led up to this separation. The reporter writes that the club had been meeting "in a hall specially fitted up in the rear of the Emmanuel Church but as there never has been anything denominational about the work of the club and this location is not specially fitted for a club that is destined to grow to much larger proportions—as this club surely will—it has been thought best to find other quarters nearer to the heart of the city." The reporter concludes that several sites are being considered and that a new location will probably be had by the fall. On 30 September 1913 the *Boston Transcript* ran an article entitled "Jacoby Club's New Rooms," stating that the new meeting quarters were to be at 127 Newbury Street, open every evening except Sunday.[205]

The reporter acknowledged Ernest Jacoby's role in the club's founding but also points out that Jacoby was a "communicant at the Emmanuel Church" and became interested in the "so-called Emmanuel Movement started by Dr. Worcester, the rector, and Dr. McComb and as a result he laid the foundations of the club which bears his name." The article makes clear the ties to the Emmanuel Movement and how the start of the club was seen as an aid to the "graduates from the Emmanuel Movement classes."

Perhaps the nondenominational nature of the Jacoby Club rankled Worcester and his associates, but this remains a hypothesis only. This schism, however, may well be seen as a fortunate event in the development of A.A. in their city. Perhaps only such a split from the otherwise overpowering Emmanuel Movement could prepare this fertile ground for the future Boston A.A. The fact is that an ineffable something occurred that is likely linked to the nondenominational aspects of the group, its emphasis on self-help (often referred to as "philanthropy"), and its increasing emphasis on helping those who were battling against alcoholism.

It is important to keep the spirit of the times in mind. While Worcester was open to the idea of treating alcoholism, the full impact of the "disease concept" was a long way off, as was anything approaching widespread social acceptance of treatment, medical or otherwise. Many still viewed those afflicted by alcoholism as abhorrent, tainted, moral failures. Worcester and his associates probably did not wish to stretch the generosity of the Emmanuel Church's parishioners too far toward the morally suspect. Nonetheless, according to one historian, "friendly relations were continued" despite the separation, including referrals from the church.[206] The group continued to grow. By 1917 the Jacoby Club was ready for another move, this time to 249 Newbury Street.[207]

The nature of the meetings can be gleaned from numerous newspaper stories of the group's success. The headlines of newspaper accounts between 1913 and 1916 give an idea as to the club's appeal to the general public. They reflect the pre-World War I, Progressive era spirit of self-help and optimism that inspired Worcester and the Emmanuel Movement, rather than the dour, hard-nosed realism of later figures such as Richard Peabody.

Some headlines of the period included: "Men Help Themselves By Helping Others," with the subheadline: "In the Jacoby Club a Man Who Is Making a Fresh Start in Life Finds Friends Who Help by Encouragement and Sympathy—Growth From Small Beginnings" (*Boston Globe*, 27 July 1913). "Down and Out?—See Ernest Jacoby,

Everyman's Friend" (*Boston Sunday Post*, 25 Jan. 1914). "'Help Yourself by Helping Others in Misfortune' Is Jacoby Club's Maxim," with the subheadline: "Unique Philanthropic Organization Plans a String of Similar Institutions in Various Parts of the City—Coercion Has No Part in Its Scheme of Mutual Assistance" (*Boston Sunday Herald*, 22 March 1914).

Another article, written in a notably hard-hitting, pugilistic style, announced: "1,400 Rescued From Drink by Jacoby Club"; its subheadline read: "Isn't This Some Record, Right Here in Boston? Brotherly Love a Winner." The lead continued the tone, with a reference to Billy Sunday. "How's this Rev. William Ashley Sunday? Here's the Jacoby Club, right here in Boston, which has rescued 1,400 men from the grip of John Barleycorn in seven years! There's hitting the trail in earnest—1,400 trail hitters and all like Billy Sunday, fighting the 'booze' curse with the bitterness that comes with the experience of the 'down-and-outer'" (*Boston American*, Sunday, n.d., Nov. 1916). A piece written by Ernest Jacoby himself around the same time also mentioned Billy Sunday, but to make a different kind of point, with the headline: "Jacoby Says Sunday Will Help Where Church Fails" (*Boston American*, 20 Dec. 1916).

An embarrassingly frank headline in an early article deserves special attention: "Drunkard's Club Has Helped Boston Men" (*Boston Sunday Post*, 28 Dec. 1913). The article quotes another writer who had covered the Jacoby Club for the *American Magazine*: "He [Ernest Jacoby] has never been a drinker himself but the peculiar helplessness of the drunkard has always appealed to him. He spends most of his spare moments trying to help unfortunates of this class. He has been remarkably successful. His method is—friendliness."[208] This "friendliness" would later become generalized in the club as a pervading sense of fellowship.

Key Features of the Jacoby Club

From these articles and from club publications, several key aspects of the Jacoby Club emerge. First, not all members were alcoholics. As mentioned earlier, the alcohol connection was veiled in the beginning, the "Drunkard's Club" headline notwithstanding. A 1913 article previously cited ("Men Help Themselves by Helping Others") listed three types of members: "those wishing to be of service to others," "those who have become victims of alcohol," and "those who have through other causes or troubles lost their grip on themselves." This third category left room for the "nervous American" suffering from the ubiquitous neurasthenia. In fact, the 1913 "Report of the Secretary" states that 183 men were "helped by the Club" during the year, and out of that number 114 were found "to be addicted to the use of alcohol."[209]

A second feature was the emphasis on serving others and thereby helping oneself. This was called sympathy, assistance, and companionship. One article cited earlier refers to the system as "philanthropic," a decidedly dated usage of the word.

A third feature was related to the second, that of taking personal responsibility for at least one other person. This adaptation of the "buddy system" was referred to as having a "Special Brother." In fact, each member upon joining received a small booklet with the Jacoby Club constitution, a place for his name and date, and a place for the name of his Special Brother.[210] (While the club repeatedly asserted a policy of nondiscrimination with regard to membership, there is no record of women joining the group.) Special Brothers, also referred to as "stepbrothers," were a key aspect of the club and were discussed in the 1916 booklet "Fighting for Others," discussed below. This special relationship was described as one in which the member would "win the confidence of his new charge, be his friend in everything, look after him in man to man fashion and without any air of patronage, in a word be his chum and his helper."[211]

A fourth feature was individual attention. While this went hand in hand with the Special Brother notion, it added the idea of a personal care as opposed to the strict application of any institutional system, code, or dogma. Each case was considered unique, each person's situation assessed and evaluated to find the best way to help the person reestablish himself in the world.

A fifth feature was the goal of rehabilitation. As Ernest Jacoby said, "He finds the companionship he needs for his regeneration here." Being in the club would provide him with a "better standard" to give him "renewed moral strength." "We go to his home, his friends, his environment. Perhaps his case is one which requires a doctor. His work may be unsuited to him, or he may be out of work. We try to get him a new position, or secure work for him."[212] The sympathy and compassion of the Jacoby Club never diminished its Progressive era optimism and confidence in eventual success. A Horatio Alger spirit lay just below the surface of the Jacoby Club.

A final feature was the emphasis on the activities afforded by the meetings. Typically mentioned are "cozy rooms," and "cheery" surroundings, complete with "reading tables, comfortable chairs, books, magazines and musical instruments."[213] Summer activities included sports and an occasional automobile outing in the country.

Example, fellowship, and sympathy are recurring words, always used in contrast to "exhortation," which was considered to be the bane of the club. Fellowship nevertheless allowed a certain amount of supervision, especially getting the newcomer in the meeting habit. If a "slip" occurred, an expression of penitence to Mr. Jacoby or the secretary David H. McPheters was sufficient to glide over the incident and have the "future...again held up to him."[214]

The Lonesome Man

The Story of the Lonesome Man was a Jacoby Club publication widely circulated in 1914 and immediately thereafter, as a means of introducing the club's work. The book was actually the club's 1913-1914 annual business report prefaced by a lengthy story. Apparently written by David H. McPheters, the club secretary, it tells the story of the Jacoby Club, giving further insight into its nature and assumptions.[215] Several club newspaper advertisements of the period invited readers to write for the book as a way to learn about the organization. The business portion mentions the move to 127 Newbury Street, the club's incorporation under the laws of Massachusetts, and its plans to open other branches in the city and region. Mention is also made of the club's cooperation with the probation department and Norfolk State Hospital and its "endorsement" by the Federation of Churches.

The Story of the Lonesome Man repeats many points already made, but several phrases and sentences are worth noting. The beginning of the story affirms the manly optimism of the period, echoing a bit of the Teddy Roosevelt roar in a time of Woodrow Wilson.

> The Club in its spirit is very much of an appeal—is an appeal in fact for the consideration of men engaged in the working out of a problem that deeply concerns our present-day civilization. It is the appeal of the man who has fallen in the fight but who is conscious that with a little sympathetic help he will be able to take his place in the ranks again and do his share of the world's work. The Club is an assertion of manhood, of right, and of justice.

These men are "conscious" of their shortcomings in that "they have been unfair with themselves" but can see the spirit of brotherhood as a way to regain their dignity and strength. The help of another, who has also been down and out and could thereby express understanding and sympathy, was critical. The lonesome state is emphasized in the context of the "big city": "One of the lonesomest places in the world is a big city.... That is one reason why the saloon flourishes; it appeals to The Lonesome Man." The Jacoby Club provides the fellowship and "can take the place left vacant by his former associates and associations." In short, it can fight the "lure of the saloon" like no other group.

Importantly, *The Story of the Lonesome Man* underscores that "brotherhood must be more than a vague theory or an ethical attraction—it must be practiced." This is linked to helping another: "There comes a spiritual strength and dignity to the helper. Why, this is the cornerstone of Christianity!" This simplistic assertion was close to the only way that spirituality or Christianity was referred to in any of the Jacoby Club literature. If any sort of spiritual dimension was mentioned at all, it was almost always in terms of fellowship and helping brothers. A detailed explanation of any religious or spiritual concept was not the business of the Jacoby Club. The fear of "exhortation" was extended into a fear that too much emphasis on religious dogmas would undermine the club. It was an extreme form of what is called classical Protestant liberalism—the theological movement led by Albrecht Ritschl (1822-89) and Adolf Harnack (1851-1930)—which was sweeping the United States during these first decades of the twentieth century.[216]

(The Jacoby Club's aversion to doctrine and dogma, it should be noted, was paralleled by Courtenay Baylor, by then working with Worcester, who was going to go even further in de-emphasizing the outwardly religious element in the Emmanuel Movement.)

Margaret Deland: *Fighting for Others*

The annual report for 1914–1915 also began with a story, entitled *Men Who Have Won*. The practice was dropped the following year, but each year's report contained an original introduction that explained the nature of the Jacoby Club and discussed its recent successes. Nonetheless, the storytelling book was continued in other ways as a Jacoby Club method of proselytizing and attracting public support in general. In 1916 *Fighting for Others* appeared, once again scarcely more than a pamphlet.[217] The author, Margaret Deland, "the well known Boston author" according to one newspaper review, offered her description of the Jacoby Club as well as an account of two rehabilitated men.

Fighting for Others begins with a foreword in which Deland tells us that "in the terms of Spiritual Economics" the Jacoby Club "has made an asset of its liabilities!" She explains that this refers to how men who have been "tempted" and fallen have recovered and are now helping others. "The Jacoby Club is a club of men who have been tempted. On their feet, now, they say to those still stumbling and falling: 'We are strong, but we were weak! There is as much hope for you as there was for us—for we, too, were tempted in all points as you are!'"[218]

The main text consists of three parts. The first explains the main work of the Jacoby Club as the reclamation of fallen men. The word reclamation is likened to its use in "economic science," thereby placing the club's mission squarely in the era's masculine business ethic. The club believes, she adds, "that out of this stupefied army [of drunkards] will come rich harvests—new dividends."[219] The fallen man will be inspired and strengthened, but not only to succeed for himself alone. He will continue the miracle by helping others. Deland stresses this altruistic aspect of the club's work; like McPheters before her, she insists that this was the "essence of Christianity."

The other two sections of *Fighting for Others* consist of the stories of Bill Bursell and Tom Kilton, two cases taken "at random" from the files of the Jacoby Club, with names, of course, changed. The stories are similar to other cases outlined in newspaper stories on the club and in its own literature: A successful man drinks, socially at first, then intemperately. His social circle rejects him, and with "the cords of the saloon tightening around him," he falls into vagrancy, or close to it. By some miracle he hears of the Jacoby Club, is accepted, befriended, and rehabilitated. He returns to the world, ready to help others who have fallen. Her story of Bill Bursell in particular could well serve as a thumbnail sketch of the life of Bill W. as it appeared in the A.A. Big Book some twenty years later.

The Club and the Climate of the Times

While *Fighting for Others* offers a familiar view of the Jacoby Club, restating its assumptions and message, the fact that it was written by a well-known author reveals a degree of acceptance of the club's mission and the place of its unique methods in pre-World War I society. While the self-help method may not have been new, the context provided by the Jacoby Club was unique. The lack of dreaded "exhortation," the simple explanation of Christianity as helping one's brother, and the treatment by peers, not professionals, was in its unassuming way a breakthrough. Despite the club's nominal ties to Emmanuel Episcopal Church and Worcester, the club was not directed by doctors, psychologists, clergy, or state officials of any stripe. The atmosphere was safe. There were no bars on the windows, no padded cells, no straitjackets. There were no tambourines, no soup kitchens, no sermons. Instead, there were comfortable chairs, reading material, and friendly faces. When compared to the regimen that the typical alcoholic-inebriate had to endure in the name of a "cure," the clubrooms of the Jacoby Club indeed must have seemed like a heaven-sent sanctuary.

It is important to remember that the Jacoby Club was prospering at the same time that Worcester and Baylor were in practice. Medical doctors and psychologists were still coming up with various theories of alcoholism, and Freud was also beginning to receive more notice in some American psychiatric circles (with effects at times on their theories about the proper treatment of alcoholism). Alcoholics were going to endure many more horrors and missteps before the formation of Alcoholics Anonymous. Strecker and Chambers were yet to appear, as were dozens of quack theories and remedies. Amidst the turbulence of the early twentieth century, however, the Jacoby Club serenely awaited its moment of destiny, when it would encounter the infant Alcoholics Anonymous.

Basil King's Down and Out Club

Most of the accounts of the Jacoby Club's actual working came from newspaper interviews with Ernest Jacoby, various reporters' interpretations, and second-hand accounts of the meetings. The club did not operate secretly and sought publicity for both acceptance and funding. Various projects required funds, whether furniture or a new phonograph; for the latter, the Club took out an newspaper ad, hoping for a donation in kind. Despite this relatively open policy, this was an age before the invasive electronic media, and a precise account of a club meeting is not available.

A novel by Canadian-born author Basil King, however, offers a valuable glimpse into the Club's operations at a deeper level. *The City of Comrades,* published in 1919, portrays the recovery of two men through their participation in a group that is unmistakably the Jacoby Club, although the book calls it the "Down and Out."[220] The book also affords a view of the literary tastes of at least one segment of the public. Often excessively sentimental and always thoroughly "proper," King writes of male companionship, a budding love affair, and the heroic participation of the United States in World War I. The book's conclusion reflects the martial spirit that seized the nation, which viewed war as an act of cleansing and growth, the heralding of a new and greater age for the nation.

Basil King (1859-1928) was born on Prince Edward Island and educated in Nova Scotia, where he later served as curate and rector of St. Luke's Pro-Cathedral, Halifax. From 1892 to 1900 he served as rector of Christ Church in Cambridge, Massachusetts. Ill health led King to leave his church career and devote himself to writing, which he did while residing in Cambridge and during his frequent trips to Europe.[221] King's literary career produced twenty novels and eight nonfiction books dealing with religious and spiritual matters based on his personal experience.

The Story

The City of Comrades centers around the adventures of Frank Melbury, a Canadian architect, graduate of McGill University, and a former student at the Beaux Arts in Paris. Frank (Francis) is well connected, his father being Sir Edward Melbury of Montreal, and his mother an American with ties to New York society. The novel is set in New York, so the plot naturally unfolds in these circles once Frank's rehabilitation is complete.

The first 116 pages are of greatest interest to us in our understanding of the Jacoby Club, the other 290 involving a tedious plot which has Frank moving in and around New York society while alternately trying to avoid and court Regina Barry, a flighty socialite who discovers herself during her service in World War I. Nonetheless, an overview of the plot sets the "Down and Out" club passages in context.

The book opens when Frank and his companion and fellow drunk, Lovey, are "on the bum," sleeping here and there, literally ragged and starving. Lovey, a cockney Londoner who landed in New York, befriends Frank, as "fellas together," vagrants eking out an existence, including Lovey's occasional petty crimes. Frank tells us that Lovey "had begun following me about, somewhat as a stray dog will follow you when you have given him a bone and a drink of water."[222] Despite the developing theme of fellowship, King resolutely writes from his class and historical period. Though copyrighted in 1919, the novel has a thoroughly Victorian flavor, all but quaint on the one hand, and on the other hand offensive to those readers more sensitive to contemporary political correctness. His sense of caste and Anglo-Saxon superiority never leaves him, Frank always treating Lovey with a certain air of patronage, despite Lovey's hopeful assertion, "we're Britishers together."

The Down and Out club is first mentioned as a place to avoid: "Once ye do that ye're done for" (7). The implication, somewhat mysteriously rendered, is that if you do enter the Down and Out, your drinking days are over. But before this possibility arises, Frank has an adventure. Having not eaten for forty-eight hours and without hope of a meal, Frank plans a burglary.

After resisting the temptations to commit acts as petty as stealing from a newsboy, our hero finally musters the nerve to enter a house "up on one of the long avenues" where "the buildings were thinning out." Frank enters, fortifies himself with some pilfered food and cooking sherry and proceeds to look for valuables. While there he eavesdrops on two women, learning that the feisty Regina Barry has been a hard-to-get woman who asserts "I don't mean to be married till I'm sure," a sort of proto-feminist assertion of independence by the author's value system. Her habit of breaking engagements has caused a bit of a stir in her social circle, but she seems unconcerned. This piques the interest of our hero, very much still a vagrant and alcoholic. In the course of stealing some jewelry he pins a note to a cushion: "There are men different from those you have seen hitherto. Wait." Just why he leaves the note remains unanswered, but in the world of King's contrived plots, we can be assured that he is the man whose true worth will impress her.

He reveals himself to Regina, who neither screams nor protests. Instead, her adventurous spirit and his gentlemanly ways facilitate an unlikely conversation. He leaves, but is thereafter haunted by the possibility that he will someday be recognized as the lowly cur who made his way into her home. Later he does meet her, and eventually reveals himself to be the burglar. The two flirt with the possibilities of love, but despite a number of meetings and periphrastic conversations regarding matters of the heart, they neither kiss nor touch. Of course, there is a love complication: Regina is already engaged to another man.

Patriotism

The passion that overrides all the potential love relationships in the novel, including a deepening of the involvement between Frank and Regina, is patriotism. The novel portrays a dizzying frenzy of nationalism in the period just prior to the declaration of war, at least as it is felt by the key characters. Frank's guiding principle becomes his "celibacy of the will," his single-minded purpose in life being to serve the cause of the war. He soon becomes a major in the Canadian army, later to return wounded, complete with a dashing black eye patch.

Regina's devotion to the cause scuttles her marriage plans, such as they were, and turns her into a "woman with the courage of a soldier" (284), the result of her having served as a Canadian nurse "in an amateur sense" (245). In addition to both Frank and Regina serving in Europe, the story includes a German submarine attack, and devotes many pages to fervent discussion of the noble task facing the United States in the trenches of Europe. Despite a separation of well over two years, the possibility of love between the two returns full force—but to no avail. The sentiment is that "We're in a world where…love and marriage are no longer the burning questions. They're too small" (400). (This is definitely not *A Farewell to Arms*.) The novel closes with Regina telling Frank that they cannot be together *yet* because they still had work to do, to "get a little farther on—not only you and I—but our country—our countries—we must give still more…before it's given back to us—renewed—purified" (406).

National devotion not only overwhelms the protagonists, it also crops up at the Down and Out club, where patriotic issues are fervently discussed. In a chapter at the novel's end, the club becomes little more than a recruiting headquarters. The spirit of the men is transformed by the very possibility of war, and fellowship is on the verge of becoming nothing more than wartime camaraderie. The chapter becomes a memorable account of prowar sentiment that links America's involvement to a moral cleansing and refitting. Participation in the war becomes a gift of oneself, a giving "that isn't to men, it's to God" (392). While this rhetoric may be of historical interest,[223] it is important to note that King could not help but use the Down and Out for his purposes. If the Jacoby Club members had any reaction to King's "famous patriotic meeting at the Down and Out" (381-392), no record of it has been found.

The Down and Out

The Down and Out club plays a crucial role at the beginning of the novel by helping Frank resume his position in the world, with Lovey tagging along as his valet-butler. According to Frank's telling, the club started when two drunks met, more or less by accident, and wound up sobering up a third man. "The third man, in gratitude for what had been done for him, went after a fourth…and so the chain was flung" (57). The idea of two men sobering each other up presages the inception of A.A. itself; the casual, almost accidental nature of the club's beginning is reminiscent of Bill W.'s meeting Dr. Bob.

The club "was not a mission—that is, it was not the effort of the safe to help those who are in danger; it was the effort of those who are in danger to help themselves" (56). In this key feature, the Down and Out faithfully represents the Jacoby Club. King tells us that the Down and Out had "no persuasions but such as a man who has got out of hell can bring to bear on another who is still frying in the fire. Its action being not from the top downward, but from the bottom upward, it had a native impulse to expansion." It is here that we see how the Jacoby Club, like the Down and Out, differed from its parent, the Emmanuel Weekly Health Conferences, and later self-help fraternal organizations such as the Oxford Group.

The emphasis is also on a self-governance that rejects outside authority and avoids any direct institutional affiliation; the fictitious Down and Out has only nominal ties to a St. David's church and owes its meeting place to the church's philanthropy. But unlike the Jacoby Club, it accepted "neither gifts of money nor contributions in kind" (59). Nonetheless, both organizations had the rehabilitation of men as their sole reason for being.

The two men, Lovey and Slim (Lovey's nickname for Frank), finally find the club and enjoy its food and hospitality. The atmosphere of fellowship is apparent: "What was more active than anything else was a blind fellow-feeling. They did little things for one another. They did little watchful things for Lovey and me. They even quarreled over their kindnesses like children eager to make themselves useful" (63). The house is sparsely furnished but clean, with worn but well-scrubbed wooden floors and wooden furniture. One can almost smell the soap and furniture polish. The house had been owned by a woman of social standing at a time when the neighborhood had been rather exclusive, and King tells us that the "rooms themselves, as was natural with an old New York residence, did not lack dignity" (64). This feeling of quiet dignity is mixed with the calm but resolute pursuit of a new life. But beneath the calm each man is aware of his tenuous hold on sobriety, an anxious position were it not for the help of his brethren.

King also explains the system of rewards, how the third floor has dormitories for club members "who had kept sober for three months or more, and who wore a star of a color denoting the variety of their achievements" (65). Other rooms, designed for recreation, were open to any one who had remained sober for three weeks. The top floor contained bedrooms for those who had "preserved their integrity for three years and more; and here, too, was the sacred place known as 'the lounge,' to which none were admitted who didn't wear the gold or silver star representing sobriety for at least a year" (65). King concludes that "the whole was, therefore, a carefully arranged hierarchy in which one mounted according to one's merit" (65-66). Lovey and Slim were outsiders who had to agree to stay a week. "At the beginning of the second week they could either continue their novitiate or go" (66).

At first Lovey thinks the men at the club are a "bunch of simps," a forlorn group without any spirit. He agrees to stick it out because of Frank—they have a mutual agreement to follow each other, as "fellas together" (68-69). Frank and Lovey slowly get to know the workings of the club, and how it is based on mutual help, including the financing, each giving according to his ability. When Frank feels compelled to tell his "dark secret" regarding his entry into Regina Barry's home, he discovers that no one really cares to hear yet another tale of wrongdoing; each man has his own volume of such experiences. Frank's secret therefore continues to weigh on his heart.

The key to the Down and Out club, Frank learns, is prayer in the form of generous action. Its theology is summed up by Andrew Christian, a cofounder of the club: "It's in trying to carry out the law of His being in doing things for others. That isn't all of it, by any means; but it's a starting-point.... Prayer is action—only it's kind action." He adds, "You yourself will be praying all through this week, in your very effort to buck up. You'll be praying in helping that poor man Lovey do the same.... Prayer is living—only, living in the right way" (77-78).

Frank and Lovey realize that nothing dramatic occurs at the club: "a kind of silent, tactual clinging together" was the only comfort besides "regular food and sleep." Importantly, Frank notes that "none of us wanted to be really alone" (81). This theme of providing a cure for loneliness looms large in the club's appeal. According to Frank, the men liked simply being in close proximity to one another, this providing a type of solace that neither tobacco nor reading could supply. At this stage, the fellowship is notably silent. "From a handclasp and a few chance sentences we got the secret of a personality which gave out its light and heat like radium, without effort and without exhaustion" (83).

Lovey and Frank learn other aspects of the Down and Out, especially its blend of religion and health, echoing ties to the Emmanuel Movement. Andrew Christian tells the men that "salvation is being normal." He adds that this was learned from the "intuitive older guys" who "saw that plainly enough when they connected the idea with health. Fundamentally health is salvation and salvation is health—only perfect health, health not only of the body, but of the mind. Did it ever strike you that health and holiness and wholeness are all one word?" (82). Andrew further explains that wholeness is a significant pun for holiness and that the true manifestation of holiness is in being an "all-around man," a whole man. It is being "sound in wind and limb and intelligence and sympathy and everything that makes power."

In this the Down and Out shares in the Progressive era ethic of manliness and optimism. Wholeness and holiness in the club are not "anemic," but instead are brimming with a vitality imparted by Andrew Christian's words. Frank begins to feel that nature could provide the necessary stimulation for growth toward the salvation described to him. Sunshine, air, and water could do it, with no other "extraordinary stimulants" being necessary (85).

During an initiation meeting, in which the two men are formally admitted as members, one of the "authorities," Colonel Straight, offers what amounts to a homily. The club, says the colonel, is more like an army than a club for amusement; membership means "entering a company" and "now it's all going to be different" (91). Whereas the men were independent before, upon entering the membership they become responsible for one another, and "you can't get drunk without hurting us, and we can't get drunk without hurting you." (91). This new responsibility includes a pledge that the men will hunt down a member who has gone astray, no matter where. Whereas the two neophytes saw the club as providing for them, the colonel stressed that the "the hundred and fifty of us you see here to-night…see two men that's coming to help us" (92).

The self-help theme that Colonel Straight intones is of a nature that a contemporary A.A. member would recognize. Unlike a temperance group or religious society that might rest more comfortably and smugly with their belief that they were securely practicing a "better way," this club is made up of men who know no rest from the task of keeping their demons at bay. Their collective plight prohibits complacence toward recovery and a casual attitude toward the fellowship itself. The colonel reminds the men:

> You look round and you see this elegant house—and the beds—and the grub—and everything decent and reg'lar—and you think how swell we've got ourselves fixed. But I tell you, men, we're fighting for our life.... we're fighting with our backs against the wall. We ain't out of danger because we've been a year or two years or five years in the club. We're never out of danger. We need every ounce of support that any one can bring to us; and here you fellows come bringing it!...and if either of you fails, you leave each one of us so much the weaker (92).

Frank and Lovey take the pledge of the newcomer. They had to pledge abstinence for a week, renewable at weekly intervals until they could pledge a month. The men were to seek work and, after obtaining jobs, they were to send three-quarters of their pay to their wives. In the meantime they were to "atone for their failure" and "do their best to strengthen other members of the club." When the men became veterans, "they were to be guardians of the most zealous activity, and shrink from no insult or injury." Their promises, we are told, were "more severe" (93).

As with the Jacoby Club, the meeting deals with the question of religion quickly: "The religious issue was shelved by asking each man to give his word to reconnect himself with the church in which he had been brought up" (93). The club's unofficial physician describes the Down and Out's attitude toward religion at one point by stating that only the term is avoided because "it's been so misapplied as to have become nearly unintelligible. If you told the men at the club that such and such a thing was religion, they'd most of 'em kick like the deuce; but when they get the thing without explanation they take it every time" (100). These words might well describe a major aspect of A.A.'s attitude toward religion.

The story of Frank Melbury unfolds from the Down and Out, Frank making contacts through the club and becoming enmeshed in New York society. Lovey becomes his man servant, hanging back, yet a sober reminder of his earlier days. The Down and Out does not disappear entirely from view; Frank thinks back on the club, most notably when he returns from his stint overseas. "There had been times when I thought I had outlived that phase, times when what seemed like a new and higher companionship, with a new and higher place in the world and in men's esteem, half-persuaded me that…the Down and Out was no more to me than a sloughed skin to the creature that has thrown if off" (273).

Frank has doubts about his role in the club, and is tempted to regard himself as cured. But he knows that this is not the case and reaffirms his fellowship: "But I always waked from this pleasant fancy to see myself as in essentials the same gaunt, tattered, hungry fellow who had come with his buddy to beg a meal and a bed…. No matter what battles I fought, what medals I won, what banquets I was asked to sit down at, my place was among them" (272). But for Frank, work with the club is not chiefly about helping men gain sobriety; it serves more to proselytize the cause of World War I. King's character has the stamp of the age upon him.

The Lonesome Trail

Basil King did not leave the Jacoby Club with *The City of Comrades*. In 1919 he provided the foreword to a club booklet entitled *The Lonesome Trail*, another Jacoby Club tract describing itself and its mission. The booklet itself is anonymous, but was likely written by its secretary, David H. McPheters, in 1919, shortly after the passage of the eighteenth amendment made it clear that Prohibition was soon to be the law of the land, but before the Volstead Act (its legal implementation) began to be actually enforced at the beginning of 1920.[224] King's foreword established the purpose of the new booklet. "Prohibition does not lay its ax to the root of the tree; it only kills the leaves." He adds that Prohibition may keep men from getting drunk, "but they won't be kept from doing other things," and he does not mean bootlegging. Just what these other actions might be is not made clear. But King adds the metaphor of water being checked by a dam, adding that "great care must be taken to see that it does not flood the land."[225] King assures the reader that the organization is not unaware of this peril: "Awake to this danger the Jacoby Club is preparing to take that care." The care they are taking is apparently working to make sure that no man is left isolated and alone, in an attempt to ride the proverbial lonesome trail, which for King and the booklet's author leads to drink and ultimate ruin. Just how the new dangers brought by Prohibition, whatever they may be, are related to a lonesome state is not clear in King's foreword.

The text of the booklet itself repeats many of the Jacoby Club ideals, claims, and aspirations, reiterating that it "seeks, and finds, a cure for the lonely life in warming, human sympathy and affection" and that it "endeavors to reclaim the waste acres and to add to the great army of world workers whose days have been fruitless and unfortunate."[226] The booklet author adds that not all men at the club were brought there by drink, but then returns the emphasis to those who were. In order to temper the tendency to view a place such as the Jacoby Club as overly solemn, or inhabited by mentally impaired drunks, the author reminds us that the club has been cited as a place where "'you'll hear higher grade conversation…than one hears in most clubs in Boston.'" For an example, he writes of overhearing two men "vigorously" discussing "Wagner's true place among composers."[227]

In an upbeat spirit, the author tells us that "The Jacoby Club has no place for tears." The issue of religion is raised and handled, as ever, with an enthusiastic simplicity, repeating the injunction of the founder and secretary: "Get near God. Pray to Him. Trust Him. He will do the rest for He needs men for His work in raising men to new life." The author adds that the "club teaches a gospel of simple, trustful faith that is like that of the

Psalmist, who wrote: 'I have been young, and now am old: yet have I not seen the righteous forsaken, nor his seed begging bread.'"[228]

The booklet concludes with the concern King himself introduced: the impact of Prohibition on the Jacoby Club. "There is a disposition on the part of many," the booklet states, "to regard the work of reclamative agencies as almost at an end" due to the impending onset of Prohibition. "There are those who seem unable to understand why or how such an organization as the Jacoby Club can continue to fill a place of usefulness."[229] For the author of *The Lonesome Trail*, the answer is twofold.

First, the club would furnish the place for those who had quit drinking to reclaim themselves; the ravages of the disease would not be instantly overcome for those who had been forced to stop drinking by the new Prohibition laws. The reclamation process would include tending to the immediate needs of those who were about to quit, particularly help in overcoming "the horror of horrors," "the suffering of a man as he recovers from an alcoholic debauch…the tossing, sleepless nights, the chills, the fever, the thirst, the aversion to nourishing food, the dread of everything, the dread of nothing, the cowardice that shrinks from the darkened room but that dares not go into the light."[230] In other words, the club, though not a medical facility, would in some way aid in the withdrawal process as well as later rehabilitation.

The second way that the Jacoby Club would maintain its purpose in a dry period was through its ongoing fellowship—the opposite of the lonesome trail, the fatal drifting off into despondency and isolation. "Saloons or no saloons, loneliness and discouragement we shall have ever with us, and against them and for their victims the Jacoby Club must continue to work." The author of the booklet recognizes that the saloon was an important social force in the lives of many men: "The saloon is more than a drinking place. In it, on its saw-dust covered floor and amid its reeking odors, a cross-section of our great democracy has found its common meeting place." And most importantly, "to take the place of the social side of the saloon something must be erected, and in this stupendous work an organization like the Jacoby Club can be, yes, must be, most helpful."[231]

Stupendous indeed. Of course, the members of the Jacoby Club had no idea how endemic the saloon would remain, transformed into the speakeasy, and how both the lure and easy availability of alcohol were to remain fundamentally undisturbed. The rhetoric of the book seems appropriately quixotic: although naively convinced that alcoholism itself would cease instantly and forever in the United States, on the very day when the new Prohibition laws were to be brought to bear (which ended up occurring at the beginning of 1920),[232] *The Lonesome Trail* concludes thus: "It is a knightly fight, this battle against loneliness, a great adventure, a high emprise. The man who would win must look well to it that his armor is without chink or flaw and his sword is bright and keen. 'One for all and all for one,' the rallying cry of the Musketeers, is the trysting call of the Jacoby Club as it summons its members and friends to the work."[233]

Chapter 6

The Jacoby Club: Stasis and Schism

The Twenties and Thirties

When the new Prohibition laws came into effect at the beginning of 1920, it turned out that alcoholics would continue to drink just as much, even if it was now illegal. It was too easy to evade the law, and there were too many Americans who would turn a blind eye toward those who were providing the illegal alcohol. Those who wanted to drink badly enough, and who did not have the money or connections to obtain liquor bootlegged in from Canada and other surrounding countries, would make homemade wine and beer, or take regular trips to visit the crude moonshine whiskey stills that had been operating in isolated parts of the United States (going back to George Washington's era and before), or patronize the local entrepreneurs who produced "bathtub gin" and similar raw but potent distilled alcohol using contraptions they had cobbled together in a garage or outbuilding.

The Jacoby Club had not been put out of business, not in the least. The alcoholics were still there. It was the American general public which had been quixotic and naively idealistic. Too many people had been in massive denial about the real strength of the alcoholic compulsion, and had assumed that the punitive approach, if the laws were absolutized, would automatically solve the problem of alcoholism.

So the Jacoby Club continued to meet and do its rehabilitative work at 168 Dartmouth Street through the 1920s, just as it had before Prohibition came into effect. While the Emmanuel Movement had already seen its zenith, the Club continued to enjoy a modicum of publicity, good will, and solid standing. Throughout the 1920s and 1930s, Rev. Samuel McComb remained on the Board of Advisers, keeping the old Emmanuel Movement connection alive. The annual reports repeated the purpose and method of the Club, each citing how its fellowship, warmth, and support rescued a man from his own destruction. Interestingly, no annual report from that period mentioned Prohibition. It had turned out to be totally irrelevant in dealing with chronic alcoholics. They had to work a little harder to find their alcohol on some occasions (though even that was not necessarily true), and the quality of what they drank was much lower, but their consumption had not dropped in the slightest.

The 1923-1924 annual report boasted that the Jacoby Club had helped a total of over 2,000 men and that its secretary, David H. McPheters, "has in the past three months had an average of about four visits per day from men—ill, discouraged, out of work, without home or food. Some have been given lodging and food, others helped to find work; some have been taken to a physician for examination, others have been placed in the hospital for treatment; some have been helped to fight the craving for alcohol, others unfortunately have been turned away for lack of funds at our disposal."[234]

While the Club maintained itself in terms of numbers, its expenses increased even as contributions remained steady. In 1928, the contributions as of April 20th were $4,080; ten years later on the same date, they had fallen slightly to $3,959. Each annual report made its solicitation message strong and emphatic, stressing that the Club was supported entirely by voluntary contributions. A 1927 publication was designed for the purpose of solicitation, stating that "The present facilities of the Club are pitifully inadequate" and "We are in urgent need of funds."[235]

The next decade, the 1930s, was a period of great national tribulation, with the Great Depression settling in on the country, as well as apprehensions and anxieties produced by the gathering storm in Europe. Within the Club, the great loss was the death of Ernest Jacoby, Sr., in 1935. Interestingly enough, there is only one oblique reference to his passing in the archival material, in a 1935 newspaper article regarding the Club's twenty-fifth anniversary.[236] The annual reports skip topical references, with the occasional exception of a reference to a newspaper article dealing with the Club or one of its own booklets. The reports themselves did not mention Jacoby's passing.

The tone of the annual reports varies from "boilerplate" writing regarding the purpose of the Club to occasional flights of sentimentality, no doubt in keeping with the spirit of the times. The 1936-1937 annual report includes the following:

> Of our Christmas Eve gatherings one of the members writes, 'Dickens would feel at home on Christmas Eve at the Jacoby Club, for on that occasion the ghosts of Old Scrooge, of Marley and of Tiny Tim walk again as they did in the purlieus of old London. There is a Dickens tang in the air when groups of talented artistes sing the angelic chants to the Babe who was born in a Bethlehem stable that moonlit night two thousand years ago. What a tale the master story-teller might write could he but see the happy faces listening with rapt attention as the singers render the songs of Christmastide. On that night at the

Jacoby Club, romance—of a spiritual kind—has the company in its thrall and for the moment they are transported to realms they never believed could exist in this material age.[237]

While A.A. was being born and nurtured in New York and Ohio, the Jacoby Club unwittingly included an ominous note in one of its annual reports (1935-1936): "Truly the Jacoby Club is 'The House by the Side of the Road.' Some of its members are now in the late afternoon of life, journeying toward the setting sun, but the heart and mind will remain young and vigorous when nurtured by the fraternal bond of fellowship extended at all times by the Jacoby Club."[238] The tension between the needs of the older men and the mission to rehabilitate alcoholics would soon dominate the Club's agenda.

The middle and latter 1930s was the formative period for A.A. The purpose of this book is not to recount the stories surrounding Bill W. and Bob S. and the birth of A.A. in 1935.[239] Several histories cover this ground well, none better than Ernest Kurtz's *Not-God: A History of Alcoholics Anonymous*.[240] Nonetheless, the story of the Jacoby Club becomes intertwined with that of the birth of A.A. in no small way.

What Kurtz refers to as the "four 'founding moments' in the history of the idea and the fellowship of Alcoholics Anonymous," all occurred during this period.[241] Establishing itself in its own right, the New York A.A. group parted company with the Oxford Group in late 1937. The midwest A.A. groups followed suit in the summer of 1939.[242] The Twelve Steps were written in December 1938; *Alcoholics Anonymous*, "The Big Book," was published in April 1939; and membership reached 100 in December 1939. By February 1940, the first A.A. clubhouse was established at 334 1/2 West 24th Street in New York City.[243]

During 1940 and 1941, several events changed the course of both the Jacoby Club and Alcoholics Anonymous. Jack Alexander's *Saturday Evening Post* article in March 1941 helped spur the growth of A.A. nationwide as well as in the Boston area. The Jacoby Club, on the other hand, underwent a profound reorganization. By July 16, 1942, a swift succession of events resulted in the resignation of its acting executive secretary and the essential end of alcoholism treatment by the Jacoby Club.

The Alcoholic Group vs. the "Older Men"

By 1940 the Jacoby Club had transferred its headquarters to 159 Newbury Street, a move that was given little or no public coverage and went without much note in the Club's internal publications. Ernest Jacoby, Jr., although just 24 on his father's death in 1935, had taken over leadership of the Club. By mid-1940 the Club had hired a new assistant executive secretary, Lawrence M. Hatlestad, whom McPheters described as "a young minister who has considerable experience dealing with the type of men who come to the club."[244] According to a report by Ernest Jacoby, Jr., Hatlestad's position was part-time.[245] Shortly after his installation, Hatlestad displayed his interest in working with alcoholics to the exclusion of the other members, referred to as the "older men." By 1941 the membership of the Club had for most practical purposes split into two groups—the recovering alcoholics and the "older men"—two factions which were composed of people with very different backgrounds, problems, and concerns.

According to Jacoby's report, Hadlestad's concern and interest in working with alcoholics attracted a group of approximately twelve people who were "young, well-educated, well dressed, and have good jobs such as salesmen, executives and accountants." He added that they were all recent members of the Club and that Hatlestad did "an unusually good job and the principle of 'helping ourself by helping another' [was] being carried out."

By this time the older men's group had already been meeting separately for six months at the Ellis Memorial, a South End Boston settlement house. When not meeting at Ellis, the group went to two other settlement houses, the Wells Memorial and the South End House. According to the report, Hatlestad did not attend these meetings and Jacoby noted that he did not think he was "suited for this type of work." Jacoby's report concluded with a list of several issues that needed to be addressed, none less important than whether the Club's mission should be to work with alcoholics or devote itself "solely to work with older men."

Dissension in the Ranks: The Steele Report

Ernest Jacoby treated dissension within the ranks rather casually, stating that three members of the Club who were neither "older men" nor alcoholic "have been very outspoken in their criticisms of Mr. Hallestad [sic] and the policy of treating alcoholism to the exclusion of others." In fact, on May 13, 1941, Malcolm Steele, a member of the Jacoby Club Executive Board, wrote a strongly worded letter to Jacoby stating that, in his belief, "the main purpose for which the club was founded is no longer being carried out." Steele, who was a Boston lawyer, soon after sent Jacoby a report dated June 12, 1941, in which he detailed charges against Hatlestad. This report outlines the issues that were splitting the Club.

There is little doubt that Hatlestad had thrown himself into the "alcohol work" as his primary concern. Correspondence affirms that he sought ties with other organizations and services to further this cause, including A.A. itself.[246] Hatlestad was trying to reach out to alcoholics with the zeal of an A.A. member doing Twelfth Step work, and his enthusiasm was becoming a cause for concern for some of the Club's leadership: people who were in fact becoming decreasingly interested in such work.

Steele's report to the Board of Governors is a harsh indictment of Hatlestad and the alcoholic enterprise. In addition to having taken over the Club's quarters "for this alcoholic group under the name of the Jacoby Club," he adds that "the only chance a member has of getting welcome at what is listed as the Jacoby Club is to get drunk and announce himself during the proper hours as an alcoholic seeking a cure." Steele states that he sees "no objection to devoting a *proportionate* [his italics] share of the club funds to their behalf," but that "the club should not be turned into an alcoholic clinic." Steele also makes a key point: the original purpose of the Club was not the sole treatment of alcoholics alone. In Steele's opinion the Club's reputation is being undermined. "We are not chronic inebriates," he angrily states.

Perhaps his harshest statements concern Hatlestad's qualifications. In an age when the medical profession was becoming increasingly interested in the treatment of alcoholism, Hatlestad's minister's credentials were now coming to be viewed as insufficient. There was an irony here: in the western tradition, for many centuries, the clergy had controlled the higher educational system and "the cure of souls" (the *psychês therapeia*, originally an ecclesiastical term for this major traditional pastoral function). In earlier times—in colonial America for example—lay people were not allowed to teach at colleges and universities, or carry out "psychotherapy," as we would call the cure of souls today. People who had personal problems were told to go to their priests or pastors for counseling. But now the new secular universities which had appeared in the nineteenth century, and the new psychiatry—which was linked to the medical profession, not the professors of theology—were declaring that the clergy were not qualified either to control the universities or carry on the cure of souls.

Hatlestad might have well benefited from reviewing the trials and tribulations of the Emmanuel Movement thirty years earlier, because even then there had been complaints from people who insisted that only someone with an M.D. degree from a medical school, or a Ph.D. (a new type of American academic degree which had been developed in the new secularly-oriented universities), or some equivalent kind of secular credentials, was qualified to work with alcoholics.

Steele was a man of the new age, the twentieth century with its new ideas of what constituted adequate qualification, and declared unequivocally that "therapeutics should be in the hands of qualified practitioners."

Alcoholism is today recognized by medical science as a disease." Clerical credentials no longer counted as adequate. Steele reminded the Board of Governors that "our acting secretary is not a psychiatrist nor even a medical doctor by his admission. If he were to start an open practice as a paid practitioner in the cure of mental or other diseases, he would be arrested as a quack."

If Steele's rhetoric seems extreme, his concerns are illustrated by two letters, one written to Hatlestad and the other by him. The first was a letter to Hatlestad, indicating that he himself was receiving prescriptions (benzedrine) from the Boston Psychiatric Hospital, apparently for use with a Club member. The person signing the letter was a social worker, not a doctor, which could only annoy the physicians even more.[247] And even in earlier centuries, clergy were not regarded as qualified to prescribe or dispense medication. Hatlestad was trying to overextend his authority quite dangerously.

The second letter was written by Hatlestad to a physician, a medical professional with an M.D. degree, reflecting his contradictory self-image as a believer in nonprofessional self-help who nonetheless was crossing deeply into the realm of medicine. The letter informs the doctor that he had had a discussion with a certain woman regarding her father's drinking problems.[248] The doctor was informed that this man would be coming to him for a "thorough physical examination." Hatlestad then goes on to describe his evaluation of the man's problem, including recommendations to avoid the "build-ups" of nervousness and irritability that seemed to precede alcoholic episodes. His recommendations include the use of apamorphine, "which can be put in his coffee and thus prevent drinking because of the attendant nausea in the presence of alcohol." He also suggests the use of a sedative for sleep and benzedrine sulphate, "which would have a tendency to lift the father out of his depression." It does not seem to have occurred to Hatlestad that attempts to tell the doctor what to prescribe might offend a medical professional or provoke serious reaction among the physicians of Boston.

It should be noted parenthetically that this was the exact period (March through June of 1941) when Hatlestad was actively recruiting alcoholics in the Boston area into what was in fact starting to become A.A. By March of 1941, Burt C. and Paddy were conducting an A.A. meeting on Wednesday nights at the Jacoby Club's 115 Newbury Street address with Hatlestad's eager backing, and until early 1942, the Boston A.A. group and the Jacoby Club were to some degree intertwined with one another and attempting to work together cooperatively.

Steele would have had no sympathy for the A.A. linkage either. He stated that religion and spirituality are not the proper cure for alcoholism and suggested, in so many words, that if the Club had funds for alcoholism it would do better to spend the amount by sending people to hospitals or clinics. So much for men helping men. The tension between an exclusively medical model of alcoholism and the view that we must deal with a triad of mind, body, and spirit had again surfaced. The very same forces of professionalism that had pressured Elwood Worcester and positively plagued Richard Peabody had descended upon the Jacoby Club, albeit through a minority report from within the membership. This was complicated by Hatlestad's confused self-image. Was he a proponent of the young A.A. program, a supporter of the Jacoby idea of men helping men, or a budding unlicensed medical therapist on the order of a Richard Peabody?

Aside from the Hatlestad issue, Steele emphasized what he felt was the need to serve the other men in the Club, the non-alcoholics, in the spirit of the founder, Ernest Jacoby, Sr., and the original secretary, David McPheters. His plan for reorganization would establish (or to his mind, reestablish) the Club as a service to a wide variety of men with a range of problems, from unemployment to health issues. Rather than one secretary, there would be a committee of six secretaries, each handling a separate area of concern. The report concludes with a concession that the Club might devote "part of its efforts to the care and cure of alcoholics, though I do not believe that Mr. Hatlestad would be recognized by medical authorities as being a capable person to handle same." His plan, of course, called for Hatlestad's dismissal as acting executive secretary. Steele would not allow for a self-help group, and clearly favored relegating alcoholic treatment to the medical profession.

Moderation Prevails

Fortunately for the Club, Steele's position was met by the temperate disposition of Ernest Jacoby, Jr. In his report, Steele stated that he knew that he was expressing a minority position among the leadership. Whether this was true or not, even another anti-Hatlestad dissenter, W. M. Dooley, leader of the older men's group at the settlement houses, remarked that Steele's May 13, 1941, letter was written "without my knowledge or approval." In his own letter to Jacoby on May 16, 1941, he mentioned that Steele had told him that "the letters were written in an impulsive moment." (There must have been more than one letter from Steele to Jacoby, or Dooley made an error). Dooley underscored his own concern "with keeping the Club together." But there was nothing impulsive at one level in the point-by-point attack on Hatlestad in Steele's June 12 report, which showed that he had been thinking about the issues deeply for some time.

By November 19, 1941, W. M. Dooley himself had a change of heart regarding the acting executive secretary. In a six-page typed letter to Jacoby, Dooley made it clear that he too had more than a few grievances against Hatlestad. Included in his complaints was the observation that "Mr. H. seems to manifest impatience with regard [to] the rank and file of the old organization, which he would like to get rid of, I believe, if he could." Dooley reiterated the complaints of Steele, adding appeals to the spirit of Ernest Jacoby, Sr., and David McPheters, who "was a pleasure to work with" and "had no adolescent psychological ideas." Dooley was particularly bitter that Hatlestad was receiving a salary of $1,800, which he considered a disproportionate amount. In fact, a Board of Governors document dated Nov. 5, 1941 indicates that Hatlestad was actually receiving a little bit more than that, $2,000 per year. To put this figure in context, it must be noted that the whole budget for the "older men's club," as it became known, was only $2,200.[249]

The Board of Governor's meeting on June 30 that was supposed to resolve some of these issues essentially never took place. Jacoby's July 14 report of that meeting to the Board of Governors notes that only one member attended and "as a result no definite action was taken." The report itself reveals a few important aspects of the Club during these decisive times. First, Ernest Jacoby, Jr., did not let the absence of other members prohibit him from using the report of the non-meeting as a vehicle to set down policy; apparently the Club had no set rules of quorum. Jacoby mentions three important issues in his report. The first was that Jacoby and another board member agreed that the older men should continue to meet at "some place such as the Ellis Memorial," as they had been doing. He added that a "separate room should be set aside for the use of the Club and the perpetuation of its name." It seems that Jacoby was willing to give the Newbury Street club over to Hatlestad and wanted to keep the Jacoby Club alive as an entity elsewhere.

The second issue was that Jacoby had talked with Stanley Cobb, M.D., on the day that the report was written. The gist of this conversation was that the alcoholic venture was worth keeping and that Cobb would supervise Hatlestad, albeit informally. A key factor in Cobb's alleged enthusiasm and Jacoby's approval was the "high type of men being helped by the Jacoby Club." The implication was that the professional and managerial types would eventually contribute to the welfare of the Club and that there was a financial soundness to continuing this aspect of the Club's program. While Cobb was unable "to state definitely whether the alcoholic work would or would not be successful," he "very definitely" supported the work for "a full year's trial."

The third issue Jacoby raised was money. The treasurer himself, Frederic L. Day, had "loaned the Club $400.00 or $500.00 each summer to enable it to continue its work." Jacoby mentions that other members had contributed money to make it possible for McPheters, the secretary for over thirty years, to take leave in order "to regain his health." The Club, he said, was on shaky financial grounds. But Jacoby also noted good news, citing a recent $500.00 gift from a "relative of one of the members of the alcoholic group." Jacoby added: "The members themselves are most enthusiastic and a gift of this size indicates that our time is not being wasted."

In short, like it or not, the alcoholic group seemed to be the money-making side of the Club, at least potentially. Furthermore, as Jacoby (quoting Cobb) noted, there were not enough institutions in Boston to handle all the alcoholic cases. The future of the Jacoby Club's alcoholism treatment program, in this sense, still looked bright.

By October 7, 1941, Hatlestad had submitted his report to Dr. Cobb. His assessment of the work with the alcoholic group consisted of a page and a half typed report and a one-page chart indicating the dry days and drinking days of men in the program. The report contained conclusions based on a mere fourteen subjects, a laughably small sample size by normal medical and social science standards. The best conclusions are the two that are most obvious: He stated that "a Test for progress in readjustment seems to be [related to] the amount of interest shown [by] prospective members for the Club." And he also noted that "a correlation [exists] between the easing of social tensions and objective results in terms of dry days." It was not a well-bolstered professional case that he laid out in his report. Hatlestad in fact had had little background or training to work with, but seemed unaware of his limitations. With Dr. Cobb now given the charge of looking over Hatlestad's shoulder, one can see already at this point that the Reverend's days were going to be numbered.

Jacoby's draft of the November 16, 1941 report to the Board of Governors essentially confirmed that there were in essence two clubs: the alcoholic group and the older men's group. The older men's group, numbering "about forty men (mostly bachelors)" was doing well and would have a new director, Mr. Maurice Armstrong. Armstrong was a graduate student at Harvard Divinity School, working for a Ph.D. in the history of religions. He was also an ordained minister with a good deal of pastoral experience.

On the other side of the Club, Hatlestad was to carry on, working with Dr. Cobb. Jacoby assured the board that Cobb "believes that this experiment is well worth while." Jacoby confirmed Cobb's interest and noted that he intended to make a definite recommendation in a year. It did not take that long. On June 8, 1942, Cobb wrote Jacoby, simultaneously apologizing for not sufficiently supervising the Club and Hatlestad, and then recommending that the Club "drop him." He wrote: "As far as I went...I should judge that Mr. Hatlestad would never be a success at organizing and making the club grow, and he is too confused by many theories to be any great hand at individual psychotherapy."[250]

Lawrence Hatlestad resigned in a letter to Jacoby dated July 16, 1942. For whatever reason, he makes no mention of any rift between himself and Dr. Cobb. Instead he questioned the likelihood of sufficient funds coming into the Club, given the war effort and the number of appeals being made on behalf of various other causes. He also noted a marked decrease in contributions and a new tax program that would make an increase unlikely. In an earlier letter to Jacoby (June 3, 1942), Hatlestad related that the Club was denied membership in the Greater Boston Community Fund, because it was "still in the process of reorganization." Based on these financial uncertainties, Hatlestad thought it best that he secure a better future for himself. Though "alcoholic work" might become his avocation, he affirmed that "it is my plan to keep on with working with alcoholics."

Hatlestad's 1941-1942 Report

A month before Cobb recommended he be dismissed, Lawrence Hatlestad submitted a report to the Club covering May 1, 1941–May 1, 1942.[251] Unlike his earlier report to Cobb, Hatlestad here reveals an approach to treating alcoholics that has startling similarities to those adopted by Alcoholics Anonymous. (It should be remembered that the newly formed Boston A.A. group began holding its first meetings at the Jacoby Club in March of 1941.) The report also offers a brief account of the early days of A.A. in Boston.

In the report Hatlestad states that the Club spent "the past two years" reorganizing along three lines: (1) "the closer defining of our field service so that our work does not overlap those of other agencies"; (2) "the creation of an active Board of Governors" and making constitutional changes "for a more effective management of the reorganization"; and (3) "the development of adequate financial support of our work." Just how any of these changes materially affected the Club is unknown. What is clear, as the report spells out, was the essential division of the Club into two groups, the older men's group, headed by Maurice Armstrong, being relocated to the Ellis Memorial House. This was old news by May 1942.

The main portion of the report, not surprisingly, concerned the alcoholic work, the provision of "expert assistance to alcoholics who wish to rehabilitate themselves." The report clearly wishes to justify the Club's work in this area: "This re-emphasis upon therapeutic service to alcoholics is in keeping with the original aim of the Club and is in keeping with the desire of Mr. McPheters, who is now on sick leave." One cannot help but hear Jacoby's moderating approach tempering many of Hatlestad's words in this report, a contrast to his own more usual strident style. The reference to McPheters is a clear reaction to the claims of W. M. Dooley that the Club had drifted far from his "common sense" approach.

Hatlestad notes that the first year of reorganization was largely involved with the establishment of A.A. in Boston. This was facilitated, he claimed, largely through his own work with Ruth Hock, the A.A. secretary in New York. Hatlestad apparently first wrote to Hock in 1940 with "favorable remarks regarding the book 'Alcoholics Anonymous.'" Hock responded with a description of the A.A. organization, adding that "only within the last month…a beginning has been made in Boston." She mentions that a Mr. Joseph Lyons had visited the New York office and was now attempting to organize a group in Boston. The hope was that Hatlestad would get in touch with him.[252]

As will be discussed later, the Jacoby Club essentially nurtured A.A. in Boston at the beginning, with the group locating in the Jacoby Club itself. In June 1941, the two groups agreed that they ought to be separate organizations. Nonetheless, twelve members of the group remained in the Jacoby Club, which then continued its program of treatment.

Hatlestad also mentions his debt of gratitude to Dr. Stanley Cobb, noting that his illness prevented him from supervising the Club as he might have. He also notes that the Club attenuated its full range of services and did not expand or publicize its alcoholic work, "preferring to test the results of our treatments."

Significance for A.A.

Perhaps anticipating Cobb's reaction to his work, Hatlestad states that the Club's work (essentially his alcoholic work) "has not been carried on for a sufficient length of time to allow us to evaluate the results with anything approaching scientific accuracy." He adds that it is difficult to determine what constitutes a cure, and that even prolonged abstinence (he mentions four years) is no guarantee of anything more than a period when "the symptom, abnormal drinking, is suppressed or symptomatic." In short, Hatlestad acknowledges the imprecise nature of alcoholism treatment, both stating the case accurately and covering his own lack of scientific data.

Despite his own limitations as a researcher, Hatlestad made several "inferences" from "our experience thus far." Several of these conclusions can be directly compared with similar sentiments from A.A. literature:

Hatlestad Report: "We believe that progress in the eradication of the disease depends more upon the progressive reorganization or readjustment of a personality. We are more concerned about the effectiveness in which a patient functions in the actual situations of life." **A.A. position:** Bill W. later wrote that "no true alky ever stops drinking permanently without undergoing a profound personality change."[253]

Hatlestad Report: "Whether or not an alcoholic will be able to make the necessary adjustments to an unusual crisis sometime during his life without resorting to the use of liquor is more than one has a right to predict with our present knowledge." **A.A. position:** Bill W. again: "We are not cured of alcoholism. What we really have is a daily reprieve contingent on the maintenance of our spiritual condition."[254]

Hatlestad Report: "Many patients drop their treatment prematurely, thinking they are cured.... we must be prepared to begin treatment again." **A.A. position:** Bill W.: "Today, though slips are a very serious difficulty, as a group we take them in stride."[255]

Hatlestad Report: Many alcoholics are "unsuited for a sustained individual therapeutic treatment. They are best handled by group work." **A.A. position:** Compare with A.A.'s first tradition: "Our common welfare should come first; personal recovery depends upon A.A. unity."[256]

Hatlestad Report: "A certain type of religious emphasis of a non-denominational nature is desirable and sometimes necessary to achieve the best results." He added that "depth psychology" should be avoided in favor of a more "personalistic standpoint, such as is held for instance by Harvard Psychologist, Professor Gordon W. Allport." **A.A. position:** Compare this observation, which touches on the spiritual heart of the A.A. program, with the second tradition: "For our group purpose there is but one ultimate authority—a loving God as He may express Himself in our group conscience."

Hatlestad Report: "Our work needs to be more self-sustaining.... Our present policy of not encouraging voluntary contributions has done more harm than good to our patients." **A.A. position:** The seventh tradition states: "Every A.A. group ought to be fully self-supporting," with the long form of the tradition adding that the groups "ought to be fully supported by the voluntary contributions of their own members."

These six "inferences" which Hatlestad drew from the Jacoby Club's experiences in treating alcoholism clearly overlapped with the A.A. philosophy on many points. But there were fundamental differences as well, particularly in Hatlestad's tendencies toward a medical and quasi-scientific approach. Hatlestad concluded his report by noting rather clinically that the previous year had seen interviews with "fifty-one different individuals, which involved approximately five hundred hours of time."

He was trying to keep himself in business as a salaried alcoholism worker, which was forcing him into elaborate time-keeping and a kind of businesslike accounting procedure. In spite of his willingness to enthusiastically back the new Boston A.A. group, that group was going to have to break its links with him eventually. The spirit of the A.A. group itself could not flourish in an atmosphere of salaried workers attempting to justify their own paychecks.

CHAPTER 7

▼

THE JACOBY CLUB AND A.A.

Early A.A. Publicity Brings Boston Alcoholics to the Jacoby Club

With the publication of *Alcoholics Anonymous* in late 1939, publicity quickly came to A.A. It was only a few years since the country had repealed Prohibition; the subject of alcohol, its abuse, and attempts at reforms, was familiar to the press. The idea of a new, strange, and secretive society involved with treating the ravages of alcohol provoked curiosity. Awakened to this new organization in its midst, articles appeared across the nation. Robert A. Erwin's "Brotherhood of Alcoholics," subheadlined "Conditional Reprieve Is Sought by Members. Admit Their Organization Does Not Aim at Cures, Try to Forget Selves in Ministering to Other Drink Victims," appeared in the *Detroit News* on April 18, 1940. On March 3, 1940, the *Los Angeles Herald Express* published Beatrice Fairfax's story "'Alcoholics Anonymous' An Unusual Liquor Cure." This article prompted a follow-up by the same author: "'Alcoholics Anonymous' Article Stirs Inquiries," printed June 6, 1940.[257]

The Denver Post, on Feb. 9, 1940, ran a story entitled "Rockefeller Helps Cure Alcoholics," subheadlined "John D. Jr. is Revealed as Financial Backer of Secret Organization Which Regenerates Habitual Drunkards Into Useful Citizens." The article was from the Associated Press, and prompted a letter of objection that appeared in the *Washington D.C. Star*: "A.A. is neither secret nor an organization…. It more nearly should be called a fellowship."

A glut of articles in 1940 celebrated the new-found sobriety of Rollie Hemsley, the Cleveland Indians baseball player who became well known as famed pitcher Bob Feller's favorite catcher. Articles included "Water Wagon Gets Hemsley Via 'Alcoholics Anonymous,'" 30 April 1940, and, by Frank Gibbens, "Hemsley Tells How He Defeated Liquor," *Cleveland Press,* 17 April 1940. As Ernest Kurtz points out, "Throughout the summer of 1940, the wake of the Hemsley publicity proved not only unthreatening but uniquely beneficial."[258]

The various articles began to generate interest on the part of potential members and their families, a condition that gave rise to the development of A.A. chapters, including one that would develop in Boston. Inquiries as to the whereabouts of A.A. activity were directed to the New York office, the visible center of A.A. activity. When inquiries were made by people who lived in Boston, the A.A. office in New York at first directed them, not surprisingly, to the Jacoby Club. As pointed out earlier, Lawrence Hatlestad had made the acquaintance of Ruth Hock, the A.A. secretary in New York, by mid-1940.[259] Whatever one may say of Mr. Hatlestad, he had clearly established himself as a central actor in "alcoholic work" in Boston. So with the New York headquarters of Alcoholics Anonymous sending Boston-area alcoholics to the Jacoby Club for help, the initial effect of the publicity over the new A.A. movement was to strengthen the Jacoby Club, not diminish its influence and public regard.

Paddy Keegan Links His Boston
A.A. Work to the Jacoby Club

In addition to Hatlestad's contacts with the New York group, Paddy Keegan, one of the two founders of A.A. in Boston, decided to link his newly formed Boston A.A. group to the Jacoby Club's already sucessful program for helping alcoholics in that city.[260] According to the history of early A.A. in Boston written later on by the Boston A.A. Central Service Committee (CSC), Paddy ventured to New York and met Marty Mann, one of the first women in the program, who apparently helped Paddy get sober in the summer of 1940. "By October Paddy was back in his home town of Boston," knowing about A.A. but without a meeting to attend.[261]

The CSC history states that "somehow Paddy found out about a place called the Jacoby Club."[262] He met Hatlestad and worked with him "from October until the first of November, when another alcoholic named Burt C. came to the Jacoby Club looking for help. Doctor Hatlestad put Paddy and Burt together, and they started to help each other." Of course, if Paddy asked anyone in the New York A.A. office about a place to go in Boston alcohol treatment, Hatlestad's name would have come up. Given its ambiance, self-help orientation, and nondenominational orientation, it was the clear choice over a hospital or mission house.

Paddy was unable to stay sober for long periods of time, but he did manage to pass on the message of A.A. Whatever his success or lack of it on the personal level, Paddy and Burt C. held the first Boston meeting of Alcoholics Anonymous on Wednesday, November 13, 1940, "both men being sober."[263] It is not known how many people attended the first meeting, nor if they were sober.

Burt C. remained sober "from the first meeting until he died." Such was not Paddy's fate. He apparently slipped repeatedly and "finally died of alcoholism." According to the Boston group's history and at least one letter from Ruth Hock,[264] Paddy was a pleasant fellow when sober and did much to carry the A.A. message to New England. When inquiries came to Boston concerning the whereabouts of A.A. following the Jack Alexander article of March 1, 1941, it was Hatlestad, Burt C., and Paddy Keegan who made the contacts.[265] Paddy's picture currently graces the Central Service Committee office in Boston.

Early A.A. in Boston

The first A.A. meetings were held irregularly, but by March of 1941, Burt C. and Paddy had settled on Wednesday nights at the Jacoby Club's 115 Newbury Street address for the official weekly group meeting. The Boston group's history adds that there were then about four or five alcoholics in the group.

The history of A.A. and its relationship to the Jacoby Club becomes a bit cloudy at this point. The Jacoby Club archival material supports two basic facts: A.A. and the Jacoby Club were intertwined for a period and then separated. The Boston A.A. group met at the Jacoby Club facilities and was melded with the Club, according to Ernest Jacoby, "for quite a while." But he adds, "Gradually, however, Alcoholics became independent and I think there was some jealousy on Hatlestad's part."[266]

In the same letter, Jacoby also describes how Hatlestad "eventually got into a real fight when he kept them [the older men who were not alcoholics] out of the Club premises on Newbury Street.... This was a really tough time for me, as I was very green and did not know how to handle Hatlestad nor did I know what was best for the Club and the men." He continues, "Now as I look back on it, probably the thing that saved the Club at this point, was the fact that the alcoholics [A.A. and the alcoholic Jacobians] pulled out and left Hatlestad alone in the Newbury Street apartment without any funds, as we were forced to shut down the Club rooms. This meant that the old men no longer could say that they were being kept out of the Club."[267]

The clear split at the financial level occurred when the Jacoby Club wrote a letter to Alcoholics Anonymous on May 31, 1941, informing the group that it "regretfully recommends that the management of each group be entirely separate and distinct from that of the other."[268] The letter cited two basic differences. First, the Jacoby Club was a charitable institution, "receiving money from and making appeals to the public." A.A., being self-supporting, did not (a self-imposed rule which would later become A.A.'s Seventh Tradition). Second, the Jacoby Club employed "a salaried man who is not an alcoholic" (Hatlestad), whereas A.A. was operated without paid professionals (the rule which was later formalized in A.A.'s Eighth Tradition). It is interesting to note that already as early as 1941, A.A. members were assuming the absolute necessity of certain organizational principles which would later be formalized in the Twelve Traditions in 1945-6.

Although the Jacoby Club letter made it clear that they no longer wanted the A.A. people telling them how to manage their business, nonetheless it was cordial in tone, including an offer to continue allowing A.A. the use of Jacoby Club rooms. The letter ended with a note of thanks to A.A. "for the opportunity [the Jacoby Club] has been given to contribute its small share to their work."

According to the Boston A.A. Central Service Committee, A.A. moved to larger quarters at 123 Newbury Street in June of 1941. The nature of the relationship between A.A. and the Club at this point is not entirely clear. Although a basic organizational and financial split is documented in the May 31 letter, the CSC history states that A.A. was "still centered at the Jacoby Club. They were not strong enough to be on their own yet." Supporting this, the May 31 letter did refer to the willingness of the Club to allow A.A. to continue to use its rooms.

Since the Hatlestad resignation was not received until July 16, 1942, it is reasonable to assume that some ties between the two groups remained during this 1941–1942 period.[269] This situation lasted until A.A. relocated at 306 Newbury Street in 1942. At this point they had found a home and were unquestionably independent. An A.A. group remained at this Newbury Street address for over twenty years. But between 1942 and September 1945, additional groups were also formed, so that A.A. quickly grew to have thirteen meetings in all, scattered over various parts of the immediate Boston area. Richmond Walker, author of *Twenty-Four Hours a Day*, an early Boston A.A. member about whom we shall speak more later, proposed the establishment of a Boston Central Committee to better coordinate the activities of these thirteen meetings in a letter to the group on 25 October 1945.[270]

Looking at the geography involved provides one good way of visualizing the continually changing relationships between the organizations during this period. Emmanuel Episcopal Church is located in the heart of downtown Boston at 15 Newbury Street, right where the street ends at the green lawns and colorful flower beds of the Boston Public Garden with its lake and swan boats, with (immediately to the east of that) Boston Common, the grassy knoll where the early colonists used to pasture their milk cows. In March 1941, the little Boston A.A. group had started meeting every Wednesday night at the Jacoby Club's place at 115 Newbury Street, which was only two city blocks west of the church where the Emmanuel Movement had begun. Everything was still contained within the same tight little geographical area. At the psychological level, Emmanuel Church, the Jacoby Club, and the A.A. group were part of the same small local neighborhood.

A.A.'s first move, in June 1941, was only to 123 Newbury Street, on the same street and at the same end of the block as the Jacoby Club meeting place. They were still practically next-door neighbors, and could wave hello to one another as they entered their separate doors.

But in 1942, A.A. moved four blocks west, to 306 Newbury Street, symbolizing a much greater psychological distancing of themselves from the Jacoby Club. From that point on, as additional A.A. groups were rapidly formed in other parts of the city, the original close linkage between Boston A.A. and the Jacoby Club was quickly lost. There were similarities to the process by which Akron, Cleveland, and New York A.A. had gradually broken their originally tight associations with the Oxford Group, a process which had also taken place in stages.

Major Publicity: Jack Alexander and the Saturday Evening Post

The publication of Jack Alexander's famous March 1, 1941, *Saturday Evening Post* article was a pivotal event in the Jacoby Club-A.A. relationship. The *Post*'s owner, Judge Curtis Bok, wanted a fair piece about the fledgling group, having recently heard friends who were medical doctors praising A.A.[271] Alexander, known for his tough-minded cynicism, was called on for the task. Alexander's initial skepticism on meeting with Bill W. later flowered into a lifelong friendship. Kurtz writes: "If Bill Wilson's or Dr. Bob's conversion marked the beginning of Alcoholics Anonymous, its nationwide diffusion was due in the first instance to a similar experience on the part of Jack Alexander."[272]

The article was marked by awe, admiration, and at times amazement. The tough journalist's endorsement was a monumental jolt that quadrupled membership from 2,000 to 8,000 during the last ten months of 1941.[273] Letters poured in to the New York office. Those requesting information for the Boston area were, at this point naturally enough, mailed to Hatlestad. It was he who had come forth and cultivated A.A. as an ally and partner in his mission to treat alcoholics. Hatlestad also had a ready meeting place, a club that was familiar with self-help, a nondenominational approach, and a history of success: the Jacoby Club.

According to the CSC history, the New York office received 63 requests for information on A.A. in the Boston area by April 1941. These were all answered by either the secretary Ruth Hock or Bill Wilson himself. The names were then forwarded to Hatlestad, and he, Paddy, and Burt C. began making the contacts.[274] Apparently the letters sent back from New York to these Bostonians included Hatlestad's name and address, because many of these 63 people then wrote letters to him asking for help or information. Two typical letters follow.

> [Addressed to Mr. L. M. Hatlestad; 14 March 1941]
> Dear Sir,
>   Your name was given me from N.Y. as the Boston representative of the group known as Alcoholics Anonymous. Any information or help you can give me will I assure you be deeply appreciated. The victim is my son who is in fair way to ruin his life and the lives of his family through drink. Hoping to hear from you as speedily as possible. I am
>
>   Sincerely,
>   [name omitted]

> [Addressed to Mr. L. M. Hatlestad; no date]
> Dear Sir—
>   Thank you for your letter. I had made inquiry of the N.Y. group after reading of the movement in the *Saturday Evening Post*. A friend of mine has the problem of overcoming a strong desire for liquor and it is for this friend I made the inquiry. It is possible that your group will be the help I so much desire—but time and my friend's co-operation are elements to be considered.
>   Very truly yours,
>   [name omitted]

Some letters to Hatlestad requested information regarding A.A. groups in surrounding communities or where other members were located, so that a new group might be formed. Hatlestad maintained what appears to be a regular correspondence with Ruth Hock.

Eric Kling

On April 21, 1941, shortly after the Jack Alexander article, Jacoby Club member Eric Kling wrote a letter to the editor of the *Boston Herald*.[275] The letter appeared in the "Mail Bag" section and appeared as a spontaneous endorsement, possibly in a positive reaction to the Jack Alexander article. The newspaper headlined the article "Typical Alcoholic Addict Curable."

Kling's letter, signed only with his initials, was a literate and insightful assessment of A.A. against the backdrop of history, citing Dickens's "The Drunkard's Death" as well as Edward Strecker's medical text, *Alcohol, One Man's Meat*. Kling's message was one of hope through self-help, stressing the willingness of members to help each other and a pervasive nondenominational spirituality. He concluded: "Any alcoholic can find us and once he has done so we will do all in our power to help him, as we have ourselves been helped." Kling was an enthusiastic member, a person who had the not atypical ups and downs of recovery. His own recovery was perhaps made more difficult by his being a merchant seaman. In one sense, he typified a new type of A.A. member, one who could and would find a universality to the fellowship: he seemed as much a member of the New York group as the Boston group.[276]

Whatever Kling's motive, the letter had an effect similar to the Jack Alexander article. Requests for further information, dates, times, and places poured in, at first to the newspaper, later to the Jacoby Club. Though Kling did not mention the Jacoby Club in the article, his address at the Club was soon released by the *Boston Herald*.[277] But the growth of A.A. soon eclipsed that of the Jacoby Club. And, as we have seen, Hatlestad's relationship with the medical profession, i.e., Stanley Cobb, was soon to make it impossible for him to continue with the Club.

Boston's Influence on A.A. in the Rest of the Country: Richmond Walker

In May 1942, a forty-nine year old Boston businessman named Richmond Walker, once wealthy and successful but now a hopeless alcoholic, came to his first A.A. meeting in the new A.A. clubroom at 306 Newbury Street. He came from a family of prominent Massachusetts business people and politicians, and at one time had lived in luxury on Beacon Hill after he and his older brother Joe had started their own successful wool business, the Walker Top Company. After drinking his share of the business away, he had gotten sober for two and a half years in the Oxford Group, but then had started drinking again in 1941 and now in 1942 was at the end of the line. He had lost wife, children, business, and his health, everything that mattered.[278]

He never had a drink after that first A.A. meeting, and quickly began putting his life back together. He became an ardent A.A. member, and played a major role in starting the first A.A. intergroups both in Boston[279] and in Daytona Beach, Florida, where he had a second home. He wrote a small book called *For Drunks Only*, and also began composing some little daily meditations for himself on small cards, drawn partly from an Oxford Group work entitled *God Calling* by Two Listeners.[280]

In 1948, some of the other A.A. members persuaded Walker to combine all this material into a meditational book which he entitled *Twenty-Four Hours a Day*, containing a simple one-page reading for each day of the year.[281] Each page had a one paragraph "Thought for the Day," a one paragraph "Meditation for the Day," and a brief prayer (usually two short sentences) at the bottom. He began printing and distributing "the little black book" from his own home, and its use among A.A. members started spreading rapidly all over the United States.

A.A. people found it the most useful meditational book, for their purposes, which they had ever encountered. A comparison of the number of copies sold with the figures for total A.A. membership shows that during the period of A.A.'s greatest growth, roughly half of the A.A.'s in the United States owned their own copy of Walker's book. Ernest Kurtz believes that there was a long period when more A.A. members may have owned copies of *Twenty-Four Hours a Day* than those who had their own personal copy of *Alcoholics Anonymous* itself (the A.A. "Big Book").[282] Numerous surviving old-timers who came into A.A. during that era report that they got sober basically on two books, the Big Book and the little black *Twenty-Four Hour* book, which many of them carried with them everywhere they went, in a pocket or a purse, for instant spiritual help in time of stress or crisis. Numerous A.A. groups to this day begin their meetings by reading the selection for that day from *Twenty-Four Hours a Day*. By unspoken agreement it has always been regarded as a basic part of A.A.'s central heritage, even though it is not printed by the New York A.A. headquarters.[283]

In 1954, after the task of mailing out up to 10,000 copies a year had grown too great for Walker to handle by himself out of his own home, especially since he was no longer a young man, Patrick Butler at the Hazelden Foundation, a treatment center in Minnesota, offered to take over the task of printing and distributing the books[284] simply as a service to A.A., even though the philosophy of the little black book was not at all a statement of the principles of the Hazelden treatment system. Hazelden did not even open its doors in fact until 1949, the year after Walker's book came out, with a small program for from four to seven patients, based in a farmhouse on a Minnesota farm. It was still a small operation in 1954, without much in the way of resources, but Butler believed that *Twenty-Four Hours a Day* was too important to A.A. to be lost, and bravely committed the little treatment center to somehow keeping the book in print.[285]

The ideas in the little black book[286] came from a number of very different sources, beginning with *Alcoholics Anonymous* (the A.A. Big Book) itself, which is quoted from liberally. One can spot the influence of

Emmet Fox in the use of technical terms such as "demonstration." One can also identify technical terms and ideas originally coming from the Oxford Group: the use of words like change and guidance, and emphasis upon the four virtues of honesty, purity, unselfishness, and love (the so-called Four Absolutes of the Oxford Group).[287]

But the overall spirit of *Twenty-Four Hours a Day* is in many ways far closer to the teachings of the Emmanuel Movement and the Jacoby Club than it is to that of the Oxford Group. Walker repeatedly emphasizes that alcoholics have to work on their underlying psychological problems as well as their spiritual needs, with both being equally necessary. He devised a more sophisticated version of the Emmanuel Movement's moral suggestion method, using guided imagery to "re-educate the subconscious minds" of his readers (January 18). In fact, one of Walker's major accomplishments was to mine *God Calling* by Two Listeners for a long series of powerful and vivid images, involving sometimes all five senses, which would quietly penetrate the subconscious, and remain there doing their healing work, even long after the reader had meditated on them. It was a version of the Rev. Elwood Worcester's early techniques of suggestion and auto-suggestion, but one which used what modern psychologists call guided imagery to have even greater subconscious effect.

But above all, *Twenty-Four Hours a Day* stressed fellowship between recovering alcoholics as one of the most vital ingredients in the therapy. That was one of the most important things which the Jacoby Club had discovered, that one needed to put the recovering alcoholics in their own separate group, and do everything possible to encourage them to form a tight-knit fellowship of mutual support, living and working together as much as possible. Perhaps because of what he had learned from seeing the bitter divisiveness which began to afflict the Jacoby Club in its latter days, Walker filled his meditational book with numerous suggestions for concrete ways of minimizing the destructiveness of disputes within the A.A. groups. And he stressed continually the need for service to the A.A. group and the importance of total loyalty to the survival of the group. He did not want to see A.A. go the way of the Jacoby Club at its end.

So although the Jacoby Club quit working with alcoholics in 1942 and finally disappeared permanently from the scene in the latter 1980s, its legacy did have an influence on the A.A. movement all over the United States, and not just in Boston, through the vehicle of the powerful meditational work *Twenty-Four Hours a Day*, which was read and used so avidly by so many A.A. members all around the country. The little black book was not a Jacoby Club publication, but it was written by an A.A. member who had learned many things from them, and who was basically sympathetic to their attempt to combine spirituality, simple psychological therapy, and the enormous healing power of fellowship among recovering alcoholics. In this sense, the spirit of the Jacoby Club still lives on, in transformed fashion, in Alcoholics Anonymous today.

The Jacoby Club's Final Phase

By mid-1942 the Jacoby Club was in a precarious financial state, and had suffered the resignation of Hatlestad, the split with Alcoholics Anonymous, and a good deal of internal strife brought about by the split within their own body between the alcoholics and the older men's group. On the other hand, Alcoholics Anonymous was growing rapidly and entering a new phase, during which the Twelve Traditions began to be officially codified in 1945 and 1946, and eventually became a rule of governance as well as a way to live out the Twelve Step program.[288] These Twelve Traditions would permanently bar them from any further institutional linkage to organizations like the Jacoby Club or the Oxford Group. The rest of the A.A. story takes us beyond the immediate subject and time frame of this work.

The Jacoby Club itself had to decide on its own fate. Without the pressure of Hatlestad and his desire to do "alcoholic work," the Club's main concern became the older men's group. Virtually no publicity accompanied the decision to disengage from the work with alcoholic men.

An article concerning the Club appeared in the *Boston Daily Globe* on June 27, 1942, eleven days after Hatlestad's resignation. The article made no mention of any changes at the Club, and in fact reaffirmed that curing alcoholism was a major part of the Club's concern and the legacy of Ernest Jacoby, Sr. himself. Citing friendliness as the method of the Jacoby cure, the article concluded that "today the work goes on in the same essential spirit that it had in its beginnings. The club has fine quarters for its meetings and its therapeutic work. Men are being cured. The club stands ready, as always, to help those who genuinely desire to overcome their problem." In some ways the older spirit of the Club may have indeed been restored. There was no need to mention that the Club was now operating without direct involvement with A.A. or that it was no longer divided into two factions, one of which was the province of Hatlestad's quasi-medical ambitions.

On October 15, 1945, Jacoby answered a letter from the Boston Committee for Education on Alcoholism. A brief portion of the letter sums up what had happened at the Club: "I am writing to advise that at present The Jacoby Club of Boston is doing no work with alcoholics, this having been given up three years ago. All the work now being carried on is in connection with an older men's group which meets at the Ellis Memorial House."[289]

A 1953 letter from Jacoby to McPheters also illuminates this transitional period. In discussing the demise of Hatlestad's alcoholic program, Jacoby mentioned the Club's split into the two groups, the affiliation with A.A., Hatlestad's alleged jealousy of A.A., and finally, Hatlestad's trouble with the older men. The letter also summarizes the progress of the Jacoby Club from 1942 to 1953, a period with little documentation. The Club met at the Ellis Memorial House, an old settlement house, where it worked out a "permanent arrangement" for weekly meetings. Jacoby briefly mentions Maurice Armstrong as Hatlestad's replacement, then adds that eventually the Ellis Memorial group developed its own leaders who took over the group's management. The Club had a weekly meeting (Friday nights) and the lounge was open from 9:00 a.m. to 10:00 p.m.

The letter has a quiet tone, a sense of resignation to a more modest task, and a certain feeling of finally meeting one's appointed destiny. After mentioning that finances were "reasonably good," Jacoby states that the Club's contributors provide enough to give the Ellis Memorial a present in lieu of rent and cover the Thanksgiving and Christmas dinners. More importantly, the state of the Club in 1953 saw "the members of the Club…trying to carry on in accordance with our motto." In keeping with their old original motto, "men helping men," the Club had active committees to visit the sick, provide entertainment, and seek new members. The men were always encouraged "to do as much for themselves and others as possible." The Club recommitted itself to caring for Boston's down-and-out, the type exemplified by Basil King's character Lovey.

1953: Another Report, Another Move

In November 1953, Jacoby wrote a report entitled "Notes Concerning the Jacoby Club of Boston, Inc." The report is a history written with a sense of denouement, almost wistfully looking back. The grandest days of the Club may have been behind it, but its mission would not be complete for another thirty years.

The report reminds the reader of the Club's beginnings with the Emmanuel Church and its origins in the mix of psychiatry, medicine, and "the teachings of Jesus Christ." Jacoby discusses the first work of the Club in treating alcoholics, stating that the early work "was very much along the lines of the work now being done by Alcoholics Anonymous, except that the four individuals mentioned above [Dr. Joseph Pratt, Ernest Jacoby, Sr., the Rev. Samuel McComb, and David McPheters] were not themselves alcoholics or former alcoholics." He also cites the Club's split from the

Emmanuel Church and its own establishment as a charitable corporation on April 21, 1913.

Jacoby reviews the split with A.A., Hatlestad's resignation, the move from the Newbury Street rooms, and the agreement with Ellis Memorial. He notes that as of 1953, the Club's members were almost entirely from Boston's South End district. He adds that "most of them live in rooming houses, are dependent upon Social Security or Old Age Assistance and have a great need for friendship, sympathy and an opportunity to be a part of the Community."

The Club moved again in the fall of 1953 to a building at 20 Union Park, owned by the South End House, another settlement project. The Club was still "under the general advice of a staff member of Ellis Memorial." In fact, the president (Jacoby) had become a member of the Ellis Memorial Board of Directors. The report concludes with a discussion of financial matters. The Club, primarily financed by three charitable trust funds and an annual appeal drive, was apparently more stable financially after divesting itself of the Newbury rooms, even though the earlier hope of funds from the "alcoholic work" of course never materialized.

An article in the *South End Citizen* (2 December 1954) was typical of the coverage the Club received during the subsequent thirty-plus years. "Jacoby Club Host to 36 on Turkey Day." A caption under a picture of several men mentions that they would otherwise be spending "a lonely Thanksgiving Day." The article emphasizes the men helping others but notes that "the majority of the members live in rooming houses, and consequently have no facilities to meet other men on a social level."

A certain tone regarding the Club developed, one verging on sentimentality and melodrama for some, a somber realism for others. Nowhere was this tone more strongly expressed than in the annual solicitation letters. The 1957 letter read:

> Dear Friend,
> The hall bedrooms of Boston's South End are lonely places. In the summer they are airless and hot. Here hundreds of elderly men, who once filled a respected place in the world, eke out a sad, declining existence. For such unfortunates the Jacoby Club is a refuge, a comfort, a place of friendliness and sociability, a builder of morale. Their needs for the Club, their own club, does not diminish with years.[290]

In 1970 the letter included the following:

> The average income of a member of the Jacoby Club is less than $2,000 per year. With this he has to pay rent, feed himself, purchase clothes and pay for all his other incidental expenses. There is nothing left for any of the simple pleasures of life which are so important to one who is living all alone in a South End rooming house. Inflation has been a severe trial for him to face and in addition he is constantly threatened by people who try to rob him of his money or steal his welfare or social security check.[291]

And in September 1979, a letter was sent which was a duplicate of one sent in July 1962:

> There is a white iron bed with sagging springs in the corner, a bureau that perhaps once graced a maid's room in a Back Bay house and a torn carpet on the floor. The window is inadequate for the summer heat and drafty in the winter's cold. An old man lives here in Boston's South End. Thanks to the Jacoby Club, however, he has some place else to go, something to do, and a chance to meet friends. This is his club in just as real a sense as the successful businessman has a club—even more so. Here life seems less dreary and there is a warmth and personal concern for his welfare which he hasn't had since his wife died many years ago.[292]

On January 8, 1985, a letter was sent to friends of the Jacoby Club, presumably written by Ernest Jacoby. The letter thanked those who had supported the Club and assured them that funds were available to continue the type of program that was being carried out with Ellis Memorial. It mentioned that in 1984, someone whom Jacoby referred to as the librarian-archivist of Alcoholics Anonymous spent a week reviewing the files for materials on a future book. This researcher was actually William Pittman, who worked at the A.A. General Service Office in New York at that time, although that was not his title there. Frank Mauser was the Archivist at that point and the New York GSO never had anyone serving as "librarian." The important thing was that someone at the New York A.A. office had recognized the importance of the Jacoby Club material for understanding the history of the early A.A. movement, and had realized that precautions should be taken to be sure that the vital information would not be lost. Jacoby's letter also mentions that the Massachusetts Historical Society was taking over the records "to preserve them for future researchers." The Jacoby Club had come to the end of its existence, but there were already those who recognized that it had played a major role in history when it was at the height of its activities. An awareness was already beginning to arise among the perceptive that the Jacobians had accomplished something significant, and had done a good job of it.

The letter spells out the Club's wish to continue its work "with the elderly and alcoholism," but notes that given the number of agencies working in the area, the Executive Committee "believed that our decision not to try to become an operating agency would be universally welcomed." Therefore, the funds were to be transferred to the Boston Foundation and set up in such a way as to distribute income to agencies "providing kindly personal help and concern for the disadvantaged, local, elderly individuals, and/or support work in the field of alcoholism and other addictive substances." This essentially meant that a central charitable funding agency would manage and distribute the funds of the Jacoby Club to organizations working with alcoholics and/or the elderly. While gifts and legacies would be added to the Jacoby Fund through the Boston Foundation, the Club as such would soon cease to exist. The historian-archivist who organized the Jacoby Club's records at the Massachusetts Historical Society wrote that the Jacoby Club terminated its programs in 1987.[293] The last recorded financial transactions occurred in 1989.

Some Concluding Thoughts

The Jacoby Club's end testified both to its weaknesses and its strengths. Despite its decline from the days when it emerged from the Emmanuel Church with the blessings of organized religion, graced with the aura of science and medicine, and propelled by the spirit of the Progressive Era, the Club maintained a quiet faith in the power of fellowship. To some the end may have seemed an ironic, sad, perhaps even pitiful conclusion, an ending with the proverbial whimper and not a bang. Yet there was no whimper, just a resignation to a task, an attempt to bring cheer into the lives of otherwise forgotten men. The Jacoby Club, and perhaps nobody better than Ernest Jacoby, Jr., realized that the treatment of alcoholics would be better carried out elsewhere.

The Club may have suffered from Hatlestad's hubris, his belief that the Club should be at the center of alcohol treatment, and that it should accumulate funds through this endeavor and garner the attendant fame, however slight. Hatlestad's ambitions clearly clashed with the original mission of the Club. Even though his program ultimately helped the infant A.A. group, a fair reading cannot entirely excuse his almost cavalier disregard for the older men's group. Similarly, even Ernest Jacoby, Jr.'s moderation in the dispute, although paternal and loving at heart, were not distinct from his desire that Hatlestad's endeavors make money for the Club.

For whatever reasons, the Club's theological convictions became quite generic. Despite an occasional passing reference to Jesus, God, and prayer, the focus of the group was decidedly here and now, earthly, practical, and functional. There is certainly nothing inherently immoral or detrimental in this orientation. Yet the spiritual element, so much a part of the A.A. program, was neglected. Perhaps the fellowship the Club provided did in fact bring forth a spirit that is not evident in the documents and other archival materials. But the paucity of references to the spiritual dimension, the almost conscious refusal to speak of such matters, evokes a sense that some critical center had dropped out of the Club.

In Ernest Jacoby's "Notes" of November 1953, his opening references to the Emmanuel Movement seem to evoke a more vibrant time and a project infused with the great passion, enthusiasm, and spirit of Elwood Worcester. No one was more earthly than he, in the sense of being focused on his mission at Emmanuel Episcopal Church. Yet Worcester's writings were propelled by a strong spiritual presence, a vibrancy that seems to be all but absent in the later days of the Jacoby Club. Perhaps it was the lack of press, the lack of society's concern that gives this notion.

The power of fellowship in the Jacoby Club nonetheless stands out. Not mere conviviality, fellowship as the Jacoby Club saw it provided access to more than survival. Fellowship allowed the person to rise from mere subsistence to a fuller and richer level of humanity. The Club attempted, with varying degrees of success, to engage men in life, in a partnership of being that could fulfill existence. In this sense perhaps the spiritual dimension was kept alive. The Club attempted to save men from a limbo where they experienced neither courage nor despair, love nor hate, life nor death: a purgatory of quiet meaninglessness.

The legacy of the Jacoby Club, then, was not only a concern for the elderly—geriatric social work—but the admission that fellowship is a powerful force for all, a necessary dimension that quickens other aspects of human existence to fruition. In an age when the social contract of the Enlightenment seems to have vanished, when people are left as isolated individuals floating in a sea of ceaseless activity, the dimension of fellowship can never be more relevant. Its power has suffused A.A. from its very beginnings. Rooted in humility and informed by a Higher Power, the strength of A.A. fellowship has endured when this fad or that had passed. The synthesis that became Alcoholics Anonymous demanded the presence of this ineffable yet vital dimension.

In New England, at an earlier time, in a chapter entitled "A Bosom Friend," another writer wrote of the friendship between two men, one a Presbyterian, the other a South Sea Islander:

> As I sat there in that now lonely room; the fire burning low, in that mild stage when, after its first intensity has warmed the air, it then only glows to be looked at...the storm booming without in solemn swells; I began to be sensible of strange feelings, I felt a melting in me. No more my splintered heart and maddened hand were turned against the wolfish world. This soothing savage had redeemed it.... And what is the will of God—to do to my fellow man what I would have my fellow man to do to me—*that* is the will of God.[294]
> —Herman Melville, *Moby Dick* (1851)

APPENDIX

▼

JACOBY FAMILY GENEALOGY

The following biographical information is drawn from the data gathered for the 1920 U.S. Census, with supplementary data as assembled in the Soundex Index and the SSDeath Index in the New England Historic Genealogical Society, 101 Newbury Street, Boston MA 02116-3007. Brookline, where Ernest Jacoby, Sr., made his residence, is a western suburb of Boston, Massachusetts. *The ages of the various people listed below are given as they were recorded on the 1920 federal census form.*

Ernest Jacoby (Sr.)

35 Allerton Street, Brookline MA
Age 40. Born in England in 1880 (he had three brothers there, all of whom served in World War I). Died in 1935 in Brookline MA.

His family
(all born in Massachusetts)

WIFE: Alice (Hovey) Jacoby. Age 38. Died in Boston in 1958.
SON: Ernest Jr. Age 18. According to SSDeath Index, born on March 8, 1911. Died on April 7, 1993, at 90027 Hollywood, in Los Angeles CA.
SON: Francis. Age 17. Born in 1912.
DAUGHTER: Joan. Age 2 ½. Born on December 18, 1917.

Notes

MHS=Massachusetts Historical Society
RIHS=Rhode Island Historical Society

1   William L. White, "Pre-AA Alcoholic Mutual Aid Societies," *Alcoholism Treatment Quarterly* 19.1 (2001):1-21.
2   William L. White, *Slaying the Dragon: The History of Addiction Treatment and Recovery in America* (Bloomington, Ill.: Chestnut Health System and Lighthouse Institute, 1998).
3   Katherine McCarthy, "Psychotherapy and Religion: The Emmanuel Movement," *Journal of Religion and Health* 23.2 (1984): 92-102; and "Early Alcoholism Treatment: The Emmanuel Movement and Richard Peabody," *Journal of Studies on Alcohol* 45.1 (1984): 59-74.
4   Howard J. Clinebell, Jr., *Understanding and Counseling the Alcoholic*, rev. ed. (Nashville: Abingdon Press, 1990), Ch. 4, "The Emmanuel Movement—Religion Plus Psychotherapy." This chapter of his book is now also available online as <http://www.religion-online.org/cgi-bin/relsearchd.dll/showchapter?chapter_id=726>.
    Sanford Gifford, *The Emmanuel Movement (Boston, 1904-1929): The Origins of Group Treatment and the Assault on Lay Psychotherapy* (Cambridge: Harvard University Press, 1998), see especially Chapters 7 and 8. Gifford adds interesting information about Baylor, and discusses the impact of Freud's visit to the United States in 1909 and his much-publicized lectures at Clark University.

5   Sydney E. Ahlstrom, *A Religious History of the American People* (New Haven: Yale University Press, 1972).
6   Ibid., 1019.
7   Mel B., *New Wine: The Spiritual Roots of the Twelve Step Miracle* (Center City, MN: Hazelden, 1991).
8   Ahlstrom, *Religious History*, 1027.
9   Ibid., 1028.
10 Mark Twain, *Christian Science,* foreword by Vic Dyong (Buffalo: Prometheus, 1986), iii. Dyong suggests that some of Twain's rage against Mrs. Eddy was his jealousy of her increasing fame and wealth.
11 McCarthy, "Psychotherapy," 92-93. I am indebted to Professor McCarthy's scholarship throughout this section.
12 Raymond J. Cunningham, "The Emmanuel Movement: A Variety of American Religious Experience," *American Quarterly* 14 (1962): 54.
13 Ray Stannard Baker, *The Spiritual Unrest* (New York: Frederick A. Stokes, 1910), 196.
14 John Gardner Greene, "The Emmanuel Movement: 1906-1929," *The New England Quarterly* 7 (1934): 496.
15 Ibid., 500. Refers to all quotes in this paragraph.
16 Elwood Worcester, "The Results of the Emmanuel Movement," *Ladies' Home Journal,* Nov. 1908, 8.
17 Ray Stannard Baker, *New Ideals in Healing* (New York: Frederick A. Stokes, 1909), 26.
18 Ibid., 25. Cf. Elwood Worcester, "The Results of the Emmanuel Movement," *Ladies' Home Journal,* Dec. 1908, 9. A subheadline reads: "Sympathetic, Friendly Advice Is All That Some Patients Require."
19 Worcester, "Results," Nov. 1908, 8.
20 Elwood Worcester and Samuel McComb, *Body, Mind, and Spirit* (Boston: Marshall Jones, 1931), xii-xiii. Cf. Cunningham, 55.
21 Elwood Worcester, Samuel McComb, and Isador A. Coriat, *Religion and Medicine: The Moral Control of Nervous Disorders* (New York: Moffat, Yard, 1908), 280.
22 Worcester, "Results," Dec. 1908, 10. Cf. Baker, *The Spiritual Unrest*, 218-219.
23 Ibid. See the beginning of the next chapter: "Acceptance and Success."
24 Worcester, McComb, and Coriat, *Religion and Medicine,* 134.
25 Worcester and McComb, *Body, Mind, and Spirit,* chapter 8, 219-238. The four curses are tuberculosis, cancer, syphilis, and alcoholism.
26 Worcester, "Results," Dec. 1908, 9.

27 Worcester, McComb, and Coriat, *Religion and Medicine*, 134-136.
28 Ibid., 184.
29 Worcester and McComb, *Body, Mind, and Spirit*, 230-231.
30 Worcester, "The Results of the Emmanuel Movement," *The Ladies' Home Journal*, Feb. 1909, 16.
31 Baker, *The Spiritual Unrest*, 212. Baker quotes Lyman P. Powell: "We often do not hypnotize our patients ...it is not necessary. Our idea, of course, is to influence their subconscious lives to replace their hopelessness and moral weakness with suggestions of power and virtue and strength." Powell directed the Emmanuel clinic at St. John's Church in Northampton, Massachusetts. Cf. Powell, *The Emmanuel Movement in a New England Town* (New York: G.P. Putnam's Sons-Knickerbocker Press, 1909), chapter 6, "The Cure of the Alcoholic," 104-126.
32 Worcester and McComb, *Body, Mind, and Spirit*, 232.
33 Ibid. We should point out that Worcester makes the distinction between "dipsomania" and "ordinary alcoholism." By his description, dipsomania sounds more like a depressive state that brings about binge drinking to offset the depression (227). He likens the overall condition to epilepsy, with periods of freedom from symptoms, followed by sudden attacks. Alcoholism is the more common condition, referring to what Powell calls the "steady drinker."
34 Ibid.
35 Worcester. "Results," Feb. 1909, 15.
36 Ibid.
37 Worcester, McComb, and Coriat, *Religion and Medicine*, 67.
38 Worcester, "Results," Feb. 1909, 15.
39 Worcester and McComb, *Body, Mind, and Spirit*, 234.
40 Worcester, "Results," Feb. 1909, 16.
41 Elwood Worcester, *Life's Adventure: The Story of a Varied Career* (New York: Scribner's, 1932), 294-295.
42 Ibid., 296.
43 Cunningham, 57. This is not an exhaustive list. Cf. McCarthy, "Psychotherapy," 101.
44 E. Brooks Holifield, "Pastoral Care and Counseling," *Encyclopedia of American Religious Experience*, Vol. 1, ed. Charles H. Lippy and Peter W. Williams (New York: Scribner's, 1988), 1587.
45 Donald Meyer, *The Positive Thinkers: A Study of the American Quest for Health, Wealth and Personal Power from Mary Baker Eddy to Norman Vincent Peale* (Garden City, N.Y.: Doubleday, 1965), 250.

46 Ibid., 251. Cf. Greene, "The Emmanuel Movement," 510-512. Greene discusses the relationship between Christian Science and the Emmanuel Movement. McCarthy also makes the response point and contributes to the Christian Science-Emmanuel Movement discussion. "Psychotherapy," 94; "Early Alcoholism," 69.

47 E. Brooks Holifield, *A History of Pastoral Care in America: From Salvation to Self-Realization* (Nashville: Abingdon, 1983), 202. The text that follows this quote in Holifield stresses the religious motivation of the group and further supports this view.

48 Worcester, *Life's Adventure*, 276.

49 Ibid., 277.

50 Worcester, McComb, and Coriat, *Religion and Medicine*, 370-371.

51 Ibid., 371.

52 Ibid., 372-373.

53 Ibid., 376.

54 Ibid., 377.

55 Meyer, 73-79. Cf. McCarthy, "Psychotherapy," 95-96.

56 Worcester, McComb, and Coriat, *Religion and Medicine*, 371. The same quote is used by Baker, *New Ideals*, vi. Baker continues: "The church has tried various remedies: among them evangelism and institutional activities; but one of the most remarkable is the new movement toward healing the sick in the churches—an attempt to minister not only to the moral and spiritual natures of men, but to cure their physical ills. This is the Emmanuel Movement ...."

57 Worcester, McComb, and Coriat, *Religion and Medicine*, 379.

58 Baker, *New Ideals*, vii; Powell, *Emmanuel Movement*, vii, 7, 77, 145; Greene, "The Emmanuel Movement," 510-512.

59 Holifield, *History of Pastoral Care*, 203-204. Cf. McCarthy, "Psychotherapy," 96, 102.

60 Holifield, *History of Pastoral Care*, 204. Walter Bromberg regards the Emmanuel Movement as one of the "sounder New Thought movements" and "an example of a sincere and conscious use of spiritual participation for psychotherapeutic purposes." Walter Bromberg, *The Mind of Man: A History of Psychotherapy and Psychoanalysis* (orig. pub. 1954; New York: Harper Colophon, 1963), 139-140.

61 Powell, *Emmanuel Movement*, 77.

62 Ibid., 145, 146.

63 Holifield, *History of Pastoral Care*, 204-205.

64 Meyer, *Positive Thinkers*, 93, as quoted by McCarthy. Cf. Meyer, 90-91.

65 McCarthy, "Psychotherapy," 98.

66 Worcester, McComb, and Coriat, *Religion and Medicine*, 27.

67 Ibid., 292.

68 Baker, *New Ideals*, 8.
69 Frederick J. Copleston, *A History of Philosophy*, Vol. 8. *Modern Philosophy: Bentham to Russell*, Part II (Garden City, N.Y.: Image-Doubleday, 1966), 102. Copleston cites James' reference to Fechner in his endnote. Cf. McCarthy, "Psychotherapy," 95: "In 1908 Worcester published a book entitled *The Living Word*, explicating Fechner's ideas, claiming that he was no longer able to distinguish them from his own." See also the long note below regarding Worcester's debt to Schopenhauer and Von Hartmann.
70 Arnulf Zweig, "Fechner, Gustav Theodor," *The Encyclopedia of Philosophy*, Vol. 3, gen. ed. Paul Edwards (New York: Macmillan and The Free Press, 1972), 184.
71 Ibid. His work was titled: "Nanna, or the Soul-Life of Plants." My paraphrase is from Zweig's article.
72 Ibid.
73 McCarthy, "Psychotherapy," 95.
74 Worcester, McComb, and Coriat, *Religion and Medicine*, 57.
75 Meyer, *Positive Thinkers*, 76.
76 Charles S. Braden, *These Also Believe: A Study of Modern American Cults and Minority Religious Movements* (New York: Macmillan, 1949), 139.
77 Worcester, McComb, and Coriat, *Religion and Medicine*, 68.
78 Ibid., 68-69.
79 Worcester discusses Schopenhauer's account of human love, with its "mystical rapture, its sublime renunciations and sacrifices" with a sense of approval and awe. He mentions Schopenhauer's Universal Unconscious Mind and Universal Will as the source of this deep emotion, and approvingly remarks that love "opens to us a new and mysterious world of rapture and despair." (*Religion and Medicine*, 36-37) For Worcester the basis for this wonderful mystery seems to lie in the subconscious, which is for him a positive force. Alas, Schopenhauer is more often than not considered to be a pessimistic philosopher who saw the horrors of life and its unspeakable suffering as something to be avoided through either a life of ascetic renunciation or aesthetic contemplation. However, Worcester's affinity for Schopenhauer may be related to his own philosophical ties to Eduard Von Hartmann (1842-1906). Von Hartmann is the direct philosophical descendent of Schopenhauer and modified his views in a number of significant ways. Yet, Von Hartmann did not escape a number of rather pessimistic conclusions regarding humanity. Worcester's optimism is thus revealed in his very appropriation of these philosophers in terms of his own views and values. Cf. Frederick Copleston, *A*

History of Philosophy, Vol. 7. *Modern Philosophy*, Part II (Garden City, N.Y.: Image-Doubleday, 1965), Chapters 13 and 14, 25-59.

80 Worcester, *Life's Adventure*, 289.
81 Nathan G. Hale, Jr., writes: "The vogue of psychotherapy and the mysterious subliminal were important aspects of the American progressive mood in the years up to 1914, and occurred during a time of prosperity and confidence and the rise of a new style of mass journalism." (238) Hale discusses the popularity of psychotherapy extensively along with the impact of mass magazine journalism. This included arousing interest in psychoanalysis and other new developments in psychiatry and neurology as well as the deleterious effects of modern industrial civilization on the "nerves" of Americans. Journalism also fostered a serious attitude concerning nervous disorders, if not insanity, especially with regard to women. Another effect included the democratization of concern for "nervous" ailments, moving such concerns from the domain of the rich to working men and women. Hale also discusses the Emmanuel Movement in general. See his *Freud and the Americans: The Beginnings of Psychoanalysis in the United States, 1876-1917* (New York: Oxford University Press, 1971), 225-249.
82 Ibid., 287. Cf. Greene, "Emmanuel Movement" 507-508. Other instances of publicity are discussed.
83 Hale, *Freud and the Americans*, 289.
84 Constance Worcester (Elwood Worcester's daughter), interview with Cary D. Friedman, 1 March 1982, in Friedman, "Elwood Worcester and the Emmanuel Movement: Psychotherapy in the Church, 1906-1929," master's thesis, Harvard University, 1982, 23. Worcester himself refers to the silence of Bishop Lawrence in *Life's Adventure*, 288.
85 Worcester, McComb, and Coriat, *Religion and Medicine*, 8.
86 Worcester and McComb, *Body, Mind, and Spirit*, 94-95. Worcester discusses automatic writing and spirit communication. Samples of Worcester's own automatic writing are located in the library and archives of the Episcopal Diocese of Massachusetts, Boston.
87 Holifield, *History of Pastoral Care*, 208.
88 Baker, *The Spiritual Unrest*, 221. Baker's "Criticisms of the Movement" addresses the question concerning the role of religion in the healing process. Worcester and McComb addressed these charges extensively in *The Christian Religion as a Healing Power* (New York: 1909).
89 Cunningham, "Emmanuel Movement," 60. Cf. McCarthy, "Psychotherapy," 102. Greene, "Emmanuel Movement" 513-514, 523. Greene (513) quotes McComb's

reply to the charges of hedonism (see Worcester and McComb, *The Christian Religion as a Healing Power*, 115-116).

90   Robert McDonald, *Mind, Religion and Health: With an Appreciation of the Emmanuel Movement* (New York: Funk and Wagnall's, 1908), 314. As quoted by Cunningham, "Emmanuel Movement," 60.

91   Worcester, *Life's Adventure*, 288. This incident is also cited by Greene, "Emmanuel Movement" 515.

92   Josiah Royce, "The Modern Psychotherapeutic Movement in America," *Psychotherapy* 3.4 (1909): 20, 33. As quoted by Holifield, *A History*, 209. Cunningham cites the same quote and adds the comment concerning William James, 60. James' discussion appears in *The Varieties of Religious Experience*.

93   Raymond J. Cunningham, "The Emmanuel Movement: A Variety of American Religious Experience," *American Quarterly* 14 (1962): 54-60.

94   Hale, *Freud and the Americans*, 225.

95   Ibid., 226. Hale adds that Freud's remarks expressed an ambiguity that extended to his very appeal in the United States. "Samuel McComb expressed this precisely when he insisted that Freud was an ally against the 'transcendental mystery mongers' as well as the contemptuous scientific materialists. It was against this accent on mystery as well as medicine that Freud protested in the *Boston Evening Transcript* interview" (Hale, 248-249).

96   Greene, "Emmanuel Movement" 501.

97   Worcester, *Life's Adventure*, 286.

98   Greene, "Emmanuel Movement" 508-509, 515-516.

99   Ibid., 524. Greene comments on negative criticism concerning the expansion of the Emmanuel method, 521-524.

100 "Emmanuel Movement Deplored by Eminent Physicians of Boston," *Boston Sunday Herald*, 12 Dec. 1908, Coriat scrapbook, Harvard University. As cited by Friedman, "Elwood Worcester," 21.

101 Baker, *The Spiritual Unrest*, 229-231.

102 Greene, "Emmanuel Movement," 531. Greene adds: "one shrewd observer recently remarked, if the work had been better organized, 'the medical profession would have been madder still.'"

103 Ibid., 525.

104 Elwood Worcester, *Making Life Better: An Application of Religion and Psychology to Human Problems* (New York: Charles Scribner's, 1933).

105 Powell, *Emmanuel Movement*, 118. One should not assume that their view of alcoholism was entirely free from earlier moralistic condemnations. Powell writes:

"While there is a sense in which alcoholism is a disease, I do not emphasize this fact in the treatment of the alcoholic. I try to build up in him the sense of his responsibility to God and man. I tell him frankly that drink is a sin, and I describe the character of sin in general."

106 McCarthy, "Psychotherapy," 94.
107 Elwood Worcester, *Life's Adventure: The Story of a Varied Career* (New York: Charles Scribner's, 1932), 253.
108 Worcester, *Life's Adventure*, 25.
109 Elwood Worcester and Samuel McComb, *Body, Mind and Spirit* (Boston: Marshall Jones, 1931), v. John Gardner Greene notes that "Craigie" was "the family name of certain of Mr. Baylor's ancestors." The selection of the name had no particular significance beyond that. Neither man wished to have his name used. See Greene, "The Emmanuel Movement: 1906-1929," *The New England Quarterly* 7 (1934): 528. The "Craigie" name did in fact avoid any ties with the Emmanuel Church or the Boston Diocese.
110 Greene, "Emmanuel Movement," 529.
111 Ibid., 527.
112 Worcester, *Life's Adventure*, 253.
113 Courtenay Baylor, *Remaking a Man: One Successful Method of Mental Refitting* (New York: Moffat, Yard, 1919), 1.
114 See Sally Brown and David R. Brown, *A Biography of Mrs. Marty Mann: The First Lady of Alcoholics Anonymous* (Center City MN: Hazelden, 2001); also Marty Mann, *Marty Mann Answers Your Questions About Drinking and Alcoholism* (New York: Holt, Rinehart and Winston, 1970), xi; and Marty Mann, *Marty Mann's New Primer on Alcoholism: How People Drink, How to Recognize Alcoholics, and What to Do About Them* (New York: Holt, Rinehart and Winston, 1958), 3, 17, 116-7, and 189-91. See also the recent book by one of Mann's early protégés: Sgt. Bill S., with Glenn F. Chesnut, Ph.D., *On the Military Firing Line in the Alcoholism Treatment Program: The Air Force Sergeant Who Beat Alcoholism and Taught Others to Do the Same*, Hindsfoot Foundation Series on the History of Alcoholism Treatment (New York: iUniverse, July 2003), espec. chapt. 15, "The Effects of Alcohol on Our Emotional Development." Bill S., the father of modern military alcoholism treatment, an early A.A. figure who developed his ideas in the late 1940s and early 1950s, gives a neo-Freudian explanation in that chapter of the subconscious neurotic roots which often help compel alcoholics to continue their pathological drinking. Although more sophisticated, the similarities to Baylor's position are particularly obvious here.

115 The parenthetical numbers in this section are page references to Baylor's *Remaking a Man*.
116 Katherine McCarthy, "Early Alcoholism Treatment: The Emmanuel Movement and Richard Peabody," *Journal of Studies on Alcohol* 45.1 (1984): 66. McCarthy's article provides a thorough exposition of Baylor's work as well as that of the Emmanuel Movement in general. The article also contains the most complete exposition and criticism of Richard Peabody to date.
117 Cf. McCarthy, "Early Alcoholism," 68. McCarthy contrasts the "dry and austere language" of Freud and his followers to the "sentimentality of the clergy." She also comments on Freud's criticisms of the Emmanuel Movement.
118 These were the terms Freud used to describe these different theoretical positions, as described in his letter to the chairmen of the psychoanalytic societies in Europe and America in 1932, asking for donations to keep alive their publishing firm, the Internationaler Psychoanalytischer Verlag. One of the original printed copies is in the Sigmund Freud Collection at the Dittrick Medical History Center, Case Western Reserve University, 11000 Euclid Avenue, Cleveland, OH 44106-1714. See <http://www.cwru.edu/artsci/dittrick/rarepages/freud.htm> (26 November 2003) for the cited section of the letter.
119 In *Body, Mind and Spirit* (1931), Worcester discusses some of his views regarding psychoanalysis, a relatively unknown body of knowledge at the time of his earlier *Religion and Medicine* (1908). He demonstrates how "religious faith and a spiritual philosophy of life" can solve the "vexatious problem" of "breaking the transfer" between the patient and physician. Worcester states that psychoanalysts "have not thought of a possible third transfer, which I have called the 'Inward Transfer,' when the seat of power and authority is felt to be within, and the physician or teacher is no longer important." It is not our purpose to discuss Worcester's interpretations of the Freudians. Rather it is important to note that he never excludes the religious element from his thinking, even when he is operating analytically on the scientific-psychological plane.
120 McCarthy, "Early Alcoholism," 66. McCarthy writes that while Baylor did not make direct reference to the subconscious, he clearly "regarded it as a vital spiritual force in redirecting a patient's attention."
121 Ibid., 61-62.
122 McCarthy, "Early Alcoholism," 61-62.
123 Richard R. Peabody, *The Common Sense of Drinking* (Boston: Little, Brown, 1931). He dedicated the book to Baylor. Subsequent references to the book will be noted parenthetically in the text.

124 Ibid., 61. His wife stated: "When I had married Richard Rogers Peabody in 1915, I had stepped right into a bonded circle of Boston hierarchs." Caresse Crosby, *The Passionate Years* (New York: Dial Press, 1953), 88. Chapter 7 gives an account of their early years of marriage.
125 Crosby, *The Passionate Years,* 58. There are two major sources of Peabody's biography : the Crosby volume and Jim Bishop's *The Glass Crutch: The Biographical Novel of William Wynne Wister* (Garden City, N.Y.: Doubleday, Doran, 1945). Wister was one of Peabody's patients who later became a lay therapist himself.
126 Crosby, *The Passionate Years,* 66.
127 Ibid., 68, 69.
128 Crosby, *The Passionate Years,* 80.
129 Ibid., 82. McCarthy states that Peabody attended the Emmanuel health classes during the winter of 1921-1922 and by 1924 was listed as a "volunteer assistant in the Social Service Department" in the church, 60.
130 McCarthy, "Early Alcoholism."
131 Greene, "Emmanuel Movement," 527.
132 McCarthy, "Early Alcoholism," 72.
133 Ibid., 61.
134 Bishop, 268-269. Also cited by McCarthy, "Early Alcoholism," 61.
135 Nathan G. Hale, Jr. *Freud and the Americans: The Beginnings of Psychoanalysis In the United States, 1876-1917* (New York: Oxford U. Pr., 1971), 431-433. Cf. John C. Burnham, *Paths Into American Culture: Psychology, Medicine, and Morals* (Philadelphia: Temple University Press, 1988), Chapter Five, "The New Psychology: From Narcissism to Social Control," 69-95.
136 Hale, *Freud and the Americans,* 431.
137 McCarthy, "Early Alcoholism," 61.
138 Bishop, *The Glass Crutch,* 143.
139 John Chynoweth Burnham, *Psychoanalysis and American Medicine, 1894-1918.* Medicine, Science, and Culture 5.4. Monograph 20. Psychological Issues (New York: International Universities Press, 1967), 81.
140 Wolcott Gibbs, "The Rover Boys on a Bender," book review of *The Glass Crutch* in the *New York Times,* 18 Nov. 1945, 4.
141 Bishop, *The Glass Crutch,* 13.
142 McCarthy, "Early Alcoholism," 69.
143 Bishop, *The Glass Crutch,* 223.
144 Ibid., 229. This thesis, with a special emphasis on the emotional immaturity stemming from "defective early training and environment," was developed by Edward

A. Strecker, M.D., and Francis T. Chambers, Jr., in *Alcohol: One Man's Meat* (New York: Macmillan, 1938). Cf. xiv-v, 83. Strecker published a number of other works in the late 1930s and 1940s. As McCarthy points out ("Early Alcoholism," 71), Strecker carried Peabody's "overprotected" and "overly spoiled" causation to an extreme in his book *Their Mother's Sons* (1946). She adds that Strecker "reached new depths in denouncing mothers for virtually every faulty male act of the World War II era, much like Philip Wylie's better known *Generation of Vipers* (1942)." Wylie coined the derisive term "Momism," one of his milder contributions.

145 Elwood Worcester, Samuel McComb, and Isador A. Coriat, *Religion and Medicine: The Moral Control of Nervous Disorders* (New York: Moffat, Yard, 1908), 127. Cf. Chapter 6 and 7. Peabody is in the Emmanuel tradition in discussing the general nervousness of his society: "In the twentieth century, with its high-pressure demands on nervous systems which have not yet become adapted to big business, mass production, telephones ...alcohol has come to play an ever-increasing part as a narcotic, rather than a mere stimulant" (*Common Sense of Drinking*, ix). Worcester writes forty-five pages on the effects of environment on nervousness in chapter 7 of *Religion and Medicine*. The "not yet" inclusion in Peabody's statement might indicate some sympathy with George Beard's notion that the future would hold a group of superior individuals who would transcend nervousness, thereby bringing about a type of evolutionary cure. Cf. Donald Meyer, *The Positive Thinkers: A Study of the American Quest for Health, Wealth, and Personal Power from Mary Baker Eddy to Norman Vincent Peale* (Garden City, N.Y.: Doubleday, 1965), 21-29.

146 Peabody addresses the role of psychoanalysis in treatment by playing both ends against the middle. On the one end he acknowledges the contributions and influence of Freud and the fact that he is acquainted with psychoanalysis itself. On the other end he states that although "the fundamental motivating cause of alcoholism may often be a conflict buried in the unconscious ...experience has shown others besides myself that methods more or less similar to those set forth in this book are in general adequate for cure without more intricate psychoanalytical investigation." In effect Peabody states that his method is sufficient, even if it fails to discover or explain the true underlying "motivating cause" buried down in the deeper levels of the Freudian subconscious. Typical of his book, he adopts a cavalier attitude with regard to documenting exactly who the "others" are or what the methods are that are "more or less similar" to his own.

147 Bishop, *The Glass Crutch*, 223.

148 McCarthy, "Early Alcoholism," 63.

149 Bishop, *The Glass Crutch*, 224.
150 Ibid., 230. Cf. McCarthy, "Early Alcoholism," 69. McCarthy discusses Peabody's ideas as related to the writings of mind-cure and self-help dating back to the 1890s.
151 Bishop, *The Glass Crutch*, 231.
152 Although we can see this tendency to regard all emotion and feeling as dangerous and destructive in many Greek and Roman authors who regarded themselves as Platonists or Stoics, Plato himself knew better, as did the more astute Stoic thinkers, such as the first century philosophers Epictetus and Seneca. It is true that in Plato's metaphor of the chariot of the soul, he says that the rational ego must "sit in the driver's seat"—which sounds like Peabody's emotionally repressive language—but the two chariot horses in Plato's image, which represent the emotions and feelings, are of equal importance for him because they supply all human motive power for doing anything at all, good or ill. Sanity for Plato means not the denial of all emotion and feeling, but learning how to balance, direct, and satisfy the emotional needs appropriately. On the Stoic concept of serenity and its role as ancestor of Reinhold Niebuhr's Serenity Prayer, see Glenn F. Chesnut, *The Higher Power of the Twelve-Step Program: For Believers & Non-Believers*, Hindsfoot Foundation Series on Spirituality and Theology (San Jose CA and Lincoln NE: iUniverse/Author's Choice, 2001) 197-8 n. 21 and 238-9 n. 16.
153 Some, but not all medieval Christian thought by any means, could teach a very intellectualized kind of spirituality. But one medieval alternative to the more rationalistic spiritual systems was the long Christian spiritual tradition deriving from the teachings of St. Macarius the Homilist, along with, of course, the teachings of Augustine, the great African saint; see Chesnut, *Higher Power* 129-30, 195-6 n. 14, 197-9 n. 21, 211-2 n. 4 (on the more intellectualizing systems), 222-3 n. 16, 230-1 n. 12, and 238-9 n. 16.
154 Cf. McCarthy, "Early Alcoholism," 70.
155 Ibid., 71.
156 Mel B., *New Wine: The Spiritual Roots of the Twelve Step Miracle* (Center City, MN: Hazelden, 1991), 124.
157 McCarthy, "Early Alcoholism," 72.
158 *Alcoholics Anonymous*, 3rd ed., (New York: Alcoholics Anonymous World Services, Inc., 1976), 59. McCarthy also cites this, 70.
159 Bill Pittman has catalogued 280 of these slogans in his *Stepping Stones to Recovery* (Seattle: Glen Abbey, 1988), 221-252.

160 *Alcoholics Anonymous*, 3rd ed. (New York: Alcoholics Anonymous World Services, 1976), 8-13.
161 Winfield Scott Downs, *Men of New England*, vol. 4 (New York: American Historical Co., 1947), 359. Biographical information, unless otherwise noted, comes from this work or from "Rowland Hazard Dead in 65th Year," *Providence Journal*, 21 December 1945, or from Steve Dalpe and Rick Stattler, "A Guide to the Rowland Hazard III Papers," Rhode Island Historical Society, 1999. I am greatly indebted to Mr. Stattler in particular for his extensive and thorough scholarship in all aspects of the Hazard research. He was also very helpful in facilitating the author's research at the Rhode Island Historical Society. Material from the Rhode Island Historical Society is cited with their permission. Such material will be noted by RIHS throughout this chapter.
162 Downs, *Men of New England*, 360.
163 Ibid.
164 See Dalpe and Stattler, "A Guide to the Rowland Hazard III Papers." A letter from Rick Stattler to Richard M. Dubiel, 8 September 2003, notes that between 1930 and 1934, "Hazard never really had one fixed address."
165 Rick Stattler, letter to the author, 8 September 2003.
166 Rowland Hazard III Papers, Series 3: Maple syrup business file. RIHS.
167 Mary P. B. Hazard, letter to Thomas P. Hazard, 24 July 1933, Thomas P. Hazard Papers, RIHS.
168 The episode is documented in his mother's letters to Thomas Hazard dated 23 February, 26 February, and 10 March 1932 in the Thomas P. Hazard Papers, RIHS. The letter from Rick Stattler to Richard M. Dubiel, 8 September 2003, adds details from other sources: Rowland "did undergo some sort of hospitalization related to this drinking …apparently at a facility called 'Doctor's Hospital' in Yorkville, N.Y.…He returned there in July of the same year."
169 Thomas P. Hazard Papers, Series 2, Subseries 3: Rowland Hazard III files. Thomas was writing in the context of his attempt to document gifts made to Roy for Federal Gift Tax purposes. RIHS.
170 Courtenay Baylor, letter to Thomas Hazard, 2 February 1934, Thomas P. Hazard Papers, Series 2, Subseries 3: Rowland Hazard III files. Baylor also referred to his own "prospecting activities in Nevada" and said that he "used to be in mining in a small way and learned much by my mistakes." RIHS.
171 Secretary for Thomas P. Hazard (handwritten signature illegible), to Courtenay Baylor, 13 February 1934, Thomas P. Hazard Papers, Series 2, Subseries 3: Rowland Hazard III files. RIHS.

172 Mary H. Dick (Mrs. John W. Dick), letter to Thomas P. Hazard, 5 April 1949, Thomas P. Hazard Papers, Series 2, Subseries 3: Rowland Hazard III files. RIHS.

173 Courtenay Baylor, *Remaking a Man: One Successful Method of Mental Refitting* (New York: Moffat, Yard, 1919), 3.

174 Ernest Kurtz, *Not-God: A History of Alcoholics Anonymous* (Center City, MN: Hazelden, 1979), 21. Also see 23.

175 *Alcoholics Anonymous Comes of Age* (New York: A.A. Publishing, Inc., 1957), 64.

176 Kurtz writes, "Bill Wilson linked James' portrayal of 'conversion' with what he had learned—directly from Dr. Silkworth and indirectly, via Rowland and Ebby, from Dr. Jung—of the necessity and role of hopelessness. Wilson's efforts over many years to give intellectual respectability to Alcoholics Anonymous sprang from his own deep need as well as from his perception of the needs of others." Kurtz, *Not-God*, 23.

177 See R. Thomsen, *Bill W.* (New York: Harper & Row, 1975), 214. As quoted by Bill Pittman, *A.A.: The Way It Began* (Seattle: Glen Abbey Books, 1988), 154-155. See Kurtz, *Not-God*, 8-10, 17-21. See especially Kurtz's endnote 308-309 n. 6. The January 1961 correspondence between Bill W. and Carl Jung is the only known truly solid documentation at present for the case that Rowland indeed had contact with Jung.

178 Thomsen, *Bill W.*, 214, as quoted by Pittman, *A.A.: The Way It Began*, 155.

179 Unlike the Jung connection, Rowland's membership and active participation in the Oxford Group is well-documented in family correspondence. See the letter from Mary P. B. Hazard to Thomas P. Hazard dated 25 February 1934 in the Thomas P. Hazard Papers; and the letters from Thomas P. Hazard to Mary P. B. Hazard dated 14 February and 28 March 1934 in the Rowland G. Hazard II Papers, both in the Manuscripts Collection, RIHS.

180 See Kurtz, *Not-God*, 8-10, esp. 309 n. 8. Also see Pittman, *A.A.: The Way It Began*, 154-155.

181 It is important to recognize at least five considerations (or perhaps one might call them warnings) regarding these materials, for those carrying out research into Rowland Hazard's contacts with Jung and Baylor. First, the letters written by his mother or brother discuss Hazard's problems obliquely by contemporary standards. The term "alcoholism" was not yet permitted in polite circles and is not used in the letters. While there are references to Roy's "problems" and "drinking," there are no details. Though Stattler notes that the "sessions with Baylor are discussed with some candor" (letter from Rick Stattler to Richard M. Dubiel, 8 September 2003), the openness consists of mentioning the sessions themselves

rather than psychological substance. Other personal matters, such as finance and health, are also treated very circumspectly. Second, Hazard, as was the case with the very rich, kept several addresses at any one time. It is difficult to track his exact whereabouts at some points. And partly because of the multiple residences, there may also be considerable correspondence that has been lost. Third, in keeping with the mores of the times and his social class, Hazard may not have discussed his personal matters with his family. His own tribulations regarding drinking, therapy, and matters of Jungian psychological introspection most likely would *not* have entered into familial correspondence. None of the letters from his mother or brother ever mention Jung, psychology, or the substance of what Hazard and Baylor discussed. Occasional references to the Oxford Group do mention God, forgiveness, direction, and the like (Mary P. B. Hazard, letter to Thomas P. Hazard, 25 February 1934, Thomas P. Hazard Papers, RIHS). But these are phrases that could have been used while discussing a conventional church service. Fourth, letters from Hazard himself are generally not available. There are only a few, all regarding business matters. And fifth, other papers in the Hazard Family Collection are still being organized according to Stattler, so we cannot be sure that additional information on some of these matters will not emerge later.

182 Letter from Rick Stattler to Richard M. Dubiel, 8 September 2003.
183 The author met with Stattler from June 30 through July 3, 1998, at the RIHS, discussing the subject of Rowland Hazard and reviewing the materials contained in the document list firsthand. The author also examined other materials in the Hazard Family Papers collection as they might relate to the Jung or Baylor issues.
184 Letter from Rick Stattler to Richard M. Dubiel, 8 September 2003.
185 Ibid.
186 Mary P. B. Hazard, letter to Thomas P. Hazard, 22 May 1931, Thomas P. Hazard Papers, RIHS.
187 Mary writes to Thomas from Villars-sur-Ollon, Switzerland: "Shall see Roy & H in a day or two and decide on our next step. They are about 50 miles from Geneva, & seem to be having a good time at Annecy." 9 July 1931, Thomas P. Hazard Papers, RIHS. (Annecy, France, is approximately twenty miles south of Geneva.)
188 See letters from Earl W. G. Howard to Frederick W. Tillinghast dated 5 May 1943 and 11 May 1943 in the Rowland Third Inc. Records, Sugarbush Files, RIHS. Rowland and Helen were divorced February 25, 1929, and remarried on April 27, 1931.
189 In a conference with the author, Stattler agreed that the references were puzzling.

190 *"Pass It On" The Story of Bill Wilson and How the A.A. Message Reached the World* (New York: Alcoholics Anonymous World Services, 1984), 381-6.

191 Ibid. 383. Letter from Glenn F. Chesnut, Indiana University (South Bend), 17 October 2003: "It is significant that Bill, in his letter to Jung, misspelled Hazard's first name as 'Roland,' leaving out the W in the middle (382). Someone from Switzerland (remembering the famous *Song of Roland* and other continental European usages of the name in that spelling) would have simply assumed that this was the correct spelling, barring any other information to the contrary. Roland without the W is in fact the only form that the spell checker in my American word processing program regards as correct. And yet Jung, in his letter of reply, quietly corrected the spelling and referred to the businessman as 'Rowland' with a W (383). This seems a clear indication that Jung either still remembered what would have seemed to him an odd spelling of the name, or had old case files to refer to. In either eventuality, Jung clearly had been in some sort of contact with Rowland Hazard somewhere along the way."

192 Jung's letter as transcribed in *"Pass It On,"* 384. The previously mentioned note from Glenn F. Chesnut, 17 October 2003, called attention to "the importance of Jung's comments on the three different paths to spiritual conversion for better understanding Rowland Hazard's personality in terms of Jung's professional assessment of the businessman's spiritual, psychological, and intellectual limitations."

193 See Kurtz, *Not-God*, 19-20.

194 Jung's letter as transcribed in *"Pass It On,"* 384.

195 The only dark spot occurred in August 1936 when Rowland had a serious drinking bout. A packet of correspondence of Rowland's brother Thomas documents the binge in New Mexico and Rowland's return trip to New York, see Thomas P. Hazard Papers, Series 2, Subseries 3: Rowland Hazard III files, RIHS. Stattler cites one letter that proposed enlisting the aid of an Oxford Grouper, Shep C. [Shep Cornell], to help Rowland.

196 Linda A. Mercadante, *Victims and Sinners: Spiritual Roots of Addiction and Recovery* (Louisville: Westminster John Knox, 1996), 12, quoting from Pittman, *A.A.: The Way It Began*, 189. Mercadante cites Ernest Kurtz when she says that "the A.A. Big Book contains no reference ...to 'meetings'" and that the Big Book was to be the central concern of the recovering alcoholic. There was nevertheless the proviso that there would be the occasion to "help other drunks" and hold gatherings at which "newcomers could ask questions and meet other sober alkies" (quoting from personal correspondence with Kurtz, 9 January 1995, 12-13).

197 John Gardner Greene, "The Emmanuel Movement: 1906-1929," *The New England Quarterly* 7 (1934): 526; Elwood Worcester and Samuel McComb, *The Christian Religion as a Healing Power: A Defense and Exposition of the Emmanuel Movement* (New York: Moffat, Yard, 1909), as quoted by Katherine McCarthy, "Early Alcoholism Treatment: The Emmanuel Movement and Richard Peabody," *Journal of Studies on Alcohol* 45.1 (1984): 64.
198 Advertisements from the *Boston Transcript*, 1913 and 1915. Unless otherwise noted, all newspaper and Jacoby Club document citations in the Jacoby Club and Basil King chapters are from the Scrapbook in the Jacoby Club collection of the Massachusetts Historical Society, Boston. These are quoted with the kind permission of the Society. All subsequent references to material from their collection will be indicated by the initials MHS after the item.
199 Various ads ran in the major Boston newspapers. Cf. the *Boston Evening Transcript* advertisements in the Scrapbook in the Jacoby Club collection of the Massachusetts Historical Society. MHS.
200 Elwood Worcester, "The Parish News," May 1910. MHS.
201 McCarthy, "Early Alcoholism," 64. Cf. Leonard U. Blumberg with William L. Pittman, *Beware the First Drink! The Washington Temperance Movement and Alcoholics Anonymous* (Seattle: Glen Abbey, 1991).
202 "Men Help Themselves by Helping Others," *Boston Globe*, 27 July 1913. MHS.
203 Ibid. MHS.
204 "Jacoby Club Quits Emmanuel Church," *Boston Transcript*, 30 September 1913. The subheadline reads "Officers in Difference with Rector, Causing Schism." MHS.
205 The *Boston Post* ran a similar article on 1 October 1913. It simply cited growth as a reason for the new rooms. MHS.
206 Greene, "The Emmanuel Movement," 526. Greene offers the following as a reason for the separation: "After several years, a newly-arrived director of social service feeling that such a club was not a proper part of the health work, it dissociated from the church, incorporated, and moved to different headquarters in another part of the city."
207 Annual Report, The Jacoby Club of Boston, Inc., 1917-1918, 1. MHS.
208 The writer quoted is Peter Clark Macfarlane. MHS.
209 D. H. McPheters, "Report of the Secretary," in *The Story of the Lonesome Man* (n.p., 1914). The book was copyrighted in 1914 under the name D. H. McFeeters (McPheters is spelled McFeeters in a number of the Club's earlier documents), but there is no other publication information. In the 1915-1916 Annual Report,

McPheters stated: "Let it also be understood that the work of the club is not confined alone to men who are victims of excessive indulgence in alcoholics [sic]. There are many men who from stress and worry from various other causes have come to that point of despondency where they feel that their usefulness to the community is at an end." McPheters remained the Club's executive secretary well into the 1940's, when ill health finally forced him to retire. MHS.

210 The booklet also included a place for the secretary's signature under the heading "Member in Good Standing," with the instructions "The above must be filled in by the Secretary every three months." The booklet itself was a miniscule at 1 3/4 inches by 4 1/4 inches. MHS.

211 "'Help Yourself by Helping Others in Misfortune,' Is Jacoby Club's Maxim," *Boston Sunday Herald*, 22 March 1914. MHS.

212 "Down and Out? See Ernest Jacoby, Everyman's Friend," *Boston Sunday Post*, 25 January 1914. MHS.

213 Ibid. MHS.

214 "Help Yourself." MHS.

215 *The Story of the Lonesome Man* does not directly attribute authorship to McPheters, but the work is copyrighted in his name. The 1913-1914 annual report (that is, *The Story of the Lonesome Man*) was apparently published and released later in 1914 since the Club's recognition by the Federated Churches of Boston and Religious Organizations in Greater Boston on January 31, 1914 was listed as news. McPheters wrote that this was an "endorsement." A *Boston Sunday Herald* article on the Jacoby Club ("Help Yourself by Helping Others") likewise used the word "endorsement" with regard to the Federated Churches but noted that it had the (mere) "sympathy of Cardinal O'Connell." McPheters did not mention the cardinal in his report. MHS.

216 Adolf Harnack, *Das Wesen des Christentums* ("The Essence of Christianity," 1900) was the manifesto of this movement. It quickly went through multiple editions in numerous languages. The English translation (1901), which was reprinted over and over again, changed the title to *What Is Christianity?* Harnack proclaimed that the "kernel" (as he called it) at the heart of the Christian gospel was *an ethical message*, seen above all in portions of the New Testament such as Jesus' Sermon on the Mount. It was not a set of philosophical doctrines and dogmas about the Trinity and similar speculative metaphysical issues. The simple teaching of the real historical Jesus, as reconstructed by the modern historical-critical method, was about doing good, helping the needy, and loving your neighbor as yourself. One of the two largest American Protestant denominations, the Methodists, were

almost completely taken over during the first two decades of the twentieth century by classical Protestant liberalism and the vision of a Christianity which dedicated itself to advancing social causes. The faculty at the Methodists' Boston University (where the great social reformer Dr. Martin Luther King, Jr., later obtained his Ph.D.) and Boston School of Theology (which was attached to the university) became some of the strongest proponents of the new movement. The A.A. movement was also going to be affected very strongly by these ideas later on: Bill W.'s picture of Jesus in chapter one of the A.A. Big Book (page 11 in the 3rd edit.) was not unlike that of early twentieth century classical Protestant liberalism: "To Christ I conceded the certainty of a great man.... His moral teaching—most excellent." The Methodist publication called *The Upper Room*, which was basically structured by classical Protestant liberal ideas, was the most common meditational book used in early A.A. prior to Richmond Walker's publication of *Twenty-Four Hours a Day* in 1948.

217   The phrase "fighting for others" had appeared in at least one newspaper ad for the Club prior to the publication of the book. The book *Fighting for Others* itself was soon mentioned in these ads, replacing *The Story of the Lonesome Man* as a description of the Club. MHS.

218   Margaret Deland, *Fighting for Others* (n.p., c. 1916), 1. The 1916 date is approximated by virtue of references to the book made in different newspaper ads and textual references to other events. MHS.

219   Ibid., 9. MHS.

220   A *Boston Evening Transcript* article states: "One popular novel, 'The City of Comrades,' by Basil King, was inspired by the club and a large part of its contents are devoted to a description of its activities." "Boston 'Anti-Suicide Club' Has Its Twenty-Fifth Birthday," 21 April 1935. MHS.

221   "Basil King" in the *Dictionary of American Biography* (New York: Scribner's, 1933), 406.

222   Basil King, *The City of Comrades* (New York: Grosset & Dunlap, 1919), 4. Subsequent references to the novel in this chapter will be noted parenthetically in the text.

223   It is partly reminiscent of a motif found centuries earlier in the sermons and songs of the medieval Crusades, where the claim was made that participation in a "holy war" could be a literally Christlike sacrifice and crucifixion of the self which would redeem and save the soul of the knight who so dedicated himself.

224   The Eighteenth (Prohibition) Amendment to the U.S. Constitution was ratified on January 16, 1919, and the Volstead Act was then passed to implement it on

October 28, 1919. Prohibition was actually not to be enforced under this act until the beginning of 1920, so Basil King would not have known yet, at the time he wrote this foreword, how futile and ineffective the attempt would be to bar Americans from any access at all to alcoholic beverages.

225 Basil King, foreword to *The Lonesome Trail* (n.p., [1919]), 3, 4. MHS. Although no date of publication is given in the booklet itself, the way it talks about the impending prohibition of all beverage alcohol in the United States indicates some point in 1919 after the ratification of the Eighteenth Amendment (January 16) and perhaps even after the passing of the Volstead Act (October 28), but before the new laws were to take force at the beginning of 1920. The last page contains this note: "The cost of producing this booklet has been provided for through the generosity of one of our friends."
226 *The Lonesome Trail*, 7. MHS.
227 Ibid., 11. MHS.
228 Ibid., 13, 14. MHS.
229 Ibid., 15. MHS.
230 Ibid., 17. MHS.
231 Ibid., 18, 19. MHS.
232 The Eighteenth (Prohibition) Amendment to the U.S. Constitution was ratified on January 16, 1919, and the Volstead Act was passed to implement it on October 28, 1919. Prohibition was scheduled to be first enforced by law under this act at the beginning of 1920. The prohibition era lasted fourteen years in all, down to December 5, 1933, when its repeal took effect.
233 Ibid., 20. MHS.
234 "The Jacoby Club of Boston, Inc. What It Is and What It Does" (n.p., 1923-1924), 3. Jacoby Club Collection, Massachusetts Historical Society, Boston. The secretary, later called field secretary, actually functioned more as a program director and counselor. McPheters held the position for over thirty years. After years of illness, he died in 1960. MHS.
235 "What Is a Club?" (n.p., [1927]), 3. Jacoby Club Collection, MHS.
236 "Boston 'Anti-Suicide Club' Has Its Twenty-Fifth Birthday." *Boston Evening Transcript*, 20 April 1935. Jacoby Club Collection, MHS.
237 *Annual Report of the Jacoby Club of Boston, Inc. 1936-37* (n.p.: 1937), 7-8. Jacoby Club Collection, MHS.
238 Ibid., 6.
239 *Alcoholics Anonymous Comes of Age: A Brief History of A.A.* (New York: A.A. Publishing, Inc., 1957), vii.

240 Ernest Kurtz, *Not-God: A History of Alcoholics Anonymous* (Center City, MN: Hazelden, 1979). See Chapters 1-4.
241 Ibid., 33. The four founding moments were "Dr. Carl Gustav Jung's 1931 conversation with Rowland H.; Ebby T.'s late November 1934 visit with Bill Wilson; Wilson's 'spiritual experience' and discovery of William James in Towns Hospital in mid-December 1934; and the interaction of Wilson and Dr. Bob Smith through May and June 1935 which climaxed in the final and enshrined 'founding moment' [June 10]."
242 *Alcoholics Anonymous Comes of Age*, 74, viii. The Rev. Samuel Shoemaker broke with the Oxford Group in 1941. See Kurtz, *Not-God*, 47.
243 *Alcoholics Anonymous Comes of Age*, vii-viii.
244 According to the official history of A.A. in Boston, Hatlestad had the title of reverend doctor, a fact that is ignored in the Jacoby Club archival material. *A History of the Boston Central Service Committee: A Brief History of Alcoholics Anonymous in Boston*, mimeographed, obtainable from the A.A. Central Service Office in Boston, prepared by their Archives Subcommittee (December 1989), 2.
245 No actual date is included on the letterhead but the report was prepared for a Board of Governors meeting scheduled for June 30, 1941. Unless otherwise noted, all documents and correspondence cited are from the Jacoby Club Collection, MHS.
246 As early as December 13, 1940, Hatlestad wrote to the Boston Dispensary ("A Unit of the New England Medical Center") inquiring whether or not the Jacoby Club "could be of service to the Dispensary in connection with Dispensary patients." The reply to Hatlestad from the Dispensary implies that Hatlestad had requested that his organization in some way become involved as an aftercare facility. The letter tersely stated that "it would be inconsistent in our opinion with good medical policy to share the responsibility for treatment with a non-medical organization." Cf. Malcolm Steele's 12 June 1941 report to the Board of Governors. By January 1941 (Invoice No. 330), Hatlestad had subscribed to the *Quarterly Journal of Studies on Alcohol*. In April 1941 Hatlestad received two replies from Stanley Cobb, M.D., a member of the Club's advisory board, concerning contacts at the Washingtonian Home, McLean Hospital, and the Boston Psychiatric Hospital. Cobb seemed supportive (letters on April 14 and 18, 1941.) Further, Hatlestad wrote and gained some support regarding his alcoholism work from at least one older member, Horatio Swasey, a former executive committee member (letter from Swasey to Hatlestad, March 4, 1941.) Further, Hatlestad joined the Research Council on Problems of Alcohol, "An Associated Society of

the American Association for the Advancement of Science" (letter from the Council to the Jacoby Club, May 1, 1941.) Also, a letter to Hatlestad from a medical doctor associated with the Peter Bent Brigham Hospital in Boston indicated Hatlestad's desire for a reprint of an article, interest in finding the *Cyclopedia of Medicine,* and a wish to have the doctor speak at a club meeting (John Romano, M.D., letter to Hatlestad, Sept. 8, 1941). MHS.

247 Boston Psychiatric Hospital, letter to Hatlestad, March 5, 1941. MHS.
248 Hatlestad, letter to Dr. Elmer W. Clark, June 18, 1941. MHS.
249 "Functions of the Jacoby Club," November 5, 1941. MHS.
250 Stanley Cobb, letter to Ernest Jacoby, Jr., June 8, 1941. MHS.
251 "Report of the Acting Executive Secretary of the Jacoby Club of Boston, Inc. May 1, 1941-May 1, 1942." MHS.
252 Ruth Hock, letter to Hatlestad, June 10, 1940. MHS.
253 Quote from a letter written by Bill W. in 1940 in [Bill W.=William Griffith Wilson], *As Bill Sees It: The A.A. Way of Life ... Selected Writings of A.A.'s Co-founder* (New York: Alcoholics Anonymous World Services, 1967), 1.
254 *Alcoholics Anonymous,* 3rd ed. (New York: Alcoholics Anonymous World Services, 1976), 85.
255 *Alcoholics Anonymous Comes of Age* (New York: Alcoholics Anonymous World Services, 1957), 97.
256 For the Twelve Traditions, see *Alcoholics Anonymous,* 564-568.
257 From a collection of newspaper clippings in the Alcoholics Anonymous Archives at their General Service Office in New York City.
258 Ernest Kurtz, *Not-God: A History of Alcoholics Anonymous* (Center City, MN: Hazelden, 1979), 87. See Kurtz for an account of Hemsley's impact on A.A. as well as the role of publicity in general in the development of A.A., Chapter 1. "Prelude to Maturity: October 1939-March 1941," subtitled "Needing Others: The Era of Publicity."
259 Ruth Hock, letter to Lawrence M. Hatlestad, 10 June 1940. MHS.
260 *A History of the Boston Central Service Committee: A Brief History of Alcoholics Anonymous in Boston* (prepared by the Archives Subcommittee of the A.A. Central Service Office in Boston, mimeographed, December 1989; obtainable at the office), 2. The information therein was verified and discussed with Eddie O., a member of the subcommittee which prepared it, in a taped interview with the author at 368 Congress Street, Boston, Massachusetts, 26 July 1996. This history and letters from the MHS are my sources for this section.
261 *History of the Boston Central Service Committee,* ibid.

262 Ibid.

263 Ibid. Paddy wrote a letter to Hatlestad on 24 March 1941 from High Watch Farm, the "A.A. farm." Paddy thanked Hatlestad for "the assistance that you gave me in getting me to come back to the farm. It's …solved many of the problems which I think were factors in my slip." MHS.

264 Ruth Hock, letter to Hatlestad, 17 April 1941. "I understand that Paddy is back in Boston and I hope he is in touch with the group and serene. I'm going to drop him a note today …give him my best regards." MHS.

265 *History of the Boston Central Service Committee*, 2, 3. According to Eddie O. (interview of 26 July 1996), Bill W. never met with the Jacoby Club and only visited Boston itself twice, one visit for a delegates' meeting and the other for the funeral of Helen Brown, an early A.A. secretary who helped Bill with the writing of the Traditions.

266 Ernest Jacoby, Jr., letter to David H. McPheters, 17 March 1953. MHS.

267 Ibid.

268 Jacoby Club, Special Committee, letter to Alcoholics Anonymous, 31 May 1941. Shortly after, Hatlestad wrote a personal letter to Paddy Keegan expressing the desire for a break between the two groups. 5 June 1941. MHS.

269 In a document titled "Report on the Affairs of the Jacoby Club of Boston, Inc.," dated October 1942, a writer, unnamed but most likely Ernest Jacoby, summarized the September 23rd meeting of the Board of Governors. Included in the report was Dr. Stanley Cobb's belief that Hatlestad would not "successfully develop and organize the further growth of the Club." He added that this reason, along with the difficulty in raising funds during a time of war, was sufficient to discontinue the alcoholic work. The report added that the Club would work out a permanent arrangement with the Ellis Memorial as a meeting place. It also mentioned that the offices at 159 Newbury Street "have been vacated and the furniture temporarily stored" for eventual use at the Ellis Memorial. The report also referred to the issue of providing for McPheters's salary, mentioning that he was currently not on active duty. McPheters' welfare was always a priority with the Club, giving recognition for his thirty years of faithful service. MHS.

270 *History of the Boston Central Service Committee*, 4. MHS.

271 Kurtz, *Not-God*, 100. See 100-109 for a complete account of the article's impact.

272 Ibid., 101. The article itself is reprinted in the pamphlet *The Jack Alexander Article about A.A.* (New York: A.A. World Services, Inc., 1991). The article is also reprinted in Igor I. Sikorsky, Jr., *A.A.'s Godparents: Three Early Influences on*

Alcoholics Anonymous and Its Foundation: Carl Jung, Emmet Fox, Jack Alexander (Minneapolis: CompCare Publishers, 1990).

273 Ibid.

274 The original lists still exist in the Jacoby Club archives at the Massachusetts Historical Society.

275 Eric Kling corresponded with Hatlestad on a number of occasions, including once from the A.A. Farm in Cornwall, Connecticut. While there he wrote to Hatlestad: "Your work in the Jacoby Club appears to be along the same lines and in the same way as that of the [A.A.] people here. Spirituality is necessary, though not necessarily of the orthodox type, and this phase I have paid all too little attention to. I thought I could conquer drinking through an intellectual approach and I, like many others, failed. I am going to start from scratch and, with your help, rebuild my personality." Eric Kling, letter to Hatlestad, 25 Sept. 1940. MHS.

276 Kling maintained a correspondence with Hatlestad and visited the A.A. office in New York. While he had at least one slip, the last observation was made by Ruth Hock: "There is certainly an amazing change in that man for I hardly knew him. He gave a talk at the meeting Tuesday night and the sincerity carried us right along with him." Letter from Ruth Hock to Hatlestad, 23 May 1941. MHS.

277 L. S. Novius, the secretary to the editor of the *Boston Herald*, wrote a letter in response to an inquiry concerning Eric Kling's address. She gave his address as that of the Jacoby Club, 115 Newbury Street. 23 April 1941. MHS.

278 Richmond Walker was born on August 2, 1892, and died on March 25, 1965, with twenty-two years sobriety. Most of the basic biographical information comes from a talk which Walker gave to an A.A. meeting in Rutland, Vermont, in 1958, which was tape-recorded. Unless otherwise noted, the information on his life given in this section is drawn from that source. There is a transcript of the tape recording in the *Northern Indiana Archival Bulletin* 4 (No. 1, 2001): 1-4 (published by the Archives Committee of A.A.'s Northern Indiana Area 22, with the editorial address given as Michiana Central Service Office, 814 E. Jefferson Blvd., South Bend IN 46617), and another transcript in [Richmond Walker], *Twenty-Four Hours a Day*, Hazelden Foundation 50th Anniversary Edition (Center City MN: Hazelden, n.d. given but must be c. 1998 or 99). There is also a brief biography written by Mel B. as a special foreword to the 40th Anniversary Edition of *Twenty-Four Hours a Day* (Center City MN: Hazelden, 1994). The most detailed biography at present is one put together by Glenn F. Chesnut, "Richmond Walker & the Twenty-Four Hour Book," which was given at the 8th Annual National Archives Workshop in Fort Lauderdale, Florida on Sept. 27, 2003; the text of this presentation

was placed afterwards on the West Baltimore A.A. history website as <http://www.a-1associates.com/aa/richmond_walker.htm> and on the AAHistoryLovers website as <http://groups.yahoo.com/group/AAHistoryLovers/>, September 2003, postings numbered 1372, 1373, 1374, and 1375.

279 A.A. in Boston had grown to thirteen meetings every week by the beginning of Fall 1945, so Walker proposed the establishment of a Boston Central Committee to better coordinate their activities in a letter to the group on 25 October 1945. *History of the Boston Central Service Committee*, 4. MHS.

280 Richmond Walker, *For Drunks Only: One Man's Reactions to Alcoholics Anonymous* (Center City MN: Hazelden, 1987 [orig. pub. mid-1940's]). *God Calling* by Two Listeners, ed. A. J. Russell, re-edited by Bernard Koerselman (orig. pub. 1935; Uhrichsville OH: Barbour and Company, 1993). The method which Walker used for composing the meditations was discovered by David W., who interviewed Florida A.A. old-timers, and also oversees the Florida A.A. archives which has one part of the Richmond Walker papers (the other portion is at the Hazelden Foundation in Center City, Minnesota).

281 [Richmond Walker], *Twenty-Four Hours a Day*, "Compiled by a member of the Group at Daytona Beach, Fla." (Center City MN: Hazelden, 1975 [orig. pub. 1948, first Hazelden edit. 1954]). Walker had one home at Cohasset, Massachusetts, a place on the coast within commuting distance of Boston, and another home in Daytona Beach in Florida.

282 The book sold 80,000 copies in the first ten years (Vermont talk, par. 24), and by 1994 had sold nearly six and a half million copies (Mel B., Foreword to the 40th Anniversary Edition). For Kurtz's estimate as to its extraordinary spread and usage, see *Not-God*, 347 (n. 13 to Chapter 5).

283 There are a few other works, which have always been and still are considered totally proper to use in American A.A. meetings, which are not published by Alcoholics Anonymous World Services in New York using A.A. conference funds, for example the *Little Red Book* (first printed edition in Minneapolis: Coll-Web Company, 1946), the Detroit Pamphlet: "Alcoholics Anonymous: An Interpretation of the Twelve Steps" (early 1940's, still obtainable from Alcoholics Anonymous of Greater Detroit, 380 Hilton Road, Ferndale MI 48220; sometimes also called the Washington D.C. Pamphlet) and the little Cleveland pamphlet on the Four Absolutes. But *Twenty-Four Hours a Day* is the only work of this sort which has achieved anything even remotely close to such a widespread and all-encompassing usage. The New York A.A. office from the very beginning had no objection at all to A.A. meetings using books and pamphlets of this sort, see the

letter from Margaret R. "Bobby" Burger (secretary at the Alcoholic Foundation, now called the General Service Office) to Barry Collins of the Nicollet Group in Minneapolis (11 November 1944) and Bill Wilson's comment to Barry Collins in November 1950, both reprinted in the Foreword to the 50th Anniversary Edition of *The Little Red Book* (Center City MN: Hazelden, 1996). The use of such works in A.A. meetings, that is, locally produced books and pamphlets which embody generally accepted A.A. teachings, is supported by long-standing A.A. tradition, going back sixty years or more at this point.

284 Mel B., Foreword to the 40th Anniversary Edition.
285 White, *Slaying the Dragon*, 201-202.
286 For a discussion of some of Walker's spiritual teachings, see Glenn F. Chesnut, *The Higher Power of the Twelve-Step Program: For Believers & Non-Believers*, Hindsfoot Foundation Series on Spirituality and Theology (San Jose: Authors Choice Press/iUniverse, 2001), 9, 81-2, 115-128, 191-3 n. 7, 213 n. 10, and 224-8 nn. 1-9.
287 "Demonstration" and "change" used as technical terms (*Twenty-Four Hours* April 22), "guidance" (Feb. 5, Mar. 14, Nov. 7 and 27, Dec. 10, 13, 18, 21, and 26). "Honesty, purity, unselfishness, love" are especially emphasized in the concluding lines of Walker's Vermont talk and passages on one or another of these virtues appear frequently throughout the *Twenty-Four Hour* book.
288 Kurtz, *Not-God*, 111. See 111-153 for the subsequent development of A.A.
289 Ernest Jacoby, Jr., letter to Mrs. Elizabeth D. Whitney, Executive Secretary, Boston Committee for Education on Alcoholism, 15 Oct. 1945. MHS.
290 Allan Riley, Jacoby Club secretary, annual appeal letter, July 1957. MHS.
291 Samuel R. Payson, Jacoby Club secretary, annual appeal letter, July 1970. MHS.
292 Letter from Marc Scullin, Jacoby Club secretary, annual appeal letter, September 1979. MHS.
293 William Pittman, "The Jacoby Club Records, Ms. Coll. N-41," MHS.
294 Herman Melville, *Moby Dick*, ed. James Baird (New York, Harcourt, Brace, 1963), 52, 53-54.

BIBLIOGRAPHY

MHS=Massachusetts Historical Society

Ahlstrom, Sydney E. *A Religious History of the American People.* New Haven: Yale University Press, 1972.

Alcoholics Anonymous. 3rd ed. New York: Alcoholics Anonymous World Services, 1976.

"Alcoholics Anonymous: An Interpretation of the Twelve Steps," see Detroit Pamphlet.

Alcoholics Anonymous Comes of Age: A Brief History of A.A. New York: A.A. Publishing, 1957.

Alexander, Jack. "Alcoholics Anonymous: Freed Slaves of Drink, Now They Free Others." *Saturday Evening Post*, 1 March 1941. More readily available as the A.A.-published pamphlet: "The Jack Alexander Article about A.A." New York: A.A. World Services, 1991.

As Bill Sees It, see W., Bill.

B., Mel. *New Wine: The Spiritual Roots of the Twelve Step Miracle.* Center City, MN: Hazelden, 1991.

_____. Foreword to the 40th Anniversary Edition of *Twenty-Four Hours a Day.* Center City MN: Hazelden, 1994.

Baker, Ray Stannard. *New Ideals in Healing.* New York: Frederick A. Stokes, 1909.

_____. *The Spiritual Unrest.* New York: Frederick A. Stokes, 1910.

Baylor, Courtenay. *Remaking a Man: One Successful Method of Mental Refitting.* New York: Moffat, Yard and Co., 1919.

Bishop, Jim. *The Glass Crutch.* New York: Doubleday, Doran and Co, 1945.

Blumberg, Leonard U., with William L. Pittman. *Beware the First Drink! The Washington Temperance Movement and Alcoholics Anonymous.* Seattle: Glen Abbey, 1991.

Braden, Charles S. *These Also Believe: A Study of Modern American Cults and Minority Religious Movements.* New York: Macmillan, 1949.

Bromberg, Walter. *The Mind of Man: A History of Psychotherapy and Psychoanalysis.* New York: Harper Colophon, 1963 [orig. 1954].

Brown, Sally and David R. Brown. *A Biography of Mrs. Marty Mann: The First Lady of Alcoholics Anonymous.* Center City MN: Hazelden, 2001.

Burnham, John Chynoweth. *Paths Into American Culture: Psychology, Medicine, and Morals.* Philadelphia: Temple University Press, 1988.

_____. *Psychoanalysis and American Medicine, 1894-1918.* Medicine, Science, and Culture. Monograph 20. Psychological Issues. New York: International Universities Press, 1967.

Chesnut, Glenn F. *The Higher Power of the Twelve-Step Program: For Believers & Non-Believers.* Hindsfoot Foundation Series on Spirituality and Theology. San Jose CA and Lincoln NE: iUniverse/Author's Choice, 2001.

_____. "Richmond Walker & the Twenty-four Hour Book." Paper given at the 8th Annual National Archives Workshop in Fort Lauderdale, Florida on September 27, 2003; the text is available at <http://www.a-1associates.com/aa/richmond_walker.htm> as of 9 October 2003.

Clinebell, Howard J., Jr. *Understanding and Counseling the Alcoholic.* Rev. ed. Nashville: Abingdon Press, 1990. Chapter 4, "The Emmanuel Movement—Religion Plus Psychotherapy." This chapter of his book is now also available online at <http://www.religion-online.org/cgi-bin/relsearchd.dll/showchapter?chapter_id=726>.

Copleston, Frederick J. *A History of Philosophy.* Vol. 7, *Fichte to Nietzsche.* Garden City NY: Image-Doubleday, 1965.

_____. *A History of Philosophy.* Vol. 8, *Bentham to Russell.* Garden City NY.: Image-Doubleday, 1966.

Crosby, Caresse. *The Passionate Years.* New York: Dial Press, 1953.

Cunningham, Raymond J. "The Emmanuel Movement: A Variety of American Religious Experience." *American Quarterly* 14 (1962): 54-60.

Dalpe, Steve and Rick Stattler. "A Guide to the Rowland Hazard III Papers." Rhode Island Historical Society, 1999.

Deland, Margaret. *Fighting For Others.* N.p.: n.p., c. 1916. Copy in MHS.

The Detroit Pamphlet: "Alcoholics Anonymous: An Interpretation of the Twelve Steps." Dates from the early 1940's, obtainable from Alcoholics Anonymous of Greater Detroit, 380 Hilton Road, Ferndale MI 48220.

Downs, Winfield Scott. *Men of New England.* Vol. 4. New York: American Historical Co., 1947.

Freud, Sigmund. Letter to the chairmen of the psychoanalytical societies in Europe and America (1932). One of the original printed copies is in the Sigmund Freud Collection at the Dittrick Medical History Center, Case Western Reserve University, 11000 Euclid Avenue, Cleveland, OH 44106-1714. See <http://www.cwru.edu/artsci/dittrick/rarepages/freud.htm> (26 November 2003) for the cited section of the letter.

Friedman, Cary D. "Elwood Worcester and the Emmanuel Movement: Psychotherapy in the Church, 1906-1929." Master's thesis, Harvard University, 1982; copy in the Diocesan Library and Archives, Episcopal Diocese of Massachusetts.

Gibbs, Wolcott. "The Rover Boys on a Bender." Review of *The Glass Crutch*, by Jim Bishop. *New York Times*, 18 November 1945.

Gifford, Sanford. *The Emmanuel Movement (Boston, 1904-1929): The Origins of Group Treatment and the Assault on Lay Psychotherapy*. Cambridge: Harvard University Press, 1998.

God Calling by Two Listeners. Ed. A. J. Russell. Re-edited by Bernard Koerselman in 1993. Uhrichsville OH: Barbour and Company, 1993 (orig. pub. 1935).

Greene, John Gardner. "The Emmanuel Movement: 1906-1929." *The New England Quarterly* 7 (1934): 496-528.

Hale, Nathan G., Jr. *Freud and the Americans: The Beginnings of Psychoanalysis in the United States, 1876-1917*. New York: Oxford University Press, 1971.

Harnack, Adolf von. *What is Christianity?* Philadelphia: Fortress Press, 1986 [orig. German *Das Wesen des Christentums* ("The Essence of Christianity") pub. 1900, sixteen lectures given during the 1899/1900 winter semester at the University of Berlin].

A History of the Boston Central Service Committee: A Brief History of Alcoholics Anonymous in Boston. Prepared by the Archives Subcommittee of the A.A. Central Service Office in Boston, mimeographed, December 1989. Obtainable at the A.A. Central Service Office in Boston.

Holifield, E. Brooks. *A History of Pastoral Care in America: From Salvation to Self-Realization.* Nashville: Abingdon, 1983.

_____. "Pastoral Care and Counseling." In *Encyclopedia of American Religious Experience.* Vol. 1. Ed. Charles H. Lippy and Peter W. Williams. New York: Scribner's, 1988.

Jacoby, Ernest [?]. Report on the Affairs of the Jacoby Club of Boston, Inc., dated October 1942. Writer unnamed but most likely Ernest Jacoby. MHS.

James, William. *The Varieties of Religious Experience.* Cambridge, MA: Harvard University Press, 1985 [orig. 1902].

King, Basil. *The City of Comrades.* New York: Grosset & Dunlap, 1919.

Kurtz, Ernest. *Not-God: A History of Alcoholics Anonymous.* Center City, MN: Hazelden, 1979.

The Little Red Book. Minneapolis: Coll-Web Company, 1946.

Mann, Marty. *Marty Mann Answers Your Questions About Drinking and Alcoholism.* New York: Holt, Rinehart and Winston, 1970.

_____. *Marty Mann's New Primer on Alcoholism: How People Drink, How to Recognize Alcoholics, and What to Do About Them.* New York: Holt, Rinehart and Winston, 1958.

McCarthy, Katherine. "Early Alcoholism Treatment: The Emmanuel Movement and Richard Peabody." *Journal of Studies on Alcohol* 45.1 (1984): 59-74.

_____. "Psychotherapy and Religion: The Emmanuel Movement." *Journal of Religion and Health* 23.2 (1984): 92-102.

McDonald, Robert. *Mind, Religion and Health: With an Appreciation of the Emmanuel Movement.* New York: Funk and Wagnall's, 1908.

McPheters, David H. *The Lonesome Trail.* N.p: n.p, 1919. Copy in MHS.

_____. "Report of the Secretary," containing *The Story of the Lonesome Man*. N.p.: n.p., 1914. This is the Jacoby's Club Annual Business Report for 1913-1914. Copy in MHS.

_____. "The Jacoby Club of Boston, Inc. What It Is and What It Does." N.p.: n.p., 1923-1924. Copy in MHS.

_____. "What Is a Club?" N.p.: n.p., [1927]. Copy in MHS.

Melville, Herman. *Moby Dick*. Ed. James Baird. New York: Harcourt, Brace, 1963 [orig. 1851].

Mercadante, Linda A. *Victims and Sinners: Spiritual Roots of Addiction and Recovery*. Louisville: Westminster John Knox, 1996.

Meyer, Donald. *The Positive Thinkers: A Study of the American Quest for Health, Wealth and Personal Power from Mary Baker Eddy to Norman Vincent Peale*. Garden City, N.Y.: Doubleday, 1965.

"Pass It On": The Story of Bill Wilson and How the A.A. Message Reached the World. New York: Alcoholics Anonymous World Services, 1984.

Peabody, Richard R. *The Common Sense of Drinking*. Boston: Little, Brown, 1931.

Pittman, Bill. *A.A.: The Way It Began*. Seattle: Glen Abbey, 1988.

_____. *Stepping Stones to Recovery*. Seattle: Glen Abbey, 1988.

Powell, Lyman P. *The Emmanuel Movement in a New England Town*. New York: G.P. Putnam's Sons-Knickerbocker Press, 1909.

Royce, Josiah. "The Modern Psychotherapeutic Movement in America." *Psychotherapy* 3.4 (1909): 20-33.

S., Sgt. Bill, with Glenn F. Chesnut. *On the Military Firing Line in the Alcoholism Treatment Program: The Air Force Sergeant Who Beat Alcoholism and Taught Others to Do the Same.* Hindsfoot Foundation Series on the History of Alcoholism Treatment. New York: iUniverse, 2003.

Sikorsky, Igor I., Jr. *A.A.'s Godparents: Three Early Influences on Alcoholics Anonymous and Its Foundation: Carl Jung, Emmet Fox, Jack Alexander.* Minneapolis: CompCare Publishers, 1990.

Stattler, Rick. "Biographical Note on Rowland Hazard," Rhode Island Historical Society Research Report, 15 January 1998.

Strecker, Edward A. *Their Mothers' Sons: The Psychiatrist Examines an American Problem.* Philadelphia: Lippincott, 1946.

_____ and Francis T. Chambers, Jr. *Alcohol: One Man's Meat.* New York: Macmillan, 1938.

Thomsen, Robert. *Bill W.* New York: Harper and Row, 1975.

Twain, Mark. *Christian Science.* Buffalo: Prometheus, 1986 [orig. 1907].

Two Listeners, see *God Calling.*

W., Bill [William Griffith Wilson]. *As Bill Sees It: The A.A. Way of Life…Selected Writings of A.A.'s Co-founder.* New York: Alcoholics Anonymous World Services, 1967.

Walker, Richmond. *For Drunks Only: One Man's Reactions to Alcoholics Anonymous.* Center City MN: Hazelden, 1987 [orig. c. 1945].

_____. Tape-recording of a talk given at an A.A. meeting in Rutland, Vermont, in 1958. A transcript of the tape recording may be found in the *Northern Indiana Archival Bulletin* 4 (No. 1, 2001): 1-4 (published by the Archives Committee of A.A.'s Northern Indiana Area 22, with the editorial address given as Michiana Central Service Office, 814 E. Jefferson Blvd., South Bend IN 46617). There is also a transcript in the 50th Anniversary Edition of his meditational book *Twenty-Four Hours a Day*, see below.

[_____]. *Twenty-Four Hours a Day.* By Richmond Walker, although to preserve his anonymity during his lifetime, he requested that it only say (at the end of the volume) "Compiled by a member of the Group at Daytona Beach, Fla." Center City MN: Hazelden, 1975 (orig. pub. 1948, first Hazelden edit. 1954).

[_____]. *Twenty-Four Hours a Day.* Hazelden Foundation 50th Anniversary Edition. Center City MN: Hazelden, n.d. given but must be c. 1998 or 99.

White, William L. "Pre-AA Alcoholic Mutual Aid Societies." *Alcoholism Treatment Quarterly* 19.1 (2001):1-21.

_____. *Slaying the Dragon: The History of Addiction Treatment and Recovery in America.* Bloomington IL: Chestnut Health Systems, 1998. Obtainable from Chestnut Health Systems, 720 W. Chestnut St., Bloomington IL 61701, telephone 888-547-8271.

Worcester, Elwood. *Life's Adventure: The Story of a Varied Career.* New York: Scribner's, 1932.

_____. *Making Life Better: An Application of Religion and Psychology to Human Problems.* New York: Charles Scribner's, 1933.

_____. "The Results of the Emmanuel Movement." *Ladies' Home Journal,* November 1908.

_____. "The Results of the Emmanuel Movement." *Ladies' Home Journal,* December 1908.

_____ and Samuel McComb. *Body, Mind, and Spirit.* Boston: Marshall Jones, 1931.

_____ and Samuel McComb. *The Christian Religion as a Healing Power.* New York: Moffat, Yard and Co., 1909.

———, Samuel McComb, and Isador A. Coriat. *Religion and Medicine: The Moral Control of Nervous Disorders.* New York: Moffat, Yard and Co., 1908.

Wylie, Philip. *Generation of Vipers.* New York: Reinhart, 1942.

Zweig, Arnulf. "Fechner, Gustav Theodor." In *The Encyclopedia of Philosophy.* Ed. Paul Edwards. Vol. 3. New York: Macmillan and The Free Press, 1972.

INDEX

A.A., xii-xv, 3, 8-12, 14, 16, 27, 33-34, 36, 38, 40-41, 45-46, 49, 52, 58, 60-61, 64-65, 69-73, 77-79, 81, 83, 85, 92, 97, 100-101, 109, 11i, 114, 119-136, 138, 140-143, 154, 160-162, 165-173, 176, 178-179
abstinence, 13, 15, 101, 120
addiction, 147, 162, 178, 180
Adler, Alfred, 58
Ahlstrom, Sidney, 2
alcohol, 12-13, 15, 41, 45, 48, 51-53, 55, 78, 82, 87, 105-107, 111, 113, 123, 125, 131, 141, 147, 154, 156-157, 162, 166-167, 177, 179
Alcohol, One Man's Meat, 131, 156, 179
Alcoholics Anonymous, x, xii, xv, 33, 38, 44, 49, 60, 65, 70, 73, 78, 92-93, 109, 119-120, 123-125, 127, 129-130, 133, 135, 137, 140, 143, 154, 158, 160-161, 163, 166-169, 171, 173-179
alcoholism, 12-15, 34-35, 38, 44-45, 47, 50-53, 55, 57-58, 64-72, 74-75, 82-83, 85, 92, 105, 107, 110-114, 117, 120-122, 125, 136, 140, 147-149, 153-158, 160, 162-163, 167, 172, 177-180
Alexander, Jack, 173
Alger, Horatio, 88
Allport, Gordon W., 121
American Magazine, 86

American Medical Association, 48
Armstrong, Maurice, 118-119, 136
As Bill Sees It, 168, 173, 179
B., Mel, xv, 3, 174
Baker, Ray Stannard, 174
Baylor, 33-49, 56, 61, 65-69, 73-76, 78-79, 90, 92, 154-155, 159-161, 174
Baylor, Courtenay, xiii, 35, 174
Beard, George, 1, 157
Big Book, 41, 79, 92, 109, 133, 162, 165
Bishop, 29, 48, 50-52, 55, 152, 156-158, 174, 176
Bishop, Jim, 174
Bob, Dr., 49, 62, 97, 129, 167
Body, Mind and Spirit, 4-5, 12-13, 25, 33, 44, 148-149, 152, 154-155, 180
body, mind, and spirit, 4-5, 12-13, 25, 33, 44, 148-149, 152, 154-155, 180
Boston, x-xii, 4-6, 8, 26, 29-32, 42, 46, 61-62, 69, 78-79, 81, 84-86, 91, 103, 109-111, 113-114, 117-120, 122-132, 135-141, 145-146, 148, 152-155, 163-172, 176-178, 180
Boston American, 86
Boston Central Service Committee, 167-169, 171, 176
Boston Daily Globe, 136
Boston Evening Transcript, 31, 153, 163, 165-166
Boston Foundation, 140-141
Boston Globe, 84-85, 163
Boston Herald, 131, 170
Boston Sunday Herald, 32, 86, 153, 164
Boston Sunday Post, 86, 164
Brattleboro Asylum, 60, 72
C., Burt, 114, 125-126, 130
C., Shep, 162
Cabot, Dr. Richard C., 31
Calvinism, 2
Central Service Committee, 125-127, 167-169, 171, 176

Charles River, 84
Chesnut, Glenn F., ix, 158, 161-162, 170, 172, 175, 178
Christ, 2-3, 7, 9-10, 15, 19-20, 27-28, 93, 137, 165
Christian, 1-5, 7, 10, 15, 18-19, 21-23, 26-27, 56, 82-83, 99-100, 148-149, 152, 158, 162, 164, 179-180
Christian Science, 1-4, 18, 21-22, 148-149, 179
Christianity, 1-5, 18-19, 25-26, 90-92, 164, 176
City of Comrades, 93-94, 102, 165, 177
Clinebell, Howard J., Jr., xiv, 175
Cobb, 116-120, 131, 167-169
Cobb, Stanley, 116, 120, 131, 167-169
Common Sense of Drinking, 46, 49, 51, 53-54, 56-58, 61, 155, 157, 178
Coriat, Dr. Isador H., 5, 31
Craigie Foundation, 33, 35, 68
Crosby, 46-47, 155-156, 175
Crosby, Caresse, 175
Crowley, John W., ix
Cunningham, 30, 148-149, 152-153, 175
Darwinism, 1
Day, Frederic L., 117
Deland, Margaret, 175
Denver Post, 124
Detroit News, 123
disease, 9-10, 13, 38, 44-45, 52, 58, 76, 85, 104, 113, 121, 153
divine, 3, 20-21, 23, 26, 30, 41, 43, 77
Dooley, W. M., 115, 119
Down and Out, 85, 89, 93-97, 99-102, 164
Down and Out Club, 93-97, 99
Dresser, Horatio, 22
Eddy, Mary Baker, 2-3, 18, 149, 157, 178
Eighth Tradition, 127
Ellis Memorial, 110, 116, 119, 136-138, 140, 169

Ellis Memorial House, 119, 136
Emmanuel Church, 6, 10, 12, 17-18, 29, 32-33, 47, 54, 68, 81-85, 128, 137-138, 141, 154, 163
Emmanuel Episcopal Church, 5, 69, 78, 81, 92, 128, 142
Emmanuel Movement, xi-xv, 1, 4-6, 8, 10, 12, 17-22, 26-35, 37-38, 44, 46-48, 50, 58-59, 61, 68, 74, 77-79, 81-82, 84-85, 90, 99, 107, 112, 128, 134, 142, 147-150, 152-156, 162-163, 175-178, 180
Emmanuelite, 28, 43, 61
Episcopal Diocese of Massachusetts, 152, 176
evil, 13-15, 23, 26-27, 30, 54
Fechner, 6, 24-25, 150-151, 181
Fechner, Gustav, 151, 181
fellowship, 2, 4, 6, 8-10, 12, 14, 16, 18, 20, 22, 24, 26, 28, 30, 32, 34, 36, 38, 40, 42, 44-46, 48, 50, 52, 54-56, 58-59, 62, 64, 66, 68, 70, 72, 74, 76-80, 82-84, 86, 88, 90, 92, 94, 96, 98-102, 104, 107-110, 112, 114, 116, 118, 120, 122, 124, 126, 128, 130-132, 134-136, 138, 140-143, 146, 148, 150, 152, 154, 156, 158, 160, 162, 164, 166, 168, 170, 172, 174, 176, 178, 180, 184, 186, 188, 190, 192, 194, 196
Fighting for Others, 87, 90-92, 165, 175
Fitzgerald, F. Scott, 50, 57, 64
Fosdick, Harry Emerson, 27
Freud, 7, 14, 27, 31, 41-43, 48-49, 92, 152-153, 155-157, 176
Freud, Sigmund, 176
Freudian, 13, 38, 42, 45, 50-51, 157
G., Cebra, 72
Glass Crutch, 50-54, 56, 156-158, 174, 176
Gordon, Rev. Dr. George, 30
Great Depression, 108
Great Gatsby, 64
Greater Boston Community Fund, 118
Greene, 33, 148-150, 152-154, 156, 162-163, 176
Groton, 46

harmonial religion, 2-3
Harvard Medical School, 31
Hatlestad, 110-122, 124-127, 129-131, 135-136, 138, 141, 167-170
Hatlestad, Lawrence, xiii, 118-119, 124
Hazard, 60-80, 158-162, 175, 179
Hazard, Rowland, xii, 60-62, 64-65, 68-71, 73-74, 76-80, 158-162, 175, 179
Hazard, Thomas, 62
Hemsley, Rollie, 124
higher Spirit, 10-11, 45
Hock, Ruth, 120, 124, 126, 129-130, 168-170
Holifield, 18, 22, 29, 149-150, 152-153, 176
Holifield, E. Brooks, 176
hypnosis, 7, 13
Jacoby, 8, 12, 34, 59, 78, 81-94, 97, 101-111, 114-120, 122-129, 131, 134-142, 145-146, 163-164, 166-170, 172, 177-178
Jacoby Club, xi-xv, 8, 12, 34, 59, 78, 81-94, 97, 101-111, 114, 116-117, 119-120, 122-129, 131, 134-142, 163-164, 166-170, 172, 177-178
Jacoby Fund, 141
Jacoby, Ernest, xi, 177
Jacoby, Ernest, Jr., 110, 115-116, 141, 168-169, 172
Jacoby, Ernest, Sr., 108, 114-115, 136-137, 145
James, William, 2, 4, 7, 177
Jesus, 2-3, 9, 14-15, 19-21, 137, 141, 164-165
Jung, 61-62, 64-65, 70-78, 160-162, 166, 169, 179
Jung, Carl, 61, 64, 70-74, 76-78, 160, 169, 179
Kant, 20
Keegan, Paddy, 125-126, 169
Kellogg, John Harvey, 2
King, 93-95, 97-98, 102-104, 137, 163-165, 177
King, Basil, 177
Kling, Eric, 131, 170
Kurtz, 70-71, 109, 124, 129, 133, 160, 162, 166-169, 171-172, 177

Kurtz, Ernest, ix, xv, 70-71, 109, 124, 129, 133, 160, 162, 166-169, 171-172, 177
Ladies' Home Journal, 8, 12, 17, 148-149, 180
Life's Adventure, 33, 149-154, 180
Lonesome Trail, 102-105, 165-166, 177
Los Angeles Herald Express, 123
MacDonald, Rev. Dr. Robert, 30
Making Life Better: An Application of Religion and Psychology to Human Problems, 33, 153, 180
Mann, Marty, 154, 177
Massachusetts Historical Society, 140-141, 147, 163, 166, 170, 173
McCarthy, 1, 4, 23, 47, 49, 54, 82, 147-158, 162-163, 177
McCarthy, Katherine, ix, xiv, 1, 4, 47, 177
McComb, 5-9, 12, 18, 24, 27-30, 32-33, 48-49, 53, 84, 107, 137, 148-154, 157, 162, 180
McComb, Samuel, 5-6, 107, 137, 148, 153-154, 157, 162, 180
McPheters, 88-89, 91, 102, 107, 110, 114-115, 117, 119, 136-137, 163-164, 166, 169, 177
McPheters, David H., 177
medical profession, 4-5, 30-32, 34, 37-39, 49, 112, 115, 131, 153
Melville, Herman, 178
Mercadante, Linda, 178
Meyer, 18, 21, 149-151, 157, 178
Meyer, Donald, 178
Midkiff-Debauche, Leslie, ix
mind-cure, 3, 34, 52, 54, 157
Morgan, J. P., 46
nervousness, 1, 12, 53, 82, 113, 157
neurasthenia, 12, 87
neurotic, 37-42, 52, 68, 154
New Thought, 1-3, 18, 21-23, 25-26, 150
New Wine, 3, 57, 148, 158, 174
New York Times, 51, 156, 176
Niebuhr, Reinhold, x, 28, 158

optimism, 5, 10-12, 24, 26-28, 57, 85, 88-89, 100, 151
Oxford Group, xii, xv, 10, 58, 60-61, 66, 69-70, 72-73, 75, 77-79, 97, 109, 129, 132, 134-135, 160-161, 167
Paddy, 114, 125-126, 130, 168-169
panpsychism, 24-25
pastoral counseling, xiii
Peabody, xiv, 34-35, 45-59, 61, 85, 114, 147, 154-158, 162, 177-178
Peabody, Rev. Endicott, 46
Peabody, Richard, xiii, 178
Peace Dale, 62-63, 68
physicians, 4, 6, 8, 31-32, 37, 48, 83, 113, 153
Pittman, ix, 140, 158, 160, 162-163, 172, 174, 178
Pittman, William, 140, 172
Plato, 158
Platonic, 55
Powell, Lyman, 178
Pratt, Dr. Joseph, 137
prayer, 3, 8-10, 15-16, 29, 45, 99, 132, 141, 158
prayers, 9
Progressive, 5, 8, 20, 85, 88, 100, 121, 141, 151
Prohibition, 102-107, 123, 165-166
psychiatrist, 5, 49, 61, 65, 71, 76, 113, 179
psychiatrists, 42, 71
psychology, 4, 6, 10, 15, 18, 21, 24, 32-33, 43, 45, 48-49, 53-54, 57, 121, 153, 156, 161, 174, 180
psychotherapy, 4, 18, 31-33, 48, 51, 76, 112, 118, 147-153, 174-178
publicity, 33, 36, 83, 93, 107, 123-124, 129, 136, 152, 168
Putnam, Dr. James J., 31-32
Rauschenbusch, Walter, 5
Reed, Ryan, ix
Religion and Medicine, 13, 19, 27-28, 30-31, 33, 148-152, 155, 157, 180
Remaking a Man, 36, 39, 42, 154, 159, 174

rest cure, 7
Rhode Island Historical Society, 61-62, 65, 69, 73-74, 77, 147, 159, 175, 179
Roberts, Jon, ix
Rockefeller, 124
Royce, Josiah, 178
Saturday Evening Post, 109, 129-130, 173
self-help, 4-5, 12, 37-38, 82-83, 85, 92, 97, 100, 113, 115, 125, 129, 131, 157
serenity, 7, 69, 158
Seventh Tradition, 122, 127
Smith, Dr. Bob, 62, 167
Social Gospel, 5, 28
soul, 4, 15, 21, 25, 29-30, 158, 165
South End, 110-111, 138-139
South End Citizen, 138
South End House, 111, 138
Spirit, 2, 4-5, 9-13, 24-25, 29, 33, 41, 43-45, 50, 54, 61, 82-83, 85, 88-89, 93, 95-96, 99, 103, 108, 114-115, 122, 134-136, 141-142, 148-149, 152, 154-155, 180
spiritual, 2-3, 5, 11, 14-15, 18-21, 23, 25-27, 29, 43-44, 48-49, 57, 60-61, 69-71, 75-79, 90-91, 94, 109, 121, 133-134, 142, 148-150, 152-153, 155, 158, 162, 166, 172, 174, 178
spiritual conversion, 61, 70-71, 76, 162
Stattler, Rick, x, 62, 65-67, 73-74, 159-162, 175, 179
Steele, 111-115, 167
Steele Report, 111
Steele, Malcolm, 111, 167
Stepping Stones to Recovery, 158, 178
Story of the Lonesome Man, 89-90, 163-165, 177-178
Strecker, Edward, 179
Sunday, Billy, 86
Swedenborgianism, 2
tenseness, 39-42
Thatcher, Ebby, 60, 65, 69-70, 72-73, 77-79

therapy, 4, 12-15, 19, 32-36, 38-39, 41, 43-45, 49, 54, 58, 61, 64, 69, 72, 134-135, 161
transcendentalism, 2
Trine, 20, 22
Trine, Ralph Waldo, 22
tuberculosis, 4-5, 17, 31, 53, 148
Twain, Mark, 179
Twelve Traditions, 38, 127, 135, 168
Twenty-Four Hours a Day, 128, 132-135, 165, 170-171, 174, 179-180
unconscious, 23, 56, 71-72, 151, 157
Unitarianism, 2
Victims and Sinners, 78, 162, 178
W., Bill, 173, 179
Walker, 128, 132-134, 165, 170-172, 175, 179-180
Walker, Richmond, 179
Washington D.C. Star, 124
Washingtonian Movement, xii, 83
Weekly Health Conference, 8, 10
Wells Memorial, 111
White, ix, 73, 147, 172, 180
White, William L., xii, 73, 147, 180
Will to Believe, 25
Wister, 48, 50-56, 156
Wister, William, 48
Worcester, xi, xiii-xiv, 4-15, 17-38, 41-44, 46-49, 52-54, 56-57, 61, 69, 79, 82-85, 90, 92, 114, 134, 142, 148-155, 157, 162-163, 176, 180
Worcester, Elwood, 152, 180
World War I, 5, 47, 63, 93-94, 102, 145
Wundt, Wilhelm, 6

0-595-30740-X